I AM
ALREADY
DEAD

David Whish-Wilson was born in Newcastle, NSW, but grew up in Singapore, Victoria and Western Australia. He left Australia at eighteen to live for a decade in Europe, Africa and Asia. He is the author of *The Summons*, *The Coves* and *The Sawdust House*, and four crime novels in the Frank Swann series: *Line of Sight*, *Zero at the Bone*, *Old Scores* and *Shore Leave*. *True West* (also featuring Lee Southern) was published in 2019 and shortlisted for a Ned Kelly Award for Best Crime. His non-fiction book, *Perth*, part of the NewSouth Books City series, was shortlisted for a WA Premier's Book Award, and in 2022 David was shortlisted for a Western Australian Writer's Fellowship. David lives in Fremantle and coordinates the creative writing program at Curtin University.

I AM ALREADY DEAD

DAVID WHISH-WILSON

 FREMANTLE PRESS

For Pete and Kerri, fierce in life and love

Prologue

Four words that'll turn a life around.

I am already dead.

Inside out and upside down.

I heard it in a line of film dialogue, delivered by a man wearing mutton-chops and a green cardigan, who dispatched another man with a knife to the heart. It was an Irish movie, played on the outdoor screen in Kings Park. Families sprawled around the grassed corridor on deck chairs and picnic blankets, but I watched from the safety of the bush. I didn't understand the movie, but the four words pierced me, lifted me on hooks. Something I already knew but didn't have the words to say.

I repeated the words aloud, making the nearest family glance at each other, and at the bush behind them, where I was hidden. They were eating fried chicken and coleslaw in little china bowls, with plastic forks. I was hungry before those words were spoken, and then I wasn't.

I repeated the sentence again, once, twice, loud enough for them to hear every emphatic word, before they became afraid and shifted their blanket closer to the others.

With the turning of the phrase, I knew that I was a different person.

That night, when I went into the city, I said it while I broke a glass Coke bottle on a cement railing. I said it to the buildings that towered in every direction.

I said it as I moved through the shadows, down the graffiti canyon behind the train station where I knew they'd be sleeping, beside the skip bins that stored cardboard, and so didn't stink. It was the best kids' camp in the Northbridge streets, taken from me by virtue of the oldest boy's bowie knife. I recognised his green sleeping bag, my own knapsack for his pillow; padded out with my clothes, and my diary. The kind of words written that will betray a girl. Beautiful words and pretty things that do not belong with another.

I did not hesitate with the broken bottle. I began to stab at his face. When he screamed and the others awoke, I turned on them, tearing at their blankets and coats, searching for skin and sinew and vein.

The boy began to cry. I began to cry. I held up my hand, to hold them back. I took the bottle and gouged my palm, from thumb to pinkie finger. I waited until the blood began to pulse, in tandem with their own.

It did not hurt. *I am already dead.*

'If you want more, I'll be at the hospital, waiting for you.'

I took my bag from the boy and slung it over my shoulder. I walked the alley. My soft footsteps on the ancient bricks. I wiped away my tears. Today was my birthday. Sweet thirteen.

I

Lee Southern hung his leather jacket on a hook in Firmin's office. The hooks in the corridor were occupied with the coats, bags and hats of the other doorman, and bar staff.

Firmin lifted his head as Lee edged out the door. Lee paused, because a look from Firmin demanded attention, despite his unlikely appearance. The owner of Club Summertime was absurdly tall behind the cheap plywood desk, cluttered with invoices and pay slips, as though he were seated at a child's table. His hands were pale and leathery, pressed together in a forced gesture of invoking calm. His nickname was Cash, after The Man in Black who people said he resembled, but to Lee the older man looked more like Samuel Beckett in his prime: the same owl eyes and face like an ancient map, etched with every road travelled and lesson learned. Firmin was an old hand in the Northbridge nightclub scene, one of the survivors, and he'd witnessed everything in his time.

Firmin's mineral-blue eyes read Lee's own, looking for meaning. 'How's the Phoenix coming along?' he asked, genuine interest in his voice.

Lee had spent the day grinding the '65 Dodge back to bare steel, as a preface to the bondo work he'd anticipated spending the night doing – filling out the minor flaws in the surface steel before sanding it with the long brick, a job requiring a good eye and plenty of patience. Earlier in the day he'd set the radio to RTR, his hands still vibrating with the grinder's impossible RPM, walking around the car shell while smoking a cigarette. Lee had a permanent corner of Gerry Tracker's mechanics workshop in Spearwood that he used when Gerry left at five, often welding, grinding and sanding through the night. It was good, meditative labour that took his mind off things, although dirty and hot under the bank of dusty fluoro lights. Every car presented a different set of problems, and every problem taught Lee a solution that he could employ next time. He had use of Gerry's hoist and welding tools, and if he got stuck with something, then Gerry was there in the morning, to cast an eye.

'It's down to bare steel. Very *Mad Max* – I like the look. Might put a few coats of clear on it and leave it that way.'

'Client go for that?'

'Hell, no. It's a stock restoration. But I can dream.'

'I trust your eye. Think that'd work on the FB?'

Firmin had a collection of old cars, stored in a Malaga warehouse that had more security than the Perth Mint. He was always threatening to throw some work Lee's way, but hadn't so far.

'The blue-and-white one? The one you want to chop down, section and hot-rod?'

'The one.'

Lee danced his head, a way of saying maybe. He didn't want to think about it now. He liked to work on one restoration project at a time, enjoying the way his mind threw out ideas at random moments. Every job demanded more than at first appeared. When he lifted off the Dodge shell a month ago, he'd discovered that the chassis was rusted through, and out of square. Some idiot had also fibre-glassed the floor pans, to disguise more rust. The Dodge looked good from the outside, but it would crumple like a paper bag on any kind of impact. It'd taken three weeks of cutting and welding supports and plate steel before the chassis and shell were any good. Fortunately, the client had deep pockets, and Lee was getting paid by the hour.

Firmin lit a cigarette, the polite conversation over. 'You're on the door with Rowdy Tim. Eight to two. I've already warned Rowdy, but when you see him, make sure he isn't carrying his revolver. I'm not sure how to do that – give him a hug or something.'

Both of them laughed. Rowdy Tim wasn't the hugging kind.

'You heard anything more on the street?' Lee asked, pretty sure the answer was no. The Hastie brothers were too smart to voice their intentions. The threat to storm the door and help themselves to a drink had been made to Firmin, and one or two other bar staff, just before closing last night, when the brothers felt humiliated at being asked to leave, even though the lights were off. They wanted a lock-in drink for old times' sake, which wasn't going to happen. Theirs was a childish threat, but even so the repercussions could be bad. If word got around that the door of Club Summertime could be rushed, or that the doormen weren't up to the job, then every hoon with a reputation would be lining up for a crack. Tonight was about saving face, and for that reason the cops couldn't be on standby, and neither could they stack the door with bouncers – it'd come across as weak.

The Hastie brothers understood the coercive power of violence.

Their MO was about escalation – doing what most people wouldn't do, so that a mere threat became effective in getting their way. The 'mad dog' was only one of the roles that the Hasties might have chosen, but having chosen it, they played it to the fullest.

Lee checked Rowdy Tim's gym bag on his way downstairs. The bag smelled of stale onions and mouldy socks, with the eye-watering fumes of Lynx rising through. The bag was heavy, and Lee located the weight. He found the revolver, an old .38 snub nose, inside a plastic lunchbox beneath a squashed vegemite and lettuce sandwich, a dented mandarin and a crushed KitKat – Rowdy Tim still lived at home with his mum. Lee opened the chamber of the revolver, thought about taking out the bullets, but decided against it.

The music battered at the heavy steel door separating the stairs from the floor of the club. As usual, tonight would be Nirvana, Pearl Jam, Beastie Boys, Pixies, Red Hot Chili Peppers and Guns N' Roses on high rotation. Lee opened the door and was hit by a wall of Billy Corgan – rising over the dancefloor singalong of what looked like a hens' night possie – just the kind of punters the Hastie brothers were hoping for. Lee nodded to the regulars and read the room as he moved through it, looking for body language that marked potential violence – the stiffness or exaggerated ease, the strange silence that accompanied predatory looks, or the sneer latched upon another. The Summertime clientele was mainly suburban kids on the tear, and the set-up was beer barn, despite the heavy cover-charge and nightclub lighting.

The place was almost at capacity, which was significant because of the Hastie brothers' threat. They'd want to cause the maximum chaos, create the most fear. The fact that doing so constituted, in the brothers' minds, the equivalent of a job interview, would be funny in any other context, except that Lee was on the door beside Rowdy Tim, who wasn't always reliable. The brothers had been away somewhere for the past year and wanted their doormen jobs back. If they could take the door, then it was, they hoped, a probable case of 'if you can't lick 'em, hire 'em'.

Lee exited the bunker-like entrance. Despite the heat he hefted his leather jacket and zipped it to his chin – the hide was a crude but effective stab-proof barrier. He wore his steel-caps and in his pocket carried a pair of knuckles, ready to be slipped on. He nodded to Rowdy Tim and looked up at the security camera, winking at Firmin, who would be watching.

2

Lisa sat in the park on a cement bench and smoked. The bench was strategically placed beneath a ye olde imitation gas lamp, whose electricity pumped a dull yellow light. The Northbridge park had been a gay beat for more than a hundred years, and the lights did little more than illuminate pools of grass and paving, threaded with dive-bombing insects. The Moreton Bay fig trees behind her were large and shadowy – there were plenty of places to hide.

Lisa watched the man. His Landcruiser stood out because of the way that it was parked. Most people parked their cars closest to the lights to discourage the attention of street kids, but the Toyota had chosen a darkened corner when there were plenty of other spaces available. This was the first thing that she noticed. The second was that in the twenty minutes she'd been watching, nobody had exited the car. Four times now the front seat had been illuminated when the man lit a cigarette. She saw him then, middle-aged and large, the windows closed despite the heat. When a patrol car swept the block, coming at him from behind, she watched the man sink deeper into his seat. The minutes passed, but he didn't climb out. For a few seconds he switched on the overhead light and dipped his head and moved his arms over something – a bag, perhaps?

Lisa looked at her watch. It was two minutes before ten. She had a feeling that the time was significant and was proved correct when at ten o'clock the man exited the car, carrying what looked like a sawn-off rifle that he slipped beneath his donkey jacket. He stood in the shadows and patted himself down, examining his silhouette against the faint light. He was tall and blond and wore his hair long. He had a thin face and a strong nose, but it was hard to get a clearer picture. He hadn't noticed Lisa, one among many within the borders of the park.

The man moved toward the club. At the edge of the park he crossed the road and entered the wash of streetlight, reaching the steps leading to the club door, waiting as a group of young women in jeans and cowboy boots, all baggy singlets and bangles down their arms, drunkenly made their exit. One staggered and braced herself on the giant doorman, who righted her and smiled, before turning her toward the street. The long-haired man now climbed the stairs. Lisa was too far away to tell if any words were exchanged with the doormen, but the man certainly ducked his head in a nod before entering the gloom behind, where he would pay his money to the booth-jockey and get his wrist stamped.

Lisa didn't know what the man was planning, and she didn't care. She was off-duty tonight, having worked the twelve-to-eight shift before changing out of her uniform into street clothes. It would be easy to get a message to a patrol car and have them stationed outside the club, but that would ruin the fun.

She wasn't there to make arrests or improve Northbridge's reputation. She wasn't there to add to some sergeant's arrest statistics either, although that would be the smart move, given her low rank.

Lisa was enjoying watching the younger doorman, who sat

relaxed on the railing beside the entrance, smoking and chatting with the other bouncer, who looked stiff and worried, checking his watch every couple of minutes. The young doorman wore a leather jacket, jeans and boots, where the bulkier man wore a uniform of sorts – black trousers and a matching polo shirt emblazoned with the words 'security' in white letters, together with fat, clumsy shoes. His trousers were too short in the leg, or the cuffs were rolled too high, revealing white socks that even from a distance didn't match.

Lisa watched the young doorman light another cigarette. In the unguarded moments between responses to the other man, he looked coolly down the street and across the park. Each time he did so he clocked Lisa, who didn't look away.

3

'Well, it's not gonna get any more broken between now and when I present at the hospital. Play the tape again.'

Firmin's fractured wrist was swelling fast. With his other hand he necked a shot of Tullamore Dew, making sure the whiskey didn't touch his mangled lip and broken teeth. One of his eyes was closed under a black welt. The split over his eyebrow where he'd been struck with the rifle butt was going to require stitches, although it'd stopped bleeding due to a self-administered splodge of vaseline.

The computer screen boxed six camera shots, none of them live. Lee had gone through the recordings to capture images of the man who'd raided Firmin's office when things kicked off outside – the same time that Lee and Rowdy Tim were occupied with the Hastie brothers. Firmin, the only other person who'd seen the man up close, sat with his one good eye near to the screen as the cameras panned across the dancefloor and horseshoe bar, the booths set around the walls and the stage in the corner, until he recognised the man and stopped the recording.

Lee pressed play on the clearest recording of the entrance. They watched as the man in the donkey jacket entered, Lee freezing the frame on his face and zooming in. Lee pressed a button and took a screen grab of the image, then saved it to the desktop. Lee, Firmin, Rowdy Tim and the head bartender, Michelle – an ex-stripper who knew everybody in the scene that produced armed robbers – watched the footage of the man entering the stairwell, opening his jacket and withdrawing the sawn-off rifle before leaving the camera frame, where the footage stopped. Just as he stepped out of frame, the man with the long hair had looked up at the camera and winked, pursed his lips in a kiss.

'Anyone?' Firmin asked.

Nobody said yes. Lee, like the others, didn't recognise the assailant who'd bashed Firmin until he opened the safe, scooping out Friday's takings and whatever else Firmin kept in there.

'I want to see him leave again.'

Firmin had been unconscious at the time. Lee fast-forwarded the entrance recording until the arrival of the Hastie brothers, then pressed pause. The time on the stairwell recording and the entrance recording were in sync. The robbery was planned around the Hastie's arrival, to the second.

Lee pressed play and the two recordings continued alongside one another. Don Hastie, the older of the brothers, a short man with greying hair and large hands clenched around a pickaxe handle, and his brother, Todd, whacking a tyre iron into the palm of his spare hand, stood at the foot of the entrance stairs. Lee had watched them emerge from the park and whistled to Rowdy. Lee then shut the door behind him, made sure he heard it latch. The street was empty. At the foot of the stairs, Don Hastie started with his slagging off of Rowdy, calling him a traitor, a dog, a company man, a mummy's boy. It was a ruse to draw Rowdy down the stairs and onto the street, but Rowdy kept to the plan. Lee watched himself brace for the charge up the stairs, but Don stared coolly while he berated Rowdy. Lee wasn't known to either man, and he assumed that the brothers were trying to get a measure of him, wear him down before the fun began. Because neither man was carrying a blade, Lee slipped into his knuckles and shrugged off this jacket. He cracked his neck and waited. Don Hastie took the first step, sneering up at them. Lee felt Rowdy flinch and moved to cover him. Todd Hastie tossed his tyre iron from hand to hand, pretended to throw it, making Rowdy duck and the two brothers laugh. Don Hastie took another step, looking solely at Lee now, and then another step. Soon, he'd be within swinging range. Lee moved into a kicking stance, his arms loose by his sides. He was trained for this, and the adrenalin that coursed his veins was controlled and constant, not interfering with his breathing, or his heartbeat. He heard Rowdy panting beside him, beginning to crack, calling the brothers on, to get it over with.

Their reluctance to rush the door was odd, but Lee put it down to a desire to maximise fear, a display of gamesmanship.

And then the door opened behind them, and a man pushed through. Surprisingly, Don Hastie didn't take advantage of the distraction and instead moved away to let him pass. Lee paid the departing man little attention, instead focussed on Don's hands, the dilated pupils in his reddened eyes, his smirking mouth.

'There … see?' Lee said.

Lee froze the frame on Don's face, then pressed slow-motion, each of them watching the little nod of recognition as the man left the steps, moved away toward the park, carrying a leather bag. The nod was merely confirmation of what they already knew, that the antics at the door were a distraction to enable the robbery, the real game and payback. After all, when confronted by the armed man, Firmin had acquiesced, as experience had taught him to do – it's never worth dying over money. The beating that followed was sustained and unnecessary. It was personal.

'What now?' Lee asked. 'You need to get that wrist looked at.'

Firmin nodded, lifted his broken forearm, which had ballooned to double its regular size, blackening around the wrist.

Firmin had drawn a blank in looking for the Hastie brothers prior to the robbery. The regular way to see off their kind was to send some bat-wielding boys to their home, persuade them of the error of their ways, or have a friendly copper plant something in their car, pull them over when they moved.

They were likely camped somewhere in the bush, or were staying out in one of the satellite towns that ringed the city. As for the man who'd bashed Firmin and then cleaned out the safe, he was a stranger, almost certainly from interstate.

'First thing tomorrow, Michelle, call my person at the city council, see if one of their CCTV cameras picked up anything. Lee – while I head to the doc's, please save some stills from that footage onto a floppy. Insurance is going to need them, as are the coppers.'

Lee began the process, having caught the wistfulness in Firmin's words. There were things in that safe that he could claim on, and things that he probably couldn't. It was the latter items that would be most valuable.

The others trooped out the door. Michelle was tasked with

making calls downstairs to see if there was anything on the street, enticing her contacts and friends with the offer of a reward. Rowdy Tim was going to take Firmin to Royal Perth Hospital. Lee was going to lock up. It'd been a long night, but at least he'd avoided getting into it with the Hastie brothers, even if they had the last laugh.

Lee saved the images onto the floppies and put them in separate manila envelopes. Officially, Firmin should have called the coppers as soon as it happened, but he had his contacts, and they would take a look tomorrow. Besides, the man had worn gloves, and Michelle hadn't recognised him, which meant that the coppers weren't going to be much help, beyond authorising the insurance company paperwork with a police report.

Downstairs, the emptied club was silent. Lee went behind the bar and opened the cupboard beneath the till where Firmin kept the good stuff. Lee had developed a taste for Lagavulin, and he poured himself a triple. Like Firmin had taught him, Lee took up a few beads of water in a glass dropper and laid them on top of the whisky. He took the glass and went round the bar, planted himself on a stool in front of the tumbler. The till said it was three in the morning. He lit a cigarette and took a mouthful of the peaty and something-else tasting liquor, unable to decide on an iodine or mushroom or oily-fish flavour, or whether its vapours just reminded him of the ocean. Either way, he savoured the mouthful before taking a drag of his cigarette. It was too late to get back to the mechanics workshop and make a start on the Dodge's bodywork. By the time he got there and prepared the bog, it'd be morning, when he'd be too tired to concentrate properly.

There was a rapping on the door, loud and harsh. Metal on glass, and Lee turned on his stool and half-expected to see the Hastie brothers, but behind the tinted and shatterproof windows was a young woman, using the rings on her left hand to hit the glass and get his attention.

Lee pointed to his imaginary watch and shook his head, but he remembered her – it was the woman in the park. He remembered her because it was dangerous for her to be sitting there under a sickly light, although she hadn't given off the potential-victim vibe, then or now.

Lee watched her, watching him approach the door. There was always a chance, of course, that she was a spotter for the Hasties, or the man who'd bashed Firmin. She didn't look nervous, holding his eye. She was dressed in jeans, boots and a green woollen jacket, fitted to shape. It was only when Lee looked past her to the street that the woman smiled and rolled her eyes.

He locked the door behind her, led her to the bar. He nodded to the taps and she smiled for the second time.

'Sure,' she said. 'I could go a dram of what you're having.'

Lee nodded, went through the ritual with the glass, the whisky and the dropper of water. He passed it to her. 'So, I guess you saw something?'

'You got a pen?'

She was a few years older than him, perhaps, and he watched as she scrawled a licence number on the back of a Cooper's beer coaster. She had blonde hair cut short and dark-blue eyes. Her cheekbones were high and her lips were full and pale. She was beautiful without trying, he decided, because there was character in her eyes. They were warm and intelligent, so unlike the jaded eyes of the models allowed to drink *gratis* in the club, which were no longer eyes but traffic lights, understandably set to red or amber.

She passed him the beer coaster. On it was written the make and year, and the licence number.

'Thanks,' Lee said.

'This is excellent whisky.' She toasted him with a mischievous smile, her voice husky and clipped. She kept her arm raised until he touched glasses. She was thin but moved with an athlete's poise, nodding toward Lee's packet of Stuyvesants. 'Sure, help yourself.'

She waited a beat for him to light her cigarette, but when he didn't, smiled and put fire to it herself. 'Yes, I saw everything. There was only one of them. Nobody else in the car. And yes, I can come back tomorrow to speak to your manager.'

Lee watched her with a new interest. No mention of going to the cops, as though she understood that Firmin would prefer to handle the recovery himself.

'There might be a few dollars in it, as finder's fee,' he said, which made her laugh.

'I don't want any blood money.' She met Lee's eyes then, and held them. 'But I'll take another Scotch. And in the meantime, if you want to thank me, go ahead and tell me about yourself.'

She was very good. Hers was a routine of sorts, but he felt it hard, knowing for certain that she had him.

4

There was a note waiting for Lee Southern on the dusty table inside the door of Gerry's mechanics workshop. Gerry had left town for a while, to visit his son in Leonora, a nine-hour drive across the wheatbelt and then desert roads. Gerry was doing it more and more often, feeling the pull of his son's family in the remote community. He hadn't talked about moving there, but it was on the cards. Gerry was an ex-pug and repeat prisoner who'd worked hard all his life. He owned his own home, a fibro shack in Hilton, and several vintage cars and trucks that were worth a lot of money, seeing them as safer investments than stocks and bonds.

The note asked Lee to finish some of the service and repair jobs in the workshop, and to keep the money. He could also, if someone turned up with an older car that needed looking at, take on the work and keep the payments, but only if he wanted to.

As another sign that he was perhaps edging out the door, Gerry hadn't adapted to the technological changes of recent years. He was strictly a carburettor-era man, who wanted nothing to do with fuel injection systems or computer run vehicles. That suited Lee fine because he felt the same way. He winched up the roller door and cast his eyes over the Rover, Ford Fairlane and Holden Torana that were parked beside the pit and hoist. Affixed to each was a sticky note describing what needed to be done, what parts had been ordered and the price that had been agreed on. The Rover was a straight-up service, the Fairlane needed a new clutch and the Torana was missing at idle – could be fuel, or it could be electrics, neither of which seemed too problematic.

Gerry's note also asked Lee to check in on Frank Swann, and see if he needed help running the boxing gym they'd set up nearly a decade ago, principally to keep local kids out of trouble. That was something Lee was already involved in, and he was usually happy to run the evening classes.

The sun was setting over Manning Ridge. Lee turned on all the lights and went to the Dodge and pulled off the canvas sheet that protected it from dust. He ran his hands over the bare steel fender, checking for oxidation. He could feel ripples and divots in the steel that weren't visible to the naked eye. He checked the angle-grinder blade and rested it on the fender. Back at the door, Lee sat on an old plastic chair and smoked a little weed, watching the sun sink over the valley. The wind dropped and the world went eerily still, the stippled reds reaching from the ocean through the Norfolk Island pines and tin roofs, sinking into the shadowed streets.

As always happened when he smoked, Lee felt a moment of panic as his senses sharpened. It was a feeling that he understood, and although he didn't enjoy it, Lee used the drift into paranoid thinking to examine his current situation, as his father had taught him, and to assess it for risk. His father had always followed the 'just because I'm paranoid don't mean people aren't out to get me' mantra, and Lee thought about the most recent job he'd completed for Frank Swann, and how his worry might relate to the violent threats made against him a month ago. It was a lonely feeling knowing that there were men in the world who wanted to kill him, aware that the coppers couldn't help until a crime had been committed. This was something that the recent job had crystalised in a way that Lee knew would disturb him forever.

On paper it'd looked a simple enough task – fly to Port Hedland and while an abusive husband was on shift at the port, escort a mother and her son to the airport, then board with them on the flight to Perth, then make sure they got on a plane to Melbourne without being observed. Given the abuse that Lee's mother had suffered at the hands of his father, he was immediately invested in the task, but hadn't expected to become so overwhelmed with murderous feelings of his own. The woman's name was Marie, and her son, Troy, was three years old. Her parents were the client, paying for the flights and Lee's time, but they'd undersold the danger Marie was in. Not only were the signs of her abuse written upon her in bruises and burns, but she was nearly mute with terror at the thought that her husband might return and catch her running away, as he'd done twice previously. He was known to be armed, and had done time for manslaughter, and Lee came prepared, staying in a nearby motel and communicating with Marie via messages thrown over her back fence, taped to a rock. She was essentially a prisoner in her own home. Her husband collected the mail at a PO box, and their phone had been disconnected. She was locked inside the house when he left for work, and only had access to a back porch which was enclosed with cyclone fencing. That first time, Lee had watched her unfold the note and read it, nodding to him while she burned the message. The next day he returned and kicked in the front door. She was ready with a packed bag, concealed in a nearby cupboard. She was worried about neighbours calling her husband, and so they hurried to the hire car parked on the street. Instead of heading directly to the airport, they'd driven to Karratha, the nearest town six hours away, and taken a flight from there. Marie had dosed the boy with Phenergan, to sedate him on the flight, but it backfired when he became agitated and then hyper, jumping and crawling and screaming for the five hours on the plane and then through the two-hour layover at Perth airport, even as Marie sat silently crying. It was only when Lee put her on the flight to Melbourne, under an assumed name, that he saw the first glimmer of hope in her eyes. The boy was still wild with energy, but he'd sensed something in her, and quieted, took her hand and boarded the plane.

Lee wasn't a drinker, but that night he got drunk. He knew that the husband would target Marie's family, and he wasn't wrong. A call from Frank Swann confirmed it – the man was already on a plane to the city. He had a description of Lee from one of the neighbours, assuming him to be a rival, a confirmation of his mad jealous fantasies. The parents were safely in the country for the next months, but they would never be safe. Lee had thought about staking out their house for when the man arrived, knowing what his father would do if a confrontation occurred, aware that his father would read the situation and conclude that the chances were strong that one day the man would force the parents to give Lee's name, knowing what that would mean. Lee would then lose the only advantage he had, that of surprise, and the man would hunt him and get him when his head was turned. But Lee hadn't gone and staked the house. Instead, he called Frank Swann, whose counsel was always wise. Swann lived eternally ready for such men, and if Lee wanted into the same line of work, then he'd have to learn to live ready too.

A gust of wind caught a loose corrugated sheet in the fence-line down the alley, banging loudly. It was a regular sound and one that Lee normally tuned out, but this time it made him flinch. He coolly examined his reaction, picturing the man hiding in the shadows and waiting for him, but laughed to himself, stood and shook it off, turning toward the brightly lit workshop where the welcome hours of labour awaited him.

5

Lee stripped to his jeans and boots and turned on the angle grinder at the wall. He put on a pair of protective glasses and leant into his work. With the edge of the blade, he ground off the last traces of paint from the rear panel, watching the sparks sleeve his arms only to spin and die midair. It was hot in the workshop, and it felt good to sweat out the remnants of his nerves but also last night's booze. By the time Lee and the woman had left the club it was dawn, a garbage truck clanking down the alleys and hefting skip bins full of bottles. Outside on the street, the air smelt of tarmac after summer rain, dusty and musty; and the sprinklers in the park ticked perfect circles of bore water over the grass and paths. There was no need for either Lee or the woman to invite the other home; they'd had their fun on a booth table and bench seat, and then again at the bar. Lee had learned that the woman was a rookie cop, which explained her confidence and matter-of-fact speech, but it wasn't until they were saying goodbye that he realised he didn't know her name. She laughed when he asked, then asked for his own. They kissed and parted ways. There was no need to exchange numbers. She knew where he worked.

Lee wasn't going to be at Club Summertime when she returned to tell Firmin the details of the man who'd robbed the club, and neither did he ask why, as a copper, she wasn't taking the information to her station. If he ever met her again, he might ask, but last night hadn't been the occasion for looking behind the surface of things, for breaking the spell of being a stranger, with another stranger.

He turned off the grinder and walked the length of the car with the hook-light close to the buffed and scalloped raw steel. He went over to the tables where the bonnet and boot, and the four doors, and bumpers were laid. Each looked as clean as could be. He removed the bumpers and took them to the front of the shop so that he wouldn't forget them. Later on, he'd take them to another workshop where they'd be getting re-chromed.

He had to work quickly now, before the Dodge began to oxidise. In a large bucket he mixed up a slurry of bog. Its pink colour and smell of heated silicone told him when it was ready. He scraped the filler onto a sheet of plywood and starting with the doors, bonnet and boot, began to spread it on with a soft plasterer's trowel, as Gerry had taught him. He worked fast and clean, switching to a rubber silk-screening squeegee to thin the bog without drawing it from the divots and scratches. He then did the same with the car shell, getting the layer as thin as possible in the knowledge that the next stage involved hours of painstaking sanding, with finer and finer grits. He finished and stood back from his work, wiping the sweat from his face and forearms. At the shop door he smoked a cigarette and waited for the bog to dry.

While he waited, Lee put on the radio to RTR, switching from Gerry's favoured 6IX, with its '60s and '70s hits. It was now midnight and one of Lee's favourite programs was coming on air, a blues roots and rockabilly set spun by a volunteer deejay whose name Lee never learned, because he didn't talk much and instead let the music play. The set started with a Charlie Patton number, as it always did, the raw and spooky vocals building over his distinctive picking and guitar-drumming style.

Lee put the Rover over the pit and drained the engine oil, which was black and thin. He ran his finger inside the sump to see if there were any metal shavings, then climbed out of the pit and did the basics in the engine bay – checking the points, plugs, belts, filters and water. When that was finished, he went and had a listen to the Torana at idle. It missed and sounded lumpy, but didn't stall, and he had a good idea what was wrong. Taking off the distributor cap he shone the lamp onto the points, pulling on the fan belt until the points were at their widest. He slipped in a spacer and observed the extra width, then cleaned the points with a strip of sandpaper. Using a flathead screwdriver, he loosened the point screws until the spacer was tight against the twin contacts, then refixed the small screw. He put the distributor cap back on and turned the engine over – she now ran fine. The work had only taken him five minutes, and he wouldn't be charging for the labour, even though he expected better of a Torana owner, handing such a basic diagnostic routine to another. Most men and women Lee knew from the Holden's era were familiar with the basics of car maintenance.

The Fairlane would require more time, but that was something Lee had plenty of. He didn't need to sleep more than four or five hours at a time, and he rarely slept during the night. He wheeled over the engine hoist, hung up the lamp inside the Ford's bonnet and began the process of disconnecting the engine from the shell and electrics. He jacked the front end onto four low chocks, then got underneath the engine with canvas slings that he attached to the hoist. The radio was playing Screamin' Jay Hawkins, which was fine by Lee. He hummed along while he pulled the engine off the transmission, just a few inches, but enough to get the clutch plate out and replace it with the parts that Gerry had ordered.

By the time Lee was finished with the three vehicles, the body filler on the Dodge had dried. He smoked a cigarette and cracked his neck, loosened his shoulders. He put on a dust mask and got to work, using a long brick of heavy grit to take off the top layer of bog on the doors, boot and bonnet. It was slow and repetitive work, but he didn't mind. The radio turned through a three-hour program of psychedelic '60s rock before blending into the morning program. Lee was tired now, and he barely noticed the light outside until the dawn chorus of wattlebirds, honeyeaters and magpies began to rise from the valley. By now he'd moved to the finest grit, and when that was done, he went over the lot with a buffing pad on a circular sander until the car shone. He paused only to smoke a cigarette before putting the Dodge in neutral and wheeling her out into the morning sunshine. He carried out and laid down the doors and bonnet, then walked around the lot, looking at everything from different angles. Only in full sunshine could he ascertain if the body work was true, and he got down on his knees and used his thumb to sight along the flanks. Everything looked good, and he put the Dodge body and parts back inside the workshop, ready for priming and painting, most likely the following night. He was too tired now to manage another few hours of precision work. He wrapped the car in plastic and canvas, turned off the shop radio and scrolled down the roller door, kicking the lock into place. He put on his shirt and washed his face and hands in the shop sink, using a towel to get at the oil and grime around his fingernails. He stretched his sore back and yawned, pleased at the work he'd accomplished, satisfied in the knowledge that now at least he'd be able to sleep, if only until midday.

6

Lee could tell there was no love between Frank Swann and the other man seated beside him, elbowing himself forward. Swann rolled his eyes but made no comment.

The man was small and tanned, with dyed-black hair. As with most people, one of his eyes was smaller than the other, and yet the difference was pronounced due to his dabbing at it with a finger, stretching the skin which fell immediately back into place. The hooding of his smaller eye gave it an expression of raptor watchfulness, while the other was as wide and unblinking as a nocturnal animal, despite the fierce sun overhead.

Water slapped against the hull of the launch, called *Current-Sea*, a reference to the man's status as a corporate accountant during the WA Inc years, perhaps, or his then transition into real estate development. The way Paul Enright told it, moored out in Melville Water, the river empty in every direction, he'd been cleaned out by the collapse of the Conlans' bank in the '80s, but had clawed his way back. He was on the *BRW* rich list, coming in at number seven in the state, and the trajectory was up. There was no embarrassment in his gravelly voice when he told Swann and Lee, apropos of nothing, that his Peppermint Grove house was recently on the cover of *Home & Garden*, as an exemplar of taste and luxury. Lee put the boasting down to the regular wankery of a small-city tycoon, with an added dose of short-man syndrome, and was grateful that he wasn't trying to charm them.

'Do I refer to you as Paul or Mr Enright?' Lee asked the man to cut him short, and it worked. A little bolt of anger hardened in his eyes, seeping across his face despite the smile.

'Want me to spell it for you, young fella? Enright. E.N.R.I.G.H.T … Paul. But like I said, you can call me Darth Vader for all I care. I'm telling you this for a reason. It can't be a coincidence that the bastards are coming at me now. I'm not too proud to say I've been a bankrupt, and not that long ago. But that fucking *BRW* listing, no more under the radar for me.'

Enright turned to Swann, who didn't try to hide the amusement in his eyes. 'Swann … Frank? Tell me why this kid is here again?'

Swann cleared his throat. 'That's simple, Dark Lord. He's my employee, when it suits him, and maybe he can help you, because I can't.'

'Can't, or won't Frank? I know we've had our—'

'You mean the time you and Mastic tried to have me killed?'

Enright blinked, looked down at his hands. 'Water under the bridge, Frank. What can I say? It was the eighties. I've already apologised.'

'Not in so many words.'

Lee watched Swann's face. Clearly, his employer was enjoying Enright's discomfort. Lee was aware of Swann's history with men like Enright, told to him by Gerry Tracker in bits and pieces, even if he didn't know the specifics.

'Talk is cheap, Frank. Deeds are what counts. I specifically came to you with this—'

'But you still haven't told us why we're here,' Swann said, 'sitting in the middle of the river, basking in the sunshine of your wealth and power.'

Enright gave Swann a sharp, resentful look. 'The others of your kind. I can't trust them with this. This needs to be kept in the strictest confidence. Most of your colleagues either work for, or have worked for, my rivals. Most have gone corporate. I might dislike you. I might have been an enemy, once. But beyond all that, or maybe because of all that, I know what kind of man you are. I know that I can trust you.'

A pied cormorant landed on the back deck, shivered its wings and sluiced a torrent of shit across the railings and deck carpet, before spreading its wings to dry. Enright looked on in horror, made to move but restrained himself.

'There's a life lesson for you, son. Keep moving, or you get shat on.' Enright laughed, but alone.

'Go ahead then,' Lee said, 'tell us what the problem is.'

Enright leaned forward, as though they were in a crowded bar and not the middle of the river, where the only eavesdropper was the sunbathing shag, which he glanced at constantly.

'Well, it's got nothing to do with my business. I've got people to take care of my business matters. This is personal. Couldn't *get* more personal. How old are you, son?'

'I'm twenty-three.'

Lee knew what that sounded like. He wasn't about to tell Enright his personal stories, or how he'd grown up faster than most.

Swann had obviously caught something in Lee's face. He pushed forward the ashtray. 'You don't need to know the whys and wherefores, Enright, except to say that Lee has more skills and experience than most men twice his age. I'm training Lee to take over my business.'

Enright grunted but nodded. 'You trust him, Frank, that's all I need to know.'

'I do trust him, Enright. It's also up to him whether he wants to work with you. I'm only here because of your daughter. Not her fault you're her father. My own daughter speaks highly of her.'

Swann hadn't told Lee much on the drive through Fremantle down to the Royal Freshwater Bay Yacht Club, except that he was introducing Lee to a potential client, and that the client's daughter, who had once been friends with his daughter Louise, was in trouble. Rather than describing the job at hand, Swann wanted Lee to make his decision based on first impressions. The job wasn't straightforward, and would likely take some time to complete, time that Swann didn't have at the moment. Another reason Swann couldn't take the job was because his face was too well known among the men of their generation, although Swann hadn't elaborated, changing through the gears of his old Brougham as they wound their way down the switchbacks toward the river, where kids and black swans paddled in the amber shallows. Lee had only caught a few hours sleep before he'd awoken to a call from Swann, saying he was outside in the street. Lee had time to slip into a pair of old Levis and a Bonds t-shirt, putting on his boots without socks, necking a glass of water before heading out into the day.

Enright put his hands on the table, and clasped them, a gesture at odds with his blokey swagger. He looked Lee straight in the eye and didn't blink. 'Frank here knows the first part of the story, but I'll recap for your benefit. I have two daughters, who I brought up on my own. My wife died in a skiing accident in France when they were little. Fifteen years ago, one of my daughters was kidnapped. It was big news at the time. They had her for three weeks. Against the wishes of the police, the ransom was paid, and we got her back – the happiest day of my life. She was traumatised and we got her counselling. She got better for a while, and then she got worse. When she was twelve, she ran away. I had men … men like you … track her down. We got her back a second time, but she didn't stay long. She took off again, and this time she'd planned for it. She took money. I knew she was over East because every few months she wired me, and asked for more. Said if I sent men after her again, I'd lose her forever …'

Enright hadn't been breathing through his words. His hands were no longer clasped but gripped tight. He paused for breath, and swallowed.

'You said your wife was dead,' Lee said. 'But you kept saying "we" throughout all that.'

Enright speared Lee with a dirty look. 'We … is me and my other daughter, Felicity. Frank's daughter's friend. May I continue?'

'Of course.'

'It's not what you're thinking. It's not … Jessica. I mean, it's not that she's gone missing. She still takes my money. Five years ago, I sent her a credit card. I top it up every month. She charges the usual things. Shops in Melbourne. I've kept to my word. I haven't gone looking for her. She's a grown woman now. Twenty-three, like you. But …'

'But?'

'Since that fucking *BRW* listing. There are photographs. Of my daughter. When she was imprisoned in the rathole they held her in. With the animals who took her. Do I need to spell it out?!'

Enright's face was full of blood. His fists were clenched. Now Lee understood why they were out on the river.

'No, Mr Enright. Not yet. But you will, if I agree to take this on. You want me to recover the images, correct?'

Enright still wasn't capable of speech. Swann leaned forward. 'Yes, that's the job, Lee. But it isn't straightforward. I've seen the letter that was sent with a photocopy of a photo, what looks like a polaroid image. It doesn't sound like it's the kidnappers who're back in the picture. It might be them, but it doesn't sound like it. Enright, get Lee the letter.'

Enright shuffled along the bench seat and went inside the cabin, rummaging in a shoulder bag.

'Does the daughter ... Jessica ... know about the photographs?' Lee asked Swann, who had time to shake his head before Enright returned, smoothing out a sheet of A4, on which were letters taken from newspaper headlines.

Lee put the paper on the galley table and began to read. The capital and lower case letters were neatly formed. The message was short, and nothing like he'd expected. At the bottom of the photocopied letter was a photo, grainy and faded. Lee held the letter toward the light but that didn't help. The photo depicted a naked child, from the back, that much was clear – the contrast between the overexposed white skin and the black shadows fore-grounded her, the only points of difference the slightly darker ponytail of hair and a thick bangle on her forearm. Her face was hidden, and so fortunately was the rest of her.

'It's definitely Jessica?'

Enright nodded. 'The ponytail, the length and colour of her hair, and the jade bangle on her arm. The antique bangle is distinctive, you can see it's too large for her. It was her mother's. She insisted on wearing it. Both of my daughters wore one.'

'It was valuable?'

'Extremely valuable. Tang dynasty. We bought them in Shanghai and had them authenticated.'

'But the kidnappers didn't know that?'

'They never made mention of it, no.'

'And it was returned with Jessica?'

'It was.'

Lee read the ransom demand once again. 'So that we're clear,' he said, 'this person isn't claiming that they'll return the images themselves. Upon the deposit of the amount mentioned, they'll provide the address of one of the people in possession of either this image, or other images. And you want me to retrieve it, or them, from that person?'

'Yes, that's about the shape of it.'

'Why not pay the amount, and then call the police in to raid the house?'

'You know why.'

Lee acknowledged the point. 'Yes, but I want to hear you say it. So that we're clear on the strategy.'

'Because it's explicit in the letter that this person isn't the only person holding an image. Assuming these people are in contact, a raid on one will alert the others. The images will be hidden.'

'The letter says that there are five images, with five different men. So I'm retrieving images from these men, not knowing yet who they are, and then I'm leaving them be, until, I assume, all of the images have been collected. And then?'

It was a fair question to ask, and Enright was ready for it. Without the evidence in their possession, it would be useless to call in the police, unless other images of children were found.

'I'll have to wait and see.'

Enright's tone was neutral, looking down at the polaroid of his daughter. Lee couldn't imagine. The picture was of such poor quality that the only kind of man who would keep such an image was a perpetrator – a man present when the image was taken. The kind of man for whom the recollection of his experience, triggered by the image, however poor in quality, was enough.

'So I take it that you'll pay the amount and wait for further instructions?'

The amount wasn't much – twenty thousand dollars, unless it was just a lure. Once Enright started to pay, Lee had to assume, the amount would increase. As well, the instruction to wire the money to an offshore account in the Cayman Islands suggested a degree of financial acumen beyond the scope of the usual wannabe.

It was just a glance from Enright across the open water, but it was a tell of some sort. Lee took a gamble. 'You're an accountant. Tell me about this bank.'

Enright grunted, looked angrily at Swann. 'Frank, you sure the kid's up to the job? That's a question tells me he isn't. He could've waited, asked you.'

'That's not correct,' Swann answered. 'Because that isn't what annoys you about the question.'

Enright looked at them both, fixed a glare on Lee. 'It was the tone. It's what was behind the question. I don't want any of that bullshit. I've got enough to worry about—'

Lee put up two hands. 'Mr Enright. If I accept this job, it means I'm happy enough to take your money. I take your money, I'm working for you. You alone.'

That seemed to please Enright. 'Alright then. That's good. Let's leave it at that.'

Lee shook his head. 'No, because you haven't answered the question. So I'll ask it again. Do you know that bank?'

'Jesus fucking Christ,' Enright groaned, before smiling. 'Bulls and china shops. Frank, I don't know where you got this kid from, but I think I like him.' Enright laughed, but Lee didn't say anything, waiting for Enright to go cold again. It didn't take long – the glare returned, he sat forward. 'Yes, I know the bank. From the old days, you understand.'

Lee sat back to avoid Enright's breath. 'So I can assume that you've made inquiries?'

'Yes.'

'And?'

'Nothing. Nothing yet.'

'Alright. Then I'm good. I get paid cash, at an hourly rate that began when I climbed aboard your launch today.'

'Fair enough.'

Lee pulled out his notebook. 'On the way back to the yacht club, I want you to answer my questions about the kidnapping.

I'm assuming that with your ... access ... you'll have all the police and forensic reports. And I'd like to speak to your other daughter, Felicity.'

'Yes to all that, except speaking to Fi. She was just a child. She doesn't know anything that my head of security, Ron Bamber, wouldn't know. She doesn't know about the picture. And I don't want her to know.'

Enright stood, put out a hand. Lee shook it, then watched him step across the galley and climb stiffly up the ladder. Lee nodded to Swann, who shook his head. 'Think I'll watch the sights from back here. You go up.'

On the bridge, Lee heard the key turn and the inboards roar to life. It was the privilege of the ultra-rich, he supposed, to have toys that worked every time, even if those toys spent their lives in the cupboard. If Lee owned a boat like Enright's, he'd want to live on it. He felt her go into gear as the powerful twin engines whined then surged the heavy vessel forward.

7

Lee turned on the radio, still set to RTR. Outside the workshop, the sun was heading for the ocean. Within minutes it would be painting the sky magenta, orange, purple and pink, drawing its warm glow from the valley, replacing it with shadows that chased one another to the west. Lee smoked a small thin joint and leaned back in his chair, waited for the anxiety to seep into him, pondering Swann's news that the man whose wife Lee had helped escape was still in the city, still looking for her. Swann had a friend at the airport with access to flight manifests, and the man hadn't booked to return to Port Hedland anytime soon. Swann was keeping an eye on him, in regular contact with Marie's parents, advising them to stay out in the country. The good news was that Marie had set herself up in Melbourne, and found day care for Troy, and that she was feeling better for the first time in years.

Lee pinched off the end of the joint, dropped it to the ground. If Marie had the strength to start again despite her trauma, and the anxiety of looking over her shoulder for the rest of her life, then by comparison he had very little to worry about.

The radio was playing a set of local bands, all post-punk and indie rock, and Lee turned up the volume and got to work. He needed to finish the priming and painting of the Dodge before tomorrow, when he'd decided to start on Enright's material in earnest, having set up a meeting with his head of security. It would be another long and sleepless night, but that was ok by Lee. He didn't have any responsibilities or any kind of calendar to clear. All he had to do was let Firmin know that he'd be unavailable to work on the door for the next while. He'd also be missing some of the university subjects he'd been informally taking, sitting in on lectures in some of the subject areas that he felt he needed a background in. Frank Swann had been training him up over the past years, but there were gaps in Lee's knowledge. Before Swann went out on his own as a citizen investigator, he had had twenty years in the force to draw upon, including being a detective in different crime squads. Swann had made his money over the past decade recovering assets for people ripped off in stockmarket scams, for a commission. Lee didn't have the Fraud Squad background that Swann did. He didn't understand how the financial systems worked, how companies tracked and reported earnings, how tax might be monitored and minimised. Lee sat in on Commerce Faculty lectures across a range of subjects. When a lecture wasn't enough, he bought a textbook, and when a textbook wasn't enough, he pretended to be an enrolled student and participated in class tutorials, just so that he could ask questions. Lee did this by finding out the names of the tutors and the times of their classes. He would turn up at one tutorial and say that he normally attended another tutorial that he couldn't make that week. Nobody ever bothered to check or to question him, as he slowly built up a store of knowledge in basic accounting, taxation and company management, as well as sitting in on psychology and criminology classes. Acting on Frank Swann's advice, he'd also started attending some first-year computer programming classes to get a basic idea of coding, and of how digital communication and the internet worked, something that was going to become important to their line of work in the future.

With the key stored in Gerry Tracker's office, Lee opened the shared door between Gerry's workshop and Tony Romano's body and paint shop next door. By arrangement, Tony let Lee use his painting tools for a discounted price, as long as Lee did the appropriate clean-up. Lee carried the heavy Dodge doors, boot and bonnet into Tony's shop, whose breeze-block walls were misted with paints that had carried in the confined space over the years. Lee hung the parts on the steel hooks in the main body of the shop, before scrolling up the roller-door that led to the alley. Next door, he put the Dodge in neutral and wheeled it out into the alley and round into Tony's shop. He jacked it up, chocked it and removed the wheels, then closed the doors to minimise dust and opened a large can of the grey primer that Tony ordered in bulk. He stirred it with a wooden tongue and tipped some into the tank of an electric paint-gun whose nozzle had been set. Lee put on his goggles and a mask and walked the paint gun over to the shell, where he did a test spray on a sheet of cardboard before getting down on his knees, beginning the task of laying down the primer. It was precise and satisfying work, and the hours passed quickly. With his mind exhausted and his body worn down with fatigue, it finally felt safe to reflect upon the day's meeting with Enright. Frank Swann had briefed Lee about Enright on the drive back, and Lee's reading of the man tallied with Swann's longer experience of Enright's wheeling and dealing, but also his ruthlessness, and willingness to cut corners to get what he wanted.

The man presented as something of a cartoon character, with his loudhailer voice and exaggerated gestures, but his impact on the Perth business scene was real. It was hard to divorce Enright's reputation from his role as a father, but that was what Lee had to do. The man was the father of a daughter who'd suffered because of his wealth and reputation, and that was all Lee needed to know.

It was hot work despite the early hours, Lee next rubbing down the primed surfaces before painting the Dodge with a specially ordered stock white, laying down the paint in long graceful sweeps of the primed steel, and yet every time he remembered the picture of Enright's daughter, so naked and vulnerable, an eight-year-old girl in the hands of deviant men, he felt a chill pass over his naked skin, watching the goosebumps rise on his forearms until the anger came and burned the cold away.

8

Lee was met by Enright later that morning at the front door of his brown-brick, three-storey office building in central Subiaco. They didn't shake hands. Enright instead gave Lee the once-over: dressed in boots and black jeans, a navy-blue Bonds t-shirt and King Gee collared work shirt, the kind of unremarkable worker's uniform that wouldn't make him stand out on the street.

Inside Enright's offices, the air was chilled and carried the scents of perfume, deodoriser, hair spray and eau de cologne. Lee noticed this because Enright paused at the entrance to the open-plan office and waited, for what, Lee couldn't tell. One by one, the men and women in suits noticed Enright, and began to stand. Once a few had stood, looking uneasily at the others, the rest lifted themselves to their feet, straightening their ties and pushing down their skirts, all of them looking at Lee and trying to hide their embarrassment.

Clearly, the rise-for-the-king exercise wasn't for Lee's benefit, or in his honour. Enright scanned the room and nodded to each of his employees, giving them permission to sit and resume work. Lee felt the stirring of laughter in his belly, rising through his dismay at the indignity Enright's people endured every time he entered the office. Considering that Lee was on time for their appointment, as was his way, Enright must have only been outside for a few minutes at most. Like a little Napoleon, with one hand in his pocket, Enright waved Lee toward the stairs and bid him to follow. Lee did, while making sure to catch the response of as many employees as possible, none of whom rolled their eyes or shrugged. If Enright was being blackmailed, his staff was a logical first place to look, but nobody appeared overly friendly or guilty in any way. The routine of standing up when Enright graced them had obviously become that – a routine.

The stairwell was carpeted an acrylic beige that matched the minimalist brown-and-white colour scheme of the offices on each floor. At the second floor, Lee watched some of the staff make to stand when Enright went past, although the great leader didn't look, and their efforts went unrewarded. Enright seemed deep in thought as he trudged up the stairs.

Heavy is the head, thought Lee, watching the man two steps ahead of him, the little squeaks of his leather shoes as he climbed. Above the third floor landing the carpet gave out to bare cement, and the stairwell echoed to their footfalls. Arriving at a steel fire-door, Enright pointed to the only room on the level – a small alcove that was essentially a roof entrance but had been furnished with a single desk beneath a wall covered with monitors. At the desk sat a man in a white office shirt with sleeves rolled to his elbows. He didn't look up while working his way through a folder taken from an open filing cabinet. There was no air-conditioning in the room, and the stuffiness was barely lessened by the roof door wedged open with a brick. Outside, Lee could hear the sounds of traffic and laughter from the nearby primary school, obviously on recess break. Lee heard the door swish behind him. Enright hadn't even stayed to make the introductions.

The man finished walking his fingers through the file, before glancing at the clock. His hands trembled as he laid the file on the desk, which Lee noticed wasn't the same model as the sleek modular furniture downstairs but was so scored and dented that it looked like it'd come instead from one of the classrooms across the road. The man leaned back in his chair, whose castors creaked. He had small dark eyes set in a doughy face. His nose was notched with a pale scar, and one of his ears was missing a lobe. His silver-grey hair was combed back over a thinning scalp, out of sync with his thick black eyebrows raised in a silent question.

'Ron Bamber?' Lee asked. There was no other seat in the room. Lee felt like he was back in school, sent to the principal's office, which he assumed was exactly Bamber's desire, letting the silence linger.

Finally, Bamber blinked, which set off a wave of incremental gestures – he scratched his nose, cleared his throat, shifted on his seat, put his elbows on the desk and steepled his fingers, all the while regarding Lee and maintaining his silence.

Lee returned the man's stare, saw the smile in his eyes, the little nod of satisfaction at a game well played.

'Well?' Bamber asked.

Lee shrugged. 'Ok. You've been a loyal employee of Enright's. Worked for him through some tough years. Did some things you might regret. But you did them. You took the cheques, because you were probably well paid for your services, and your discretion.

You know a lot. Probably too much. Too much to fire you, but that doesn't mean he wants you around. Wants to see you, I mean. So you're up here. Doing not much. Hard to tell if he trusts you any longer, but I suppose he doesn't have a choice.'

There were other, less complimentary things that Lee might have said, but he'd played along in order to see if Bamber might give him something; an opening or a hint of betrayal that he might use later.

Bamber gave him nothing but a respectful nod. 'No doubt Frank Swann told you a few things.'

'Not much. Now it's your turn.'

Bamber chuckled, but his eyes were cold. 'I don't think so, son. I might not be "doing much", but that doesn't mean I like to waste my time. I've made some calls. There's little on you. Your father, on the other hand ...'

It was a question, but Lee shrugged it off, looked at the file on the desk. 'Is that the CIB file?'

'All yours. They put their best people on it, as you can imagine. But nothing. The fuckers who took Jess were ghosts.'

'How were the ransom demands made?'

'By phone, from public booths around the city. In those days, nobody had security cameras, so even the phones weren't any help.'

'How was the ransom paid?'

'Cash drop. I was overseas. Enright did it himself. Expressly against police instructions. But their agenda isn't always pure, as you probably know.'

'Meaning, in that specific case?'

Bamber inclined his head, regarded the file on the desk. 'They don't like ransoms to be paid because they don't want to encourage further kidnappings, for example. They also don't want to look like they can't do their jobs, and fail to retrieve the victim. None of which has anything to do with the best interests of a little girl in a bunker, in a fucking backyard somewhere, scared out of her brain.'

'Were there any other political aspects at play? Business rivals? Unpaid debts? People Enright had screwed, lives destroyed et cetera?'

'Too many of those to fucking count, son. But nothing that looked likely. In those days, I had a team. Ex-D's, like myself. Fine-tooth comb, and more.' Bamber looked at him directly now. 'In the course of our inquiries there were legs broken. Men hung by their ankles over long drops. Bullets in kneecaps. You get the picture. Nothing came of it. There was nothing on the street. Like I say, *ghosts …*'

An exhaustion had crept into Bamber's voice. He was looking down at his hands again, lost in the memories.

'Did you know the daughters? Well, I mean.'

That got Bamber's attention. A rigidity rose up through him, setting hard in his eyes. 'Yes, as a matter of fact. Great kids, both of them, until …'

'It was you who Enright got to chase down Jessica, the first time she ran away.'

'Yes, it was. She was a resourceful girl. I half-expected to find her trapped again, taken advantage of, used and abused, you know what I mean. But it wasn't like that. She surfaced in Adelaide, where she was working regular shifts in a shoe store. Should have guessed that one. Shoes, something she knew a lot about. She was fourteen, but tall for her age.'

There was genuine admiration in Bamber's voice. Lee changed tack. 'Did the daughters feel loved?'

Bamber blinked, too late to stop the reflexive snort, the sneer in his eyes. Here was the opening that Lee was looking for.

'Bit of an ask, don't you think? Loved? You're fucking kidding me. Their mother, on the other hand. She had her flaws, but at least she was a mother to them.'

'Thanks for your honesty. I'm aware that the kidnapping might have nothing to do with the current situation – the blackmailing. But, am I wasting my time looking in the file for something that isn't there? Enright doesn't think the two things are related – the historical kidnapping and the current demand for money – beyond the existence of the polaroid.'

'Listen to it,' Bamber said, cold mockery in his voice. 'The arrogance of youth. Your job, in case you need reminding, isn't to solve what better men than you haven't been able to solve. It's to use those long limbs of yours to climb drainpipes, get in the window on the second floor. Or to bat your pretty eyelashes, charm your way into some animal's confidence. That's it, son. That's your role here, and nothing else.'

Lee nodded, reached over and took up the heavy file.

9

Lee put the file on the bonnet of a Nissan Cedric that Gerry Tracker used for a table, propped up on sawhorses. Instead of returning home, Lee'd gone to the workshop so that Gerry's clients could collect their repaired vehicles. He scrolled up the roller door and backed the three cars to the bays outside the entrance. He kept the door open to let in natural light, but also turned on the fluoros nearest the table. He opened the CIB file and spread the contents, according to their sections, across the steel. Despite Gerry using a Main Roads steamroller to flatten the bonnet-table after a client failed to return to collect his car, it wasn't entirely level, and bobbed when he put weight on it.

Lee began by making a pile for the medical examiner's report on Jessica's condition at the time of her release from captivity, then another for the detectives' logbook of events, another for crime-scene photographs, another for the stack of interview transcripts and a final one for the correspondence between the police departments and civilians who'd sent in tips and suggestions.

Lee started with the photographs. The first photograph contained a scrawled address of a property in Baldivis, a bush-block suburb to the south of Fremantle. The photographer had studiously catalogued the road into the property, the view from the fibro house raised on a concrete slab, pictures taken from various windows and angles, and finally a door to the bunker in the yard hidden by a rusted sheet of corrugated iron. The handwriting on the rear of the photograph dated the bunker to the late '70s, suggesting a possible cold-war nuclear shelter or bushfire refuge. Following photographs documented the vertical entrance to the buried shipping container, the ladder welded to a side wall, the long shadowy space of the insulated chamber, the single mattress with sleeping bag and battery-powered lamp, illuminated for the camera, and a bucket in the corner for a toilet.

Jessica had been kept down there for the duration of her kidnapping, according to her statement. There was nothing for her to do, except scratch off the days in the dust by the furthest corner, as demonstrated by a flashlit shot from above; the twenty-three strokes crosshatched in clusters of five days.

Lee's childhood had been tough by any measure, but looking into the chilly gloom of the container that'd been Jessica Enright's home for three weeks, he knew that even now, with all of his training, he would struggle with the silence, darkness and lack of stimulation for that length of time, never mind the fear that each day might be his last. Jessica had been ripped from privilege – a world of yacht clubs and private schools, of cleaners picking her dirty clothes off the floor, a social life made up of sleepovers and weekends at the beach with friends whose futures were as golden as her own.

Plunged into darkness and dread. According to her statement, the man who came into the lightless dungeon once a day was tall and thin, wearing on every occasion blue overalls, leather work gloves and a black sack for a hood, with eyes cut out but no mouth.

This didn't matter because the man never talked, and it was too dark to gauge the colour of his eyes. He brought food and changed the batteries in the lamp and took away her bucket of waste, replacing it with a second bucket. He smelt bad – like chemicals. Jessica described the smell as something like the eczema cream that she used, or like the fumes that blew on the southerly from the Kwinana aluminium smelter. This description and the man's height and the blue overalls had sent the police, after her release, on a search throughout the refineries of the industrial area to the west of Baldivis, but they'd come up with nothing.

Missing from Jessica's twenty-page statement, detailing the moment of her capture to the moment of her release, was the fact that according to the polaroid photocopy now in her father's possession, she'd been stripped naked and made to pose for her captors, at the very least, and probably much worse. This omission might have been Jessica's own, or it might have been done by the interviewing officers, in deference to a superior officer, or to Enright, due to the possibility of leaks to the press.

Lee flicked through the file looking for any record of a policewoman being involved in the investigation or the rescue, or the questioning, or even the transporting of Jessica from A to B, but there was nothing. That alone might account for Jessica's omission when passed along what amounted to a chain of male custody, surrounded by men both uniformed and detective, none of whom implied there was more to Jessica's story than she was telling. This second omission might again be political, in deference to her father's status and power, or it might have been instead an omission by ignorance, a not-reading of cues that a policewoman or counsellor might have noticed.

Lee scribbled – policewoman, counsellor, psych – on the margins of the page, then stopped before his thoughts took over. Reading the file had raised many questions, some of which included the fact that nowhere in the file was it written who owned the Baldivis property, which was odd, unless he'd missed something. He looked up at the wall clock and saw that the time was past midnight – he'd been engrossed in the file for much of the day, and long since the repaired vehicles had been collected. He hadn't even noticed the change from day to night. The hubcap ashtray beside him was littered with butts.

The main question that bugged Lee wasn't something that was likely to be in the file anyway – why Jessica Enright had subsequently run away to live on the streets, moving interstate, never to return. The obvious answer was trauma, and the thought that everyone in her circle of friends and family saw her as a victim, when her actions following her departure over East showed that she was anything but. Many children lost or taken from their families, he imagined, upon being reunited would cling to their loved ones, and be clung to, relishing the love and safety of the family unit once again – nobody taking it for granted any more. You saw it in the faces of the parents and the children lost in shopping centres or in crowds, even if that separation lasted only a few minutes.

Perhaps Jessica's home life had never offered that stability and safety, that sense of enveloping love. Perhaps in the trauma of her kidnapping and imprisonment she'd come to understand that such safety and stability was illusory, that it could be taken in a moment. Perhaps she'd opted for self-reliance or was angry at her father for failing to protect her, or perhaps she was so damaged by the experience that nothing mattered anymore, including herself.

Lee collated the photographs and files, then leaned forward on the table and put his head in his hands. Bamber was correct, anyway – Lee's job was just to retrieve the image or images from one or more men. Enright himself didn't seem too concerned about the identity of the mysterious letter-writer, as long as it led to the images of his daughter. Lee could understand that. Whoever was demanding twenty thousand dollars wasn't breaking any law that Lee was aware of. It wasn't a crime to offer information for a financial benefit, although the maintaining of anonymity behind the photocopied letter, and the Caymans account, might suggest a darker motive, or a more personal knowledge of what had happened to Jessica Enright. Time would tell, and Lee took up the folder, ignoring the Dodge parked in the shadows of the workshop, turning off the banks of lights one by one until he was alone in the swelling darkness, feeling a little shiver of revulsion at the thought of Jessica Enright's underground prison once the batteries in her lamp had died.

The image of her that he'd been pushing away since opening the file stayed with him on his walk to the car. He sat behind the wheel and lit a cigarette, staring at the tin fence in front of him, and it was then that the memory of him and his father caught up with him, or ambushed him, it felt more like it. He hadn't thought about it for many years, and certainly not enough to raise it with his father on their rare meetings.

In the memory Lee is about ten or twelve years old, sitting alongside his father in their old Ford truck, staring through the windscreen at a wall of sand dunes being dug by an excavator. The sun is hot above them, and the light is fierce, reflecting off the white sands. Beside the excavator are three policemen, watching on. It is only a short memory, punctuated by Lee's father turning to him and saying, 'When I was in the hospital, a broken leg. You were only four or five years old. For one night, I left him in charge of you. When I got home you were unresponsive, sleepy, couldn't wake you up. A few days later you developed a fever. I took you to the doctors. You had the clap. Around your mouth. They fixed it with antibiotics.'

In the memory, Lee doesn't understand, doesn't know who 'he' is. He asks his father, 'Why are we here?'

His father doesn't respond, keeps looking at the excavator, the three policemen. Beside the policemen is a large sign, with a grid-map of streets laid out, papered over with large red letters – NOW SELLING.

Lee's knuckles were now white on the steering wheel. He knew that the memory was real, even though he'd pretended that it wasn't, had always ignored it when it crawled into his head. He knew that it was real because that was how his father talked, about things that he thought Lee needed to know. He knew that it was real because he remembered not knowing what the word 'clap' meant, and because by the time he knew what it meant, he didn't want to ask his father about the memory. Most of all, he knew that it was real because of what his father didn't say, in answer to Lee's question, and the behaviour of the three policemen – the burdened silence of what he would never say when asked about a crime, and that told Lee everything.

10

Lee recognised his mother's troop carrier as soon as he rounded the corner into McLeery Street. He was tired, so tired that he'd pushed the memory of his father away, replaced by his joy at seeing his mother again. His mother was an early riser, as she put it, but the truth was that she had trouble sleeping past three am. She lived alone in the country and slept lightly, and once she was awoken, the thoughts began to intrude along with her worries and cares, and that was that for another night.

None of the lights were on in the old limestone cottage that Lee rented, which meant that Carol was sleeping in her car. He cut his headlights and cruised past in neutral, not wanting to wake her. Sure enough, she was reclined on the driver's seat with a sleeping bag over her body and a truckie's cap over her face, while Maggie, her black-and-tan kelpie, slept on the passenger seat. Carol must have forgotten to pack her spare key again, and because of his line of work, Lee didn't keep a copy outside.

Lee parked his borrowed Fairlane down the street and quietly pushed the driver's door shut. He took up the Enright file and his cigarettes and went inside his house, which smelt of the takeaway curry that he'd eaten two nights ago. He turned on the kitchen light and started brewing a pot of coffee. He'd planned on getting a few hours sleep, but that wasn't going to happen. Sure enough, he soon heard Maggie bark and the front screen door open.

The Italian espresso pot started to hiss while Lee waited for his mother, who always liked a long embrace. She entered the kitchen yawning and rubbing sleep from her eyes, smiling when she saw him. Lee stepped to her and put his arms around her. He felt her hands press against his hips, his ribs, his shoulders, making sure that he was all there.

Lee and his mother had been separated for most of his life, due to his father's jealousy and desire to make Lee into a copy of himself. They'd been reunited five years ago when Lee was on the run, from the law and his father's influence. There was subsequently no evidence to convict Lee on the charge of abetting Daniel Southern's escape from custody, and the charge had been dropped. When Lee's father subsequently handed himself in, his three-year stretch in Fremantle Prison gave Lee time to spend with his mother, both down on her block south of Pemberton and on her regular visits to the city.

The coffee pot continued to hiss. Lee's mother let him go and he turned it off and took two mugs from the mantel above the old Metters stove. The rental came with a gas burner in the corner, but Lee mainly used the original wood-fired stove. He'd spent half of his life outdoors, cooking on a campfire, and the smell and sight of burning wood was a comfort to him, as well as amply heating the room in winter.

Lee poured the two coffees and added milk, sniffing the carton as an afterthought, which made his mother laugh.

'I'm sorry,' he said, remembering that his mother now took her coffee black. It was only a small thing, but he supposed was yet another reminder that he didn't know her as much as he should. He would certainly have remembered that his father took his coffee with milk and three sugars, stirred for a good amount of time.

His mother sipped on the hot brew. 'It's good,' she said. 'I've been using your gift every day. Something to look forward to when I'm out in the bush.'

Like most Australians of her generation, Carol had grown up drinking instant coffee, in her case International Roast with condensed milk from a tube. It was only recently that Fremantle's Italian, Greek and Portuguese coffee cultures had seeped into mainstream Australia. Frank Swann had taught Lee how to use the stovetop Italian espresso coffee maker, and Lee'd bought two from Galati & Sons' grocery store around the corner, gifting one to his mother.

'How are the flowers looking this year?' Lee asked.

'The melaleuca are out, and the wattle too. The marri won't be far away.'

Carol was a beekeeper, with hives on various farmer's properties that ringed the national parks protecting the karri forests and coastal woodlands near her block, close to the mouth of the Donnelly River. What started as a hobby and a means of observing creatures she was fascinated by had led to a productive small business. Good quality bush honey was rare, and she got a fair price for it in the wholefood stores around the city, visiting them every month to resupply. Doctors had also recently discovered the antiseptic qualities of jarrah honey in particular, something that Lee had known since he was a child, when his father had applied honey salves to his scrapes and abrasions when they were out camping.

'How's your father?' Carol asked, as though reading his mind.

'Haven't seen him for a few weeks,' Lee answered, not looking at her. Both of them knew where he was – out tending the marijuana crops he planted on crown land around the Gascoyne region of the Mid West – a dry area that meant regularly topping up the water beads laid around the base of each plant. He was particularly busy this time of year, even if the presence of aerial surveillance made the ventures risky. But Lee's father wasn't going to change his habits anytime soon. He was a war veteran who needed to keep the adrenalin running, to match the excitements he'd earlier found in combat. He'd made peace with this reality, and he had no fear of jail.

Lee looked closely at his mother, sipping on her coffee and glancing around the kitchen at the neatly organised spice rack and knife board, the washed dishes in formation on the drying rack and the tea towels folded over the oven door. He knew that Carol recognised Daniel Southern's hand in Lee's desire for order and simplicity – the military training passed from father to son. Carol's own kitchen was permanently disordered, with unpaid bills and broken crockery laying around that she hadn't got around to fixing, everything covered in a layer of dust, the smells of old fruit and veg in the chook bucket.

If Carol saw aspects of Daniel Southern in Lee, she was polite enough to not say anything, even though the imprinting must have been hurtful to her. During one of his psychotic episodes, Lee's father had terrorised her and driven her away from her only child, and all of her friends, forcing her on threat of murder to leave her hometown and move from the Mid West to start again. Lee and his mother had talked it out, all those years ago now, when he'd lived with her for three months until his father was back in jail. Lee had rightly expected her to be angry and bitter at the treatment she'd suffered, but he hadn't expected the weight of shame and guilt that she carried, despite everything, for leaving him behind.

Lee had always been told that his mother had run out on them. It wasn't true, and finding her felt like a miracle, and he knew that she felt the same way. They often caught each other slyly watching, and then they would laugh.

Lee realised early that he needed to demonstrate to Carol that he was ok, and that he was nothing like his father. He'd worked alongside her in her gardens, listening to her stories and taking her advice, and had helped her move the hives closer to flowering plants and trees, learning to scrape the honey and prepare it for market. Hers was a good life, he decided, something that he was pleased about, although it was far from perfect. She struggled for money, for one thing, and then there were her nearest neighbours at the time, a family of three sons and a matriarch who rented the weatherboard and fibro shack nearest the estuary, and who seemed to spend all their money on booze and bullets. Before Lee arrived to live with his mother, Carol had come into conflict with the family, having asked them to stop swimming in her dam, which was the source of all her drinking water. She'd found cigarette butts and food wrappers in the tannic water. The day following her complaint she discovered a dead kangaroo, shot and eviscerated, floating in the middle of the dam. When she complained to the boys' mother, the tyres on her troop carrier were knifed. She called the police, but was told that nothing could be done, unless she had evidence that the boys were the guilty party.

Carol told the stories to Lee one night when they were seated by the pot-bellied stove in her lounge room, drinking rum out of tin mugs. She was a bit drunk, and there was a tremor in her voice, and so he'd put his arm around her. What she told him next made up his mind. One morning following her visit to the police, her kelpie had come home limping, a .22 bullet in its back leg. The vet bill alone had nearly bankrupted her. Then she found that several of her hives had been toppled, and smashed, the queen bee dead and the worker-bees departed. The hives were each well hidden, and could only have been found if she was followed, by car and then on foot. The thought of that made her hand tremble, which in turn made Lee's blood boil. When he stood and she saw the look on his face, she grabbed his hand, making the point that nothing had happened in the past weeks.

'Probably because I'm here,' he said quietly. 'An extra witness, or just a general deterrence. Either way, what happens when I leave?'

Carol let go of his hand. 'How are we going to do it?'

Lee had already established that the family rarely left the property. The boys went into Pemberton on a Friday night, but the mother stayed at home, smoking and drinking on the sleep-out porch where she lived, shielded from the elements by a wall of flyscreen.

'Is there only the one rifle?' Lee asked, and his mother nodded.

'I know it isn't registered,' she said, 'because the coppers told me. They weren't about to come search for it though.'

The next night Lee sat on the roof of his mother's Toyota and watched the three sons spear down the dirt track in their Kingswood ute, the sound of John Mellencamp hanging in the still air, until their tail-lights were lost to the forest gloom. It was hard to say how much distance they'd get before the engine seized. Last night while they were sleeping, Lee had drained all the oil out of the engine. Whether the brothers made it into town didn't concern him, because the engine would be a write-off, and so he had plenty of time.

Lee and his mother walked down the hill, the kelpie at their heels. While Carol hid in the trees off to the side of the sleep-out, signalling to him that the mother was on her couch, the firefly glow of her cigarette flaring up behind the flyscreen, Lee entered the house via the back door. It didn't take him long to find the rifle, leant against the television in the lounge room. He could see why their mother preferred to live outside. The place smelt of mould and stale smoke. Lee made sure that there was a bullet in the breech, then put the rifle on the kitchen table. He filled a pot with the vegetable oil he'd brought and turned on the burner. He poured the rest of the oil on the benchtop and curtains above the sink. He lit the oil in the pot and watched it flare up. He carried the pot and put fire to the curtains, then the tea towels, then the wooden legs of the kitchen table. Because of the grease on every surface, the kitchen went up fast. Lee replaced the pot on the stove and wiped the handle of his prints and exited the back door. He watched the table roaring with fire and knew that soon the cartridge in the rifle would fuse as the table formed a pyre for the .22. Smoke was billowing out of the windows now and he went and joined his mother. She would be glad to hear that there hadn't been anything homely in the property – no family prints on the walls or trophies on the mantel, or crocheted blankets thrown over the couches.

They watched from the forest as flames burst the rear windows and smoke roiled above the rooftop. They waited until they heard the woman shout, fearing only that she might run back inside the inferno, but she soon emerged from the sleep-out carrying a cheap television and a sleeping bag over her shoulders. She stood barefoot in the dirt of her front yard and watched the house burn, listening to it sigh and creak and fracture in small explosions and feathery whispers as the jarrah frame caught and the wood and asbestos cladding fell away.

Lee and his mother went back up the hill. They got in Carol's Toyota and drove down to collect the woman, who seemed eerily calm. It wasn't her house, she said, and it was a pigsty anyway. Now she might get to live in town, away from her sons, who only stayed with her so they could bludge off her disability pension. She was on a shortlist to get a state commission flat in Albany, and now they'd bump her up the list for sure. A flat of her own was all she'd ever wanted.

They drove the long way into Pemberton, through the dirt roads of the state forest, the ghostly karri trees tall, pale and silent around them. They left the woman at the police station, where they made their statements. The police sent off two uniformed constables in a divvy van, who Lee assumed would find the rifle when they entered the remains of the house. He doubted that he'd ever see the three sons again, and in this he was correct, even though for the week following he slept on the front porch, his pistol within reach and his ear searching for the sound of tyres on the gravel roads.

Once the burning-out of the family was done, he and Carol didn't talk about it. It was understood that the action taken was necessary, and that they'd shown restraint compared to Lee's father, who would certainly have bashed the sons, or worse.

Lee topped up his mother's coffee, pausing on his way back to the stove to scratch the kelpie's ears. The kelpie liked to sit at the table like a human, leaning against the backrest and watching them both, waiting for the magic words of 'let's go', although Carol wouldn't be taking her companion driving around the city today. The dog was born to the southern forests and became agitated amid the welter of city sounds and smells. Better it rest out the day amid the parched grass and limestone bones of Lee's backyard, sleeping beneath the wattle trees.

Carol didn't look like she'd just slept in a car. She was somewhere close to turning forty-five, her body toned with hard work and her skin glowing in the weak sunlight. People commonly assumed that she was Lee's older sister when they went out together.

Lee went to her now, and put his arms around her shoulders. She smelt, as usual, of wildflower honey. The dog began to whine and skipped over the empty seats between to nudge them both, trying to prise free a hand that might pat it. 'See you for dinner at Ruocco's?' Lee asked. 'Warm enough to sit outside, so pup can come.'

'That'd be nice. I've been living on oats and lentils for the last month.'

Lee's pager began to vibrate and buzz. He lifted it from his belt and looked at Bamber's number.

'Work?' his mother asked.

Lee nodded, reluctant to leave her, knowing that she'd been alone for long periods since he'd returned to the city. He thought about ignoring the demand to call Enright's fixer, and instead walk to the beach for a swim before spending the day with his mother. There was only one reason Bamber would call him, however – the demand had been paid, and the blackmailer had provided a name. Lee lifted the phone off the receiver and began to punch in the numbers.

I I

Lee parked in the bays under a sprawling banksia, whose finer branches were studded with dried cones that rattled in the wind. The oval before him was empty and the streets were quiet. This was a new dormitory suburb on the northern edges of the city, and everyone was either at work or school. Toward the fringe of the oval, behind some practice nets, was a small patch of remnant bush that ran beside a power relay station full of steel towers and ceramic insulators. The electricity structures ticked in the charged air, although it didn't appear to bother the flock of pink-and-grey galahs congregated on the grass before him, chomping banksia cones, observing Lee with the curiosity of kids eating popcorn and watching a movie. Lee knew that the galahs mated for life, and that their lifespan was similar to humans'. He watched them eat, and he saw that the galahs were paired off in mating couples.

Lee heard the dinky Corolla suspension jolt as it entered the carpark, hitting the same pothole as his Fairlane had done. Lee had borrowed the Fairlane from Gerry Tracker's workshop, where Gerry used it as a client car for those needing transport while their vehicle was under repair. The Ford was boxy and white, had the look of a generic fleet vehicle, and so was perfectly suited to the job at hand.

The equally nondescript Corolla pulled up alongside, making the galahs lift their heads with renewed interest. Lee's window was scrolled down and Bamber nodded for him to come and join him. Lee walked around the two cars and went to Bamber's window. The man had just eaten a takeaway kebab, and the torn wax-paper on his lap was littered with scraps of lettuce. Bamber rolled it all up and passed it to Lee.

'Put that in the bin over there, would ya?'

It was the tone in Bamber's voice that made Lee ignore the wrapper. 'What have you got for me?' he asked. 'What's in the folder?'

Bamber shrugged, dropped the wrapper on the bitumen. He took up the folder on the passenger seat, a strange smirk on his face.

'Something funny?' Lee asked.

'Yes,' Bamber replied. 'Situation like this, working with a young fella, just starting out, I'd like to be in a position to say "You remind me of myself, when I was your age". But I don't see it.'

'Yeah, well,' Lee said. 'I appreciate the compliment. The address in there?'

'It is.' Bamber handed it over. 'The guy's harmless by the look of it, unless you're a fucking child. No form, or red flags. Lives alone. Works in the city as a town planner.'

Lee looked around at the black roofs and the treeless, levelled contours of the suburban streets around them. 'He responsible for this vision of utopia?'

'Perhaps you're looking at the wrong things. Perhaps the virtues of this place are to be found in the minor details we aren't privy to, as non-paedophiles – the creep's view of the school playground for example.'

Lee opened the folder and scanned the address, circled on a photocopied map. Gavin Drew did in fact live opposite a primary school.

Bamber had no reason now to hang around. Lee watched his fingers clenching and unclenching on the steering wheel. Part of Bamber's anger toward Lee, and the job he'd been given, he realised, was likely because Bamber wanted to ignore orders and take a hammer to Mr Gavin Drew's head.

'I'll take it from here,' Lee said. 'Call you as soon as I have it.'

Bamber's eyes flickered over Lee's face. 'You do that,' he said. 'And not a second fucking later.'

12

The primary school presented a problem. It was lunchtime, and hundreds of kids in red uniforms scampered around the play equipment and basketball court, sliding down railings and playing brandy with a tennis ball. There were no teachers on duty that Lee could see, but either way, a man parked on such a narrow street was going to attract attention. Nor were there any shops, or civic buildings to give him cover. Lee circled the block in the Fairlane, glancing at the houses he passed, looking for security cameras or people in the front yards, but there was nothing and nobody. He parked on the street around the corner from the school behind a Hiace van that he'd noticed had flat tyres. On the weedy front yard of the house were two cheap cars, one of them without wheels.

Lee cracked the trunk of the Fairlane and removed his shoulder bag, heavy with iron, but padded out with a hoodie and a towel to stop the load from clanking. He pulled his cap lower, locked the car and proceeded back toward the school. The lunchtime siren sounded, and by the time he arrived, the schoolyard was deserted. Lee went straight toward Drew's house and rang the doorbell. There was no car in the bare concrete driveway, skirted with odd-looking cacti and other succulents he couldn't name, and it was no surprise when the door wasn't answered. Neither was he surprised to see that there was no direct view from the front porch to the windows in the adjoining houses. The buildings were all of a type – Lego-blocks with a townhouse feel, designed, he supposed, to create an artificial village atmosphere. The frames in the windows were cheap black aluminium, which decided him against forcing the front door. If possible, his orders were to avoid tipping Drew to the fact that he'd been burgled.

Lee stepped off the entrance alcove and took a bricked path down the shadowed side of the house, glancing at the darkened windows in the building beside. The gate to the backyard wasn't locked, and Lee closed it and placed a nearby spade, handle down, against it. If the gate opened when he was inside, he'd hear the clatter of the steel mouth against the bricks.

The backyard was a small astroturf rectangle. There were no trees or shrubs in the yard, which made the gardening shed in the corner a strange addition, and therefore a good place to start. The small shed was rivet-skinned with cheap steel and empty except for a filing cabinet and some miscellaneous tools leant into a corner. There was barely enough room for him to stand inside, and Lee opened the trays of the cabinet and poked among the usual tubes of silicon and cheap Bunnings tools, bags of fertiliser and pots of test paint with dried-out brushes. The shed was floored with concrete pavers and he knelt and lifted one, looked under its edges, then the next. He stood and shifted the filing cabinet around until he had access to the pavers beneath. Lee didn't know if Drew had owned the house since new, but in case he hadn't, Lee was looking for a hiding place that if discovered, could be argued as belonging to a previous owner. Sure enough, beneath the paver that'd been concealed by the filing cabinet he found a plastic tackle box, in a small dugout. He popped the lid of the box and opened its trays. It was too dark to make out the images and so Lee cracked the shed door wider, casting a sunlit wedge over the stacks of photographs. Among them was a single VCR cassette and a small stack of floppy disks, none of them marked or named.

Lee felt his heart rate climb as disgust warmed his face. He needed a cigarette but fought the urge; in the windless backyard the smoke would linger. Mostly, Lee hoped that Drew would return now, so that he might do something constructive with the anger he felt, looking at the hundreds of images before him. He had been told to retrieve images of the Enright girl, Jessica, and to return everything else. Holding the stacks away from him, looking at each photograph briefly, and from an angle he hoped would make it hard to see the children clearly, he began to thumb through the piles. The photographs were black-and-white, and colour, some taken with polaroid cameras and some developed in a home darkroom – either over- or underexposed. Lee worked through the pictures as quickly as he could, but that didn't stop the eyes of the children staying in his mind. Even though he tried to scan the pictures, it was like the children were looking for him, had been waiting for him, still there in the frames of the photographs, pleading to be rescued. He began to feel nauseous, and then he was outside, leaning against the cold brick wall, emptying himself. Lee didn't know if Drew had taken the photographs himself or had bought them off others; many of the children were Asian, looked Thai or Filipino, their faces startled and flashlit in darkened rooms framed with cheap mattresses and bare concrete, even if the bodies of the adult men were European, their faces hidden but their bellies and backs pale.

Lee took out a cigarette and smoked deeply, not caring any longer about being noticed. He wanted to shout loud enough to bring down the walls around him, but instead went back to the sliver of light inside the shed door and began to flick through the images again, smoke rising through his fingers and into his eyes.

He found the polaroid of Jessica in the second stack of photographs. That there was only one image suggested it wasn't any more important to Drew than the others, which was odd given the circumstances in which they were taken, following Jessica Enright's widely publicised kidnapping. Perhaps Drew wasn't aware of who the captive was, or perhaps to him she was just another abused child, naked and afraid. Either way, it didn't matter. Lee pocketed the image as well as the floppy disks and the VCR cassette – he didn't have the means to examine them now, and so took them just in case. He didn't replace the tackle box just yet either. He still had to search the house but suspected that he'd come up empty. If so, he was going to make sure that when the cache was discovered, as it would soon be, that there was no way Drew would be able to say he was unaware of it, or that it belonged to a previous tenant. As insurance, Lee was going to plant something that clearly identified Drew as the owner, taken from inside his house. Lee didn't know what yet, but knew that he would find it.

13

Lee watched Paul Enright's face as the man drank his whisky and smoked a cigarette taken from Lee's pack of Stuyvies. They were on the back deck of the *Current-Sea*, moored in the yacht club, surrounded by the bobbing launches and yachts of the rich and famous, the sea breeze rattling teak doors and singing through wires and lines. A row of pied cormorants sat like wise old men on the pylons that stretched into open water, their white chests dazzling in the sunshine, oily wings like blankets thrown upon their shoulders.

The sunlight was fierce on the leathery skin of Enright's face too, but it couldn't match the heat from his eyes.

Bamber, Enright's fixer, was in the galley, watching the screen of his laptop and the television which played the video cassette. The sound on both devices was muted, but every few seconds Bamber groaned or swore or retched like he was being worked over, which in a sense he was.

Enright clearly didn't feel like speaking, which was alright by Lee. Underneath the glass ashtray the polaroid of his daughter was placed facedown. Lee had searched Drew's house over the course of two hours, pulling up carpet and opening duct outlets, feeling around the various mattresses and couches for hidden pockets, looking under and behind every drawer, opening every book on the three separate bookshelves, checking in the cisterns of the two toilets and finally climbing up into the ceiling space. He hadn't found another image, cassette or disk, which confirmed Drew's high degree of caution. There was a charging cable on a downstairs benchtop, which meant that Drew had his laptop with him, but Lee doubted that such a cautious man would use a computer he took to work to store incriminating material. From a bedroom Lee had taken a couple of photographs of Drew from a photo album, clearly taken somewhere in South-East Asia, innocently sitting astride a tuktuk and drinking a Singha beer at a beachside table and, together with some hairs taken from Drew's steel comb, he slipped them among the cache of filth out in the small shed, replacing everything as it was before he'd arrived.

'Oh come on,' Bamber groaned again, this time hitting something inside the galley that splintered, sending glass breaking onto the floor.

'You about finished in there?' Enright snapped, the fingers of his non-smoking hand wrapped around the heavy ashtray, as though he too wanted to break something.

A long minute passed. One by one, the cormorants opened their wings to the sun, revealing bony chests.

The laptop slapped shut inside the galley, followed by the sound of the VCR cassette being ejected beneath the television, while Enright put ice into a new glass, and poured.

Bamber winced as he emerged into the light. 'She's not on the disks, or the cassette. Watch your feet in there, boys, there's broken glass everywhere.'

Bamber's face was unnaturally pale, and his voice had some

edge to it. He was about to speak again, but Enright raised a hand. 'No, Bamber. The answer is no.'

'But I'll make it look like an accident. A gruesome, painful fucking motor accident. Nobody will know except us, and more importantly, him …'

'Can't risk it, so don't do it. Not until we know what the fuck is happening. His time will come.'

Lee didn't know what was on the disk and the cassette, didn't want to know, because Bamber wasn't the type to shock easily, and yet there he was, slipping from white-hot anger into something more dangerous, and more terrifyingly sad. There were tears starting in his eyes, and the expression on his face was morose, bereft, disbelieving – a mask of unexpected trauma.

This was a man who'd held people by the ankles over the edges of tall buildings, who had put bullets into kneecaps, any number of other cruelties.

His bug-eyes fixed on to the photograph beneath the ashtray. 'Paul, can I do it? Please. I need to do it.'

Enright lifted the ashtray and Bamber snatched at the polaroid, taking Lee's Zippo before giving fire to the corners, which bubbled and then caught in a bright golden flame. Bamber held up the fire to the sun until it had burned down, then flicked it into the river. He put his hands on the table and leant forward, looking at them both. Lee could smell the sour gastric acids on his breath.

'What do we do now?' he asked them.

Lee looked at Enright, who was too angry to speak.

'We wait,' Lee said. 'For the next address.'

One by one, the cormorants lifted off their pylons and flew into the sunlight shearing off the river, settling in the distant waters off the spit where they disappeared beneath the surface, and resumed their hunt.

14

Club Summertime wasn't due to open for another couple of hours, but its front doors were open as cleaners vacuumed and mopped, and behind the bar, pipes were flushed, and bottles restocked. The familiar blast of stale yeast met Lee as he slipped inside. He waved to the security camera in case Firmin was in his office, and nodded to the various staff going about their business. He pushed the door at the foot of the stairs but it didn't budge. It was only then that he noticed the security punch-pad incompetently set into the plaster wall beside.

Lee muttered and turned to the bar, where Michelle was watching with a smile.

'Zero. Zero. Zero. Zero,' she shouted through cupped hands.

Lee shrugged and punched in the numbers. The door clicked and he pushed it open. He gave a finger to the security camera inside the stairwell and trudged the stairs.

'Condition of insurance policy,' Firmin greeted him, 'met retrospectively. And it might've made the difference on the night in question.'

'You set it yourself?' Lee asked, knowing the answer.

Firmin beetled his brow. 'Yes, why?'

'There's enough gap in the plasterboard for me to reach behind and pull it out, trigger the setting manually.'

'Well, haven't finished it yet, mate. Tube of Selleys "no-more-skills" and some frame, it'll be grand.' Firmin nodded toward the drinks trolley but Lee shook his head.

'You paged me,' Lee said.

'Just wanted to keep you apprised. Turns out there was a witness to the hoon who did me over. Young woman out in the park. Gave us a car rego and a perfect description.'

'Oh yeah?' was all Lee said, hoping that Firmin hadn't looked at the security footage from the night, subsequent to the armed rob.

Firmin couldn't help himself, and cracked a smile, revealing his set of whitened teeth, uniformly flattened by years of grinding in his sleep. 'Yes, very clever, observant and helpful. Very pretty, too.'

Despite himself, Lee began to colour. So Firmin had watched the footage. 'Is that relevant?'

'The young lady didn't want payment, or any kind of reward. She did make me promise to give this to you, though. Said she watched you on the door, thought you were … cute.'

Firmin tossed over a scrap of paper, on which was written a phone number. Lee glanced at the first few numerals and saw the code for the CBD. Perhaps Firmin hadn't watched them after all.

Lee pocketed the number and leaned back in his chair. 'And? What came of the information? You get a line on the fella?'

'Plates were stolen from a Great Eastern Highway fuck-motel. Council eyes confirmed the model of landy as it drove down Lake Street, got a couple of glimpses of the driver, but nothing substantial, and that was about it. The young lady gave us a very skilled, almost identikit-quality sketch, which I took to Central, but there's nothing there in the coppers' database that matches.'

'You reckon he's gone back East, or up to Darwin?'

Firmin shrugged, glanced again at the drinks trolley and this time couldn't help himself, used a walking cane to hook the edge and pull it toward him. Lee watched him pour his regular daytime tipple of three fingers of Pusser's Rum, the original spirit doled out to British and Australian navy servicemen at the end of every shift – the rum was strong, sweet, and had a narcotic effect after only a few sips.

'Something to consider,' Lee said, 'if you've got a good sketch. Going on the rumour that the Hastie brothers were either working on a goldmine or working a lease of their own. Maybe run the picture by some of the larger companies out there or by the hiring agencies here in the city?'

Firmin liked the idea, nodded his approval, although he kept his eyes closed as the rum seeped into his pain. His broken wrist was cast up to his elbow, and the bruises beneath his fractured eye socket and cheekbone were still livid and black.

Lee saw the question on Firmin's lips, and stood to leave. 'I'm working on a job, looks like a couple of weeks, so I can't work the door.'

'Even in an emergency?' Firmin asked, his eyes still closed, savouring the drift of rum into his limbs, feet and hands.

'Even in an emergency. But I'll keep an ear out for the Hasties.'

Firmin didn't see a lot of sunlight, working the nights in his clubs and sleeping through the day, but right at that moment, glass of rum in his hand, the lines on his forehead smoothing as his face became slack, the old man looked like a giant reptile, basking in a tropical sun.

15

Lisa parked the Ford Transit on the street opposite the old semidetached bungalow, climbing behind the front seats into the bay area of the van, whose windows were tinted beyond the legal limit, making it impossible to see her from outside. She was short enough to stoop inside the van and she lifted the tripod assembly and settled its rubber feet in the tray grooves. She took out the camera from the cushioned bag and fixed it to the tripod, clicking the zoom lens into place. She made a seat of a milk crate that contained snacks and bottled water, and dialled in the focus on the camera, pleased by the clarity of the image that emerged from the fuzz – a front room complete with ratty couch and television, casting a blinking light over the windows.

Now all she had to do was wait. She couldn't park there for long, not in this neighbourhood – a semi-industrial rural estate on the southern edges of the city, spreading away to the foothills of the Darling Range. There were some remaining horse ranches in the area, marked by solid wooden fences and empty paddocks, but most of the dairy pastures and market gardens had been turned into warehouses, depots and scrap merchants. The business behind Lisa sold pet meat – roo, horse and bones – advertised in handpainted road signs that were placed two hundred metres either side of the property.

A nondescript white van parked on the street opposite the three men was exactly what they'd be looking for, especially a van with darkened windows, so she didn't want to linger.

Lisa scanned the front rooms of the old house, her eye catching on tiled surfaces and lurid wallpaper, and the cement lions and faux-Doric columns framing out the front porch. The building was undoubtedly made for Sicilian or Calabrian immigrants – the front yard was sectioned into flowerbeds that hosted long-dead rosebushes, set amongst trellis gardens that would have carried tomatoes and beans. Against the broken and leaning asbestos fence were several *bastardoni* prickly pear cacti, which Lisa knew were edible.

A shadow movement streaked across the lounge window, a preface to someone standing. Lisa had set the camera to semi-automatic and she pressed the trigger as a tall man with long hair, naked but for his jocks, stood and stretched his back. He lifted a leg to fart in the direction of someone off-screen, and was hit by a small cushion. Lisa zoomed closer and got some good images of the man's face. He was the man who'd arrived in the Landcruiser on the night of the Summertime robbery, and he caught the cushion and threw it back. Another man, one of the pair who were clearly brothers, stood and pushed him out of the way, crushing a beer can as he passed, both of them moving out of frame into what Lisa assumed was the central corridor in the house.

Lisa unclipped the zoom lens from the camera, then unscrewed the camera from the tripod. She packed the camera and lens away and laid down the tripod, climbing into the front seat of the van, turning the key and quietly engaging the gears with the engine at idle. She slipped the car into first and then second, keeping the revs low and making a point of not turning to look at the house.

Beside her on the front seat was the small video cassette taken from the Belmont motel, whose recording captured the numberplate of the Landcruiser that had entered the carpark solely to steal the plates from a Nissan Patrol. Lisa had taken the cassette as evidence, she'd told the motel night manager, although she hadn't logged it. She'd then made a plate search on the RTA database, coming up with the property address listed as belonging to a Mrs Irene Hunter, now deceased.

Back at her apartment, Lisa planned to twice copy the cassette and develop three prints each of the three men. One copy for her, plus a copy for safekeeping – as insurance.

One copy was for them.

16

Lee saw the kid's back foot lift and he leaned away as the right hook swished past his chin.

'Try an overhand right next time,' Lee said, before gassing himself through his nose. 'Same set-up, but an overhand right. You telegraph your big rights with your feet, but at least an overhand will follow me.'

It was a lot of words after an hour of sparring, and he felt the faintness in his head as he sucked air through his nostrils, making sure that it settled deeply in his belly.

The kid took his orthodox stance again, looking at his gloves. Lee could see the cogs turning in his mind as he recreated the choreography that Lee had just taught him.

The kid's name was Silas, and he wore the summer uniform of South Fremantle Senior High School – grey shorts and shirt. He was barefoot, as was Lee, and one of the buttons of his shirt was missing. He wore his hair short at the back and sides, with a tight pillbox shape on top, mimicking one or another of the gangsta rappers going around, but whose music was never played in the gym. It was a big part of Gerry Tracker's MO when training up the mainly Noongar kids from the local housing estates to remind them that the African-American experience wasn't the Australian-Aboriginal experience, and that they were better off finding their own forms of expression from their own culture. But Gerry was fighting a losing battle so far as Lee could tell, and once Lee had even overheard one of the kids making up a lyric that gently mocked Gerry behind his back, which Lee had silenced with a look of disapproval, even though the rhyme was pretty damn funny, sung to the tune of Bill Withers' 'Ain't no Sunshine'.

Silas was a new student who had plenty of natural talent. Lee hadn't spoken to him beyond general conversation, and so didn't know his family story or his personal circumstances. Some of that story was there, however, when Lee pushed Silas with jabs to his forehead and shortened body-shots that the kid wasn't able to see coming. Then Silas's face would darken as the pent-up anger overwhelmed his minimal training, and he would explode in a flurry of roundhouse swings that Lee ducked, and dodged, until the kid's fury was spent.

Silas's friends would laugh from outside the ring when this happened, but Lee made sure to never smile. After all, he'd had the same experience in the same ring with Gerry Tracker, who'd tested his boxing chops but mostly his temperament on the first day he'd walked through the doors. Lee had stuck around after that first experience of frustration and powerlessness because he'd seen something in Gerry's self-control and gentle encouragement that he wanted, and needed.

Silas was one of the many neighbourhood kids who came to the gym hoping to learn to fight better, primarily so that he could win more fights. It was expected that the boys and girls of Silas's community knew how to scrap, to defend themselves and their family name. Some of the kids survived on wit and bluster, and some of them were outright thugs, but each of them was found out in Gerry's makeshift ring, as Lee had been too. The things they learned from day one were that there are no shortcuts to preparation, and that self-control leads to seeing things clearly, meaning that your confidence has a sound foundation and so doesn't need to be performed.

Not all of the local kids appreciated the lesson, but those who did tended to stick around for many years, and plenty became mentors to those following.

Lee hoped that Silas would become that kind of kid, as he hoped for every one of them that had the courage to walk through the doors, whatever their motivation.

The training was good for Lee, too.

In the hour spent taking on each of the kids, one following another while Frank Swann led the remainder in cycles of bag-work and weights, Lee's legs becoming heavier and his chest tighter; he hadn't once thought of the photographs in Drew's garden shed. He needed to concentrate when sparring, to avoid getting hit, and to maintain the fitness and good humour sufficient to offer advice and encouragement.

Silas started jabbing with his left, from head to body, as Lee had shown him, before feinting at Lee's solar plexus and stepping left, telegraphing with his defensive heel again but this time launching a long overhand right that followed Lee as he swayed back, rolling his jaw and lifting his left shoulder to protect him from the blow that if he didn't know was coming, might've caught him flush.

The smile on Silas's face said it all. They bumped gloves and Lee nodded to the girl who was next, leaning on the top ropes. She had

Māori ancestry and he remembered that her name was Moana. She was a regular now, and although she was funny and enjoyed teasing some of the boys, she was game as hell. Lee could tell from the look in her eyes that she'd been watching Silas and that she wanted to try the same move.

He would test her, as he tested all of them, but only because she'd be expecting it. He felt a blush of tenderness, the same as he'd felt toward Silas and the students who'd preceded him, each of them exiting the ring exhausted but exhilarated. He liked being a teacher, he realised, something that had surprised him at first. It was only now, while Moana fitted her mouthguard and tightened the velcro straps on the headgear, and while Silas drank deeply from his water bottle, that Lee remembered there were men such as Gavin Drew in the world, driven by desires they were either unable, or unwilling, to control.

Moana began shaping up before him, but Lee had to raise a hand and turn to the wall until he'd swallowed the anger.

17

Lee sat opposite his mother at an outside table while they waited for their Ruocco's pizzas. The pockets of darkness on South Terrace were as deep as the height of the buildings around them. The sky above the terrace was still dark blue, despite the sun having set, and faint lines of mauve and orange traced each of the high clouds that filigreed the eastern horizon.

It was a good thing that he and Carol were seated outside – the night was hot and still. The steady rush of traffic was loud enough to dampen their words. On her third glass of house red, Carol was in high spirits, having confided to Lee that she'd met someone. Her eyes scanned his face as she described Greg, a former firefighter in the city who'd damaged his neck when hit by a collapsed ceiling, but who, like Carol, had moved to the country to reinvent himself. He worked now as a blacksmith designing and forging ornate garden features – gates, benches and light columns. The man could turn his hand to anything, really, and he had seriously beautiful hands too, by the way.

'Unlike these old things,' Carol added, 'worn-out and chipped.'

Lee smiled as Carol held out her hands for him to examine. They weren't at all worn-out or chipped, surprising considering how hard she worked. He ran his fingers over her smooth palms, took one hand and stroked his stubbled right cheek to compare, before returning them to her.

'You mean you have sensible nails.'

Carol pretended to be miffed, as he knew that she would. 'Sensible, eh? I suppose they are. Been a while since I had talons or put on the war paint.'

'You don't need that stuff. You're just fishing now.'

'Yes, and? You care to rephrase that?'

Lee grinned. 'You don't need that stuff because you're very … sensible.'

Carol shrieked, balled and threw her napkin at him. Lee ducked and the napkin sailed over his head, catching Enzo, the waiter, who had three pizzas up his arm. He didn't flinch, laying down two of the pizzas on their table, topping up Carol's glass and smiling at her before moving to the next table.

'You see?' said Lee. 'Even Enzo flirts with you, and he's gay.'

'Well, that will have to do, I suppose. Let's eat – I've been looking forward to this for weeks.'

Carol slid out a slice of her Tony's Special – a vegetarian number with pine nuts, spinach and pumpkin, and put it on his plate. Lee did the same with his margarita with extras, sectioning out a piece with olives, chilli and anchovies, putting it onto Carol's plate. They settled down to eating, Lee made especially hungry by the boxing, replacing the calories his body had burned through. Pretty soon, he anticipated, Carol would ask him what he was working on. Neither of them were in a rush, and he thought about what he might say, then decided he'd say nothing, not wanting to spoil his mother's mood. He'd talk about the cars he was working on, and what was happening down at Gerry and Frank's gym. He'd talk about what he was learning at the university, perhaps, anything except the story of Jessica Enright and what had happened to her. Carol was smart, and more importantly, worldly beyond her years, and she'd have solid advice to give, and good questions to ask, but that was a conversation for another day. Lee looked down at his plate and saw that he'd already finished his first slice. He gulped down a mouthful of red and reached for the pizza he'd ordered. He needed salt, and knew that the margarita wouldn't disappoint.

18

Lee followed Louise through the sleep-out and onto the back deck of the old fibro cottage, leaving his mother with Frank and Marion. It was Tuesday night at the Swann house, meaning all of the children and grandchildren were there for dinner, served at the small kitchen table clustered with three different types of chairs and stools. Louise's two sisters, Sarah and Blonny, were on the front porch drinking white wine. It was a warm night and all the windows in the house were open. From the houses around Lee heard the regular sounds of suburban life – televisions, radios, laughter and children arguing, an angry parent, a car door slamming shut.

Lee offered Louise a cigarette but she shook her head. She was the Swanns' eldest daughter and the first in their family to go to university. She worked as a lawyer on St Georges Terrace, but had shed her suit for her regular denim shorts and tank top. Her dark hair, cut short on the back and sides, was still combed into a stiff side-peak, however, catching the glow from the neighbour's security light.

'You can guess what this is about, right?' Lee asked.

Louise nodded. 'You were asked not to, but you want to speak to Fi, about Jessica.'

'That's about it. Is it going to be a—'

'Of course not.' Louise grinned. 'She'll call. I've already teed it up. She'll suggest meeting away from the house, naturally.'

Lee pinched the end off his cigarette. 'Thanks. But about her. You knew her through uni, but did she ever talk about what happened to her sister?'

Louise had a way of looking into Lee's eyes that used to unnerve him. He still wasn't accustomed to it but knew better than to look away. It was only for a few moments this time, but Lee figured it out – it was her natural concern that Lee might lack the good grace to proceed cautiously, sensitively, as the occasion would clearly demand.

'Ok, I get it,' he said. 'What about you? Did you tell her about what happened to you when you were a teenager?'

Louise gave him that look again, but her mouth pursed, a little nod. 'Yes, I did. The full story. Nothing left out.'

When Louise was fifteen, she'd run away, then got caught up in one of her father's cases. She was forcibly taken across the country to Brisbane, where she was held in a Fortitude Valley brothel room by the local coppers, until the Perth coppers gave the all clear.

'Do you think that's what might've happened to Felicity's sister, Jessica? Collateral damage in one of Enright's shonky deals?'

'Hard to say. The men who took her kept to the script of total silence except when giving her orders. She didn't talk much about it. There wasn't much of a chance to talk. I never got the chance to meet her.'

'Do you think Felicity knows where her sister is?'

That look again, and Lee didn't glance away.

'Fi is pretty hard to read. Close cards and all that. I've never asked her directly, assumed she'd tell me if she wanted me to know. But I don't think so. The sisters weren't close, according to Fi. Jessica was apparently pretty "out there", a dominant kind of person like her father, whereas Fi is shy and quiet. I don't think Fi ever got over the loss of her mother when she was nine. The sisters didn't seem to bond over their shared grief. They were very similar looking, but different personalities. Fi withdrew into herself, while Jessica apparently began to act out, against everyone and everything.'

Lee nodded. It was good background. 'If I proceed the right way, what do you think I'll learn from speaking to Felicity?'

Louise chuckled. 'That's an odd question. General and specific, tapping into my gut-reading of the whole thing. You sound like my dad. A compliment of course.'

'And that's a good answer, though a non-answer. Interpreting my question rather than answering it.'

'Fair enough,' Louise replied. 'Though I think you already know the answer to the question. I think you'll learn something about Paul Enright, your employer. The question is – why do you want to look in his direction?'

Lee smiled. 'I'm learning my trade. Following in your dad's line of work, people like Enright will often be my employer, or my target for investigation. I don't usually get to observe corporate sharks like Enright from up close, how they work, where they live, what their strengths and weaknesses are. On this job I'm just a glorified burglar, and possible bagman, but that doesn't mean I can't get something out of it, for down the track.'

Louise gave him a shrewd look as she tapped him on the belly, a big-sister gesture of encouragement before they turned toward the sounds of laughter and music coming from the Swanns' kitchen.

19

Carol was asleep in the spare room, guarded by her kelpie, who watched Lee as he smoked at the kitchen table. It was near midnight and he wasn't tired. He thought about heading to Gerry's workshop to finish painting the Dodge, but there wasn't enough time before dawn. Lee remembered the phone number in the pocket of his jeans, and stood and emptied his pockets of coins, knuckles, five and ten dollar notes and the scrunched phone number of the young woman he'd met at Club Summertime. He opened out the piece of paper and looked at the number she'd passed on to him. He thought again of her face, and her voice, the sense that she was always in control, entirely comfortable with herself. Calling her was what Lee wanted to do, but it was late, and he didn't know if she had a boyfriend, or a husband. He didn't know anything about her except her name, and the fact that she was a rookie cop. He didn't know if these things were true, either, not that it mattered. He wanted to call her with an urgency that made his heart beat faster. He looked at the number and made to stand, but the pager on the table began to trill. The number was Bamber's, and Lee muted the pager and carried it over to the phone in the hallway, punched in the numbers.

Bamber answered on the first ring. 'Good boy. Beck and call, or call back, in record time. You ready to work?'

'Sure. What's the story?'

'The story? This a game to you?'

Lee didn't answer, waited for Bamber, who let the silence hang before clearing his throat, speaking through what sounded like gritted teeth. 'Not over the phone. Meet me at the lighthouse, South Mole, soon as you can.'

Lee hung up. On the pad by the phone he jotted a message to his mother, telling her he'd be out overnight and possibly through the day. In the kitchen he knelt and tucked the note inside the dog's collar. She was used to being their go-between, and she licked the back of Lee's fingers. He ruffled her neck and ran fingertips over her silky ears. At the kitchen table he re-pocketed the knuckles, the cigarettes and cash. His bag of tools was still inside the Fairlane's boot. He looked around the kitchen and did a quick accounting of what else he might need. He had an extendable baton and an unlicensed .38 revolver in a toolbox beneath the floorboards in his bedroom, as well as mace and a bag of cable ties pre-shaped into cuffs, which his father had taught him to make when he was a boy. He didn't need any of that stuff. He filled a water bottle and took the empty two-litre milk bottle beside the bin, in case he needed a toilet.

It was cool out on the street. He pulled up the collar of his work jacket and took out the beanie from the side pocket, which when needed, rolled out to form a balaclava. He drove the Fairlane down the hill toward the port, the sulphur lights of container terminals glowing behind the silhouette of Victorian-era buildings with tin roofs and chimneys, the west-end streets empty except for a prowl car by Fishing Boat Harbour and the parked cars of port workers. The narrow road out to South Mole caught the full brunt of the gusting southerly, whipping up silver horses in the bay and carrying the iodine smell of seaweed and old bait. There were a few hardy types fishing for mulloway on set-lines in the lee of the wind, facing grimly out at the harbour mouth while the tips of their heavy rods traced silver into the black waters. At the head of the mole where the small lighthouse blinked to the west, Bamber was parked in his Corolla, facing east as Lee approached. His was the only sedan parked at the headland and Lee muttered to himself, 'Don't do it, don't flick your headlights,' just as Bamber flicked his headlights. Lee pulled through the turnaround and parked alongside Enright's fixer. He left his keys in the car and killed the lights, walked around the ticking engine bay and climbed inside the Corolla, which smelt no longer of kebab but instead of hot chips. Bamber nodded to the box on the dash.

'Help yourself, son. Captain Munchies. They double-fry the fuckers. That's Italian attention to detail, applied to the humble spud. Changing the oil more than once a decade probably helps too.'

'I'm good. Just ate.'

Bamber seemed insulted. 'I left some for you. Could've had them myself, while they were hot.'

Lee noticed the file on Bamber's lap. 'I just had pizza. Italian pizza. That the file?'

Bamber handed it to him, didn't let go of it. 'This one isn't going to be so easy.'

Lee tugged the manila file and Bamber let it go. 'So Enright made the payment, via the Cayman's bank. How long until this new one came through?'

Bamber laughed. 'You don't need to know about any of that, son.'

Lee nodded. Bamber had tomato sauce on his shirt; a red exclamation point on the grey silk midway down his chest.

'I understand. But I'd like to know how it works.' Lee put on his best earnest-face, but it didn't wash with Bamber.

'Son, if you started out like the rest of us, on the force, you'd know that the first years in the job are spent polishing shoes and wiping blood off your knuckles. You young blokes think there are shortcuts for everything. They're called the hard yards for a reason.'

There wasn't any point pushing it further. Lee flipped open the file, saw A4 blueprints stapled together, opened the folds and held them closer to the dim overhead light.

'This pervert is an architect. Award-winning architect, why I got the plans to his house so easy – they were published in a journal and available in the city library. He lives in a five-storey over there in North Freo. Two of the storeys are underground, carved out of the limestone, I guess for when the sheep ships are in port and the westerly's blowing. The fucker works from home, by all accounts, which makes getting in there trickier than the last one. I don't know the layout of the place beyond the blueprints there, or where he might hide nasty shit. My guess would be in the deepest level – what's called the basement on the plans but in reality, might be a dungeon of some sort. Who knows with these creeps—?'

'I'll head over there now and take a look,' Lee interrupted, because otherwise Bamber would go on all night. Lee understood his anger, but the mad-uncle routine was wearing thin. Before he left, though, he wanted to try something out. 'I'll get in there and take some photos. You want me to email them to you?'

Bamber looked at him appreciatively. 'Yes, son, that'd be good. You have a digital camera?'

Lee nodded. 'While I'm there, if I can put it on account, I could also bug the place.'

Bamber shook his head, watching an old man leave the rock wall carrying his rod and bucket, which he placed in the tray of his Hilux ute, clearing his nostrils with the bushman's blow on the limestone. 'In and out, son. In and out. We don't want to twig them to anything.'

Lee put out his hand. 'What's your email address?'

Bamber scribbled the numerals and letters on the file cover. The man didn't appear to be suspicious. When he'd finished writing, he looked down the mole and put one hand on the ignition key. 'If you can't get into the house, or can't find the picture, I'm told that the pervert drinks at the Rose Hotel every afternoon, from five to six. You might need to chum the water a bit, get yourself invited back home. You have any mickies?'

'I've got some Rohypnol. That'll work. Tranquillise a rhino if you do it right. I'll be in touch. In the meantime, this guy's an architect. The last guy was a town planner. You reckon that's a coincidence?'

Bamber smirked. 'Good try, son. Now off with you.'

Lee cracked his door. The old man before them backed up his ute and turned down the mole. The seagulls that had awoken to follow him from the rock wall turned hopefully toward the two sedans as Bamber turned his engine over, and Lee climbed out of the bucket seat into the stiff breeze. He was just around the front when Bamber hit the high beams, and the nearest seagulls began to screech and hover over the cold chips he'd thrown onto the bonnet, slowly pulling into gear and rolling onto the road. The cloud of gulls dive-bombed his car while he swerved to try to hit them.

20

Lee drove the silent streets of the riverside suburb, circling the mansion that fronted the verge footpath without a fence, or even a letterbox that Lee could identify. Two streets away from the highway, the building faced the port to the west, the garden roof no doubt catching the full glory of the ocean sunsets, unlike its Federation-era neighbours on either side. The building was made of recovered bricks and red oxidised steel, some of whose larger sheets were structural, giving the façade the appearance of a rusted tank. Other sheets were laid across the brickwork in a honeycomb pattern that softened the overall impression of an abandoned bunker, or something from another civilisation plonked down in the middle of leafy suburbia.

There were no lights on in the house, and the nearest streetlight was filtered through the branches of a row of peppermint trees. Lee parked underneath them, scrolled down his window and listened to the clanking from the port, and behind him from the river, where some male magpies were plaintively singing to the night, as they did this time of year. He was out of sight of the building's tinted floor-to-ceiling windows, and the balconies on each floor, and so he lit a cigarette and turned on the overhead light, began to read through the file given to him by Bamber, which was a comprehensive series of documents considering the limited time available. A photocopy of Mr Brian Laver's driver's licence. A printed list of prescriptions filled at a nearby chemist – valium, Zoloft, morphine sulphate in pill form, each at quite a high dose. A bad back and a troubled mind? Lee didn't know, and the scripts didn't tell him. The next photocopy was a list of properties owned by Laver, taken from a LandCorp database – twenty-three in all, spread across the Western Suburbs. Lee didn't recognise the name Laver, but then again, he didn't know the old families, didn't know whether Laver's wealth was new money or old. The man had no criminal record, not even speeding tickets according to an RTA printout. His immigration record was interesting, however. Extensive overseas travel, most recently to Cuba and other ports in the Caribbean. Many trips every year to the Philippines and to Thailand, Laos and Cambodia. Occasional trips to Sri Lanka and the Maldives. Very occasional flights to Europe, and then mostly to the Eastern Bloc. Lee didn't know whether these trips were work related or for pleasure, although in the dossier at the back of the file was a list, including photographs, of many of Laver's buildings, most of which were in Perth, with a few in Melbourne, Broome, Darwin and Singapore, each of them characterised by the use of oxidised steel as a structural and decorative element.

Lee reclined his seat a little, closed his eyes to lessen the burn. He thought about Laver inside his self-designed fortress, sleeping soundly or perhaps awake and staring at the ceiling, listening to the same industrial echoes from the port and the same magpies. He was respected in his wider circles, hiding his true nature from all but those like him. If he was the man Bamber painted him to be, moving like a chameleon through the world, how many others were like him? How many men were tainted with the desire to hurt children? How many men felt the desire but didn't act upon it? There was no way for such men to fulfil their desires without hurting children, either directly or indirectly – that much was a fact. Such men knew this, but still acted upon their desires, not caring about the harm they were doing, seeking others who also didn't care. That was the unforgivable crime, the reality that bleached out all of the moral shades of grey rising from questions of genetics, or of conditioning. It was the unforgivable crime that explained Bamber's reflexive hatred, the revulsion Lee felt when he contemplated the idea of Laver sleeping safely behind fortress walls, bringing forth again the uneasy memory of Lee and his father watching the disinterring of a body, back when Lee was a child. The lack of emotion in Daniel Southern's voice when he described finding Lee unresponsive, sleepy, impossible to wake after he'd left him in another's care, watching the man's bones pulled out of the loose, dry sand, before starting the truck, backing away into the impossibly white light of long ago.

Lee pushed away the memory, brought his focus back to Jessica Enright, the photograph of the bangle on her arm, the dungeon where she'd been imprisoned. If he was successful in retrieving the next photograph of Jessica from Laver, according to the photocopied letter there were three others who possessed a copy. Lee wondered who those men were, and whether they slept soundly, or whether they knew that someone was coming for them. It was the nature of predators to be aware of their prey, but also other predators.

21

She watched the young man make a U-turn in the narrow street, his headlights off until he was distant from the architect's home, and headed for the highway that would take him back across the river. She knew where he lived, and so didn't need to follow him, just yet.

Reaching for her water bottle, she realised that the young man's visible tension had become her tension. Her shoulders were tight, and she stretched her neck, heard the familiar creaking punctuated by an audible crack. She pushed down on her jawbone with one hand, felt the tension leave the joints, the tendons where she'd been gritting. She joined her hands and flexed her wrists, enjoyed the relief as her arms stretched, before shaking her hands out.

Sunlight was filling out the shadows in the street. She was surprised that the young man, whose name was Lee, hadn't stayed to watch the house, to see if the architect had routines that might provide an opportunity. She looked at her watch and, sure enough, there was the usual Hyundai sedan entering the head of the block, windows down to enable the driver, a young man wearing a Sikh headdress, to toss the rolled morning's papers over the car roof and into the front yards. The Hyundai reached the architect's house and stopped, the driver leaving the car and walking to the front door, depositing the paper through a special steel flap that funnelled it inside the house. The driver returned to his car and continued past her, invisible behind the van's tinted windows.

Out of habit, she glanced at her watch, although she needn't have. The architect didn't leave the house because of numbers on a clock, but according to the time when the paper was delivered. As usual, the front door now cracked and the architect emerged in his regular white speedos and t-shirt, a towel slung over his shoulder and the paper under one arm. He aimed his keys at the Audi parked on the verge opposite, whose lights flashed as it unlocked. The architect got behind the wheel of his car and checked his face in the rear-vision mirror, scratching some sleep from his eyes and running fingers through his wavy grey hair. If the architect was worried, he didn't show it. He pulled the car onto the road and headed toward the highway, which he crossed as he made his way past the steel silos and colourful stacks of shipping containers, turning north on the coast road away from the port, taking his time as the sunlight broke over the first dunes and settled upon the clear blue waters of the Indian Ocean.

She kept the van a good hundred metres back, not needing to keep pace, knowing where the architect met his friends: in the shallows before the whitewashed walls of the Leighton Beach surf lifesaving club. There the men waded to chest-deep water if the swell was gentle, or otherwise let the waves slap their thighs and buffet their legs as it fizzed up the shoreline. They never swam together, although each wore the swimmer's costume of speedos and racing goggles, pushed back on their heads. The men were tanned, and they were pale, overweight or fit-looking, tall or short, some were bald and some were not. Their vehicles in the carpark suggested their different classes or attitudes toward keeping up appearances.

Standing there in the ocean, arms folded against the morning chill, hands shielding eyes from the glare coming off the dunes, it wasn't possible to hear what was being said, and this, she supposed, was the purpose of their meeting this way. So too their near-nakedness had a rationale, she assumed, by excluding the possibility of one among them recording their conversation, as did their huddle separate them from the joggers and genuine morning swimmers, entering and leaving the water around them.

Many of the men and women who met regularly to swim together at this beach, and the dozens of others along the coast-line, had given themselves club names, such as the Iceberg Club, or the Shark-baits, the Silver Foxes, Washed-ups, the Oceanics or the Coffee Club. She shuddered to think what these men might call themselves, if given the chance.

She watched the architect enter the water, the champagne foam bubbling at his legs, reaching down and splashing water over his shoulders, arching his back as a cold wave washed against his belly. He didn't smile or shake hands with the four other men in the white-water foam. Even with the binoculars pressed against her burning eyes, she couldn't lip-read the men's conversation. They leant toward one another when they spoke, as though whispering in church. Without their knowing, she'd done everything in her power to put them at ease, to not startle the horses, to keep herself concealed, although the fact remained that their numbers were down two from last year, and one from last week. As a consequence, the men who normally met monthly were now meeting once a week.

She kept the bins fixed upon the men, hoping to read a snatch of phrase, or to catch a word. She had no fear of them noticing her, unlike the young man, Lee, who'd sensed her gaze back at the architect's house. Science said that it was merely foolish superstition, what was called *scopaesthesia*, the feeling of being looked at – the prickling awareness that a predator has eyes upon you, a remnant instinct from when humans were more hunted than hunter. While she had sat invisible behind the tinted windows of her van, watching the young man as he smoked and scoped the house, several times he'd broken off from his surveillance to look at her, directly, sensing her eyes upon him, even though he couldn't possibly see her.

She would have to be careful of him, she realised. He wasn't like the other men, out there in the waves, thinking themselves safe, hidden in plain sight.

22

Lee caught a few hours sleep, sprawled in his king-size while the sun rose across the clear morning sky. He awoke at midday, the hot easterly making his bedroom curtains exhale. In the kitchen he made himself some honey toast and a cup of coffee, before sitting on the back step and looking over the exposed limestone bones of his backyard that sloped to the traffic on Hampden Road. A djiti-djiti was loud in a nearby banksia tree, darting away to peck at a crow sitting on the sagging asbestos fence, the crow pretending not to notice.

Lee shaved, showered and got dressed in jeans and a collared work shirt. He slipped on his socks and boots and filled his thermos with coffee. Only now did he open the letter from his mother, perched between a jar of melaleuca honey and a salt shaker. He knew what the letter contained, had been trying not to think about it, but his heart still sank as he read the news that she'd returned to the South West. She had hives to move and combs to scrape but would be back sometime near the end of the month. It wasn't long to wait, but Lee was still disappointed. He loved his father and his mother, but experience had taught him that his volatile father couldn't be trusted. If Lee was in danger, his father would be there, but that wasn't the same thing as the confidence his mother inspired with her quiet words and good example.

It hadn't happened overnight, but had dawned on him one day, that the reason he felt comfortable around her was because of something he'd never felt toward an adult before – he trusted her completely.

Lee rolled up the dog blanket near the front door and nudged it into a corner. He set out into the heat and sunshine of a postcard summer day, the wind on the cusp of cooling as it turned southerly. If the wind maintained, the evening would be chilly, but if it dropped it'd be hot and sticky. He took a jacket just in case and threw it and the thermos onto the front seat of the Fairlane, turned the ignition and pulled from the kerb.

Connor Baird was waiting for him at their regular table in the university tavern. It was where they'd first gotten to know one another, over jugs of warm beer. Connor didn't know it, but Lee had observed the surly young man for many weeks before approaching him outside the lecture theatre, asking for a light. The Wednesday advanced computer programming class that Lee sat in on was filled with keen students, but none of them looked likely. Connor, however, was different from the others, from his camo jacket with anarchist symbols to his unkempt hair and shaggy beard. On Connor it wasn't the regular grunge fashion, but instead something that Lee suspected the man lived and breathed. Connor never asked the lecturer questions, or answered them either, unless he was directly asked, and then he knew the correct answer every time. Baird gave the impression of someone as knowledgeable about the course materials as the lecturer, an overweight man who wore a badly fitting suit, no matter the temperature. Lee had approached Baird and they'd had chatted

I AM ALREADY DEAD

about Errico Malatesta, in particular, and Lee liked how Connor's initial wariness had dissolved into open relief as he realised Lee Southern couldn't possibly be a special branch operative looking into student radicals because he knew too much about the subject. They'd gone to the tavern where they chatted until closing time, Lee holding his drink while Baird got progressively drunker, although even when he was fall-down drunk, as Lee had secretly hoped, he hadn't spilled the reason he was so paranoid about undercover cops befriending him. This came out in subsequent meetings. Just as Lee suspected, Connor Baird's politics and his brilliant mind when it came to computers worked in tandem, in the privacy of his garage den beneath his father's two-storey stucco townhouse in Claremont. But Lee was wrong when he'd assumed that Baird knew as much as his lecturer in the advanced programming lectures – in fact, Baird knew more – in the same way that a safe-cracker knows more about the workings of a safe than a safe-installer. Baird was a hacker, just as Lee had guessed when he'd observed him in the preceding weeks. Lee initially felt bad for cultivating Connor's friendship for his own ends, although that didn't matter as the friendship became genuine, and the respect mutual. Lee had things that he could teach Connor Baird too, namely the workings of the stockmarket that Swann had schooled him in. Baird was very interested in the stockmarket, but not as a player, more a disruptor. He was discreet enough not to talk in detail, but the man's intentions were clear enough – he wanted to redistribute wealth in the best way he knew how, by stealing it and depositing it in unexpected and worthy places.

Lee took a mouthful of the warm beer and watched Baird's eyes

113

flicker as he looked at Bamber's card. 'This'll be enough, I reckon.'

'It's all I've got,' Lee said. 'He's an old guy, so I don't imagine that his passwords will be extra clever. But I don't have time to dig around on him – footy team, pet names, nicknames etc.'

Baird emptied his glass, wiping froth from his moustache and chin. He was bug-eyed and sleepless, as always, and with his beard combed out and nightclub tan, he looked like a Viking who'd been drained of blood. 'Don't think that'll be necessary. I'll put on my man voice and call the company direct. Ask for Paul Enright's secretary. Her email address will likely use the same structure. I'll send her a Trojan message, ask her to click on a link etc., and then I'll be in. The fact that they're using this email service tells me security is an afterthought. If Bamber's their head of security, and he's an old guy like you say, I doubt they'll see it coming.'

Lee and Baird touched glasses, swallowed their beers. The tavern was quiet and smelled of beermats, but it was pleasant enough in the dappled light of the courtyard. Baird was also a font of absurd stories, gleaned not from his own life, but from the intercepted communications and surveillance he spent his life undertaking, watching people when their guards were down, not knowing that they were being watched. For Baird, it was an aspect of *Know Thy Enemy*, but there was personal pleasure to be had, too, in reading what the CEO of an oil and gas company really thought of the environmental regulator, in between watching porn on his company desktop and emailing his wife to say that he'd only been able to secure one ticket to Melbourne for the conference next week, even as he searched the internet for the names of Victorian escort agencies. Baird was fascinated by getting a reading on the true faces behind the masks that everyone wore, and hacking was going to be, he thought, a revolutionary means of showing what really goes on in the minds of the powerful and greedy, behind the various misdirections. Lee didn't share Baird's optimism, but he couldn't fault his friend's commitment. He filled Baird's glass a final time and patted his shoulder, leaving through the courtyard into the carpark, enjoying the alcohol cooling his blood, softening the burn of the afternoon sun.

23

The Rose Hotel sat off to the side of the North Fremantle town centre, isolated from the rest of the Victorian-era buildings by a highway channelling trucks to the port. Lee stepped into the cool chamber of the front bar and left the fumes, heat and traffic outside. It was 4.30 and the bar was empty apart from a couple of men in bowling whites drinking pony glasses at the horseshoe. As Lee approached, they turned and checked him out, and he nodded, and they nodded back. They had cash on the bar and the bartender, an older man with a drinker's nose and keg-belly, saw that their glasses were empty and filled them, taking the separate two-dollar coins and turning to the till, swiping out the change. By the time he'd turned, the men had finished their ponies, which they turned over on the beer mat, as per the ritual of their generation. They pocketed their change and without a word picked up their bowling bags and made for the door.

Lee was now the only customer, and when the bartender finally met his gaze he nodded toward one of the empty ponies, and the man nodded back and slid a hand onto the tray beneath him. It only took a second to fill the fresh glass. Lee gave the man a five dollar note and took a stool on the corner of the bar, where he could watch the door but also make conversation with potential customers either side of him. Like the old men had done, Lee left his cash on the bar mat, signalling that he expected it to be refilled as soon as it was empty. This was done deliberately to detain the bartender, who looked Lee over before asking, out the side of his mouth, 'You passin through? Haven't seen you before.'

Lee finished his pony glass of ice-cold Swan Draught, which had gone down nicely. 'Normally drink at The Railway, or The Swan,' he replied, to which the bartender nodded, but didn't meet his eye. The Rose was one of three pubs within walking distance of one another. The Railway and The Swan serviced the dock workers and student crowd when they put music on, which was often, while The Rose had a more suburban clientele.

'You workin or livin in the area?' the older man asked, not out of curiosity but just as something to say.

'Living,' Lee said. 'Just round the corner. The flats past the bowling club.'

The bartender gave Lee a stern look and nodded, content in the knowledge that the tenants of the nearest flats were generally transient, and broke, and probably not worth the effort of cultivating.

Just to play, Lee added, 'Finished two years on the mines at Paraburdoo. Bugger all to do up there except drink down by the waterhole, water's the same temperature as an iced beer, bloody beautiful.' As though exhausted by the words, Lee paused. 'Gonna buy myself a house, a troopy and a fucking big boat. You know anybody—'

'Matter of fact I do,' the bartender replied, taking Lee's glass with renewed enthusiasm and filling it. 'All of those things. Got a lot of cousins. And my cousins have got a lot of cousins. Boats, cars, houses ... guns, girls, goey or dirty pictures, you name it, mate.'

Lee raised his glass just as the door bumped open, letting in a blast of noise and light, by degrees. Whoever was pushing the doors wasn't strong, but instead of an elderly man or woman, Lee recognised the punter as Laver, the architect dressed in chinos and polo shirt, a pink jumper wrapped around his neck, boaters on his feet. The man's silver hair and deep tan matched the outfit, but the impression that Laver had magically walked off the streets of Milan and into the Rose was ruined by his visible lack of disappointment. Instead, he ran hands through his mane of hair, and smiled a big beaming smile, his teeth white and even.

'Guvnor, a pint of your finest ale, if you please.'

The bartender smiled back, although the smile was strained. He took out a pint glass from inside the misted fridge and put it under the draught tap.

Laver continued playing the country gent, or the boatie wanker, Lee couldn't tell which. 'Oh well, lager will have to do then.'

Laver had the length of bar to choose from, but he sidled up to Lee and whispered under his breath, 'Cat's piss,' just loud enough for the bartender to hear. 'And whatever my friend here is drinking. Oh, lager too.'

It couldn't have worked out better for Lee. Despite Bamber's suggestion that Lee ingratiate himself to Laver, and get himself invited back home, Lee couldn't see himself making small talk with the man. He only had to think of the photos in Drew's shed and he was liable to lose it. But he smiled. He would be as quiet as possible and play along as best he could. When Laver went to the toilet, as every pint drinker must, Lee would take his opportunity.

So that the bartender didn't feel the need to hang around, Lee turned over his pony glass.

'I'll have a pint, too,' he said, 'and a shot of Jameson. If he's paying.'

24

Lee followed Laver at a distance, and from across the road. He had left The Rose right after he'd slipped Laver the mickey – three crushed Rohypnol tablets pre-mixed with water. He knew that Laver took meds for depression or anxiety, and that he likely had a tolerance for tranquillisers, and so the dose was pretty high. On top of three pints of beer and two shots of Jameson, he knew that the surge would come quickly. Lee kept his cap pulled low and watched Laver for signs of wobbliness or distress. He didn't want the architect to keel over until he was around the corner and onto his quiet street – he didn't want to have to carry him while there was still daylight.

Laver turned the corner into the narrow street. There was nobody about, as Lee had hoped, watering lawns or washing cars, setting off to walk the dog or checking their mailbox. It started with a stiffness in Laver's step, soon followed by a spongy rhythm as the man's feet splayed, staggering a little on both sides, putting his arms out instinctively in case he fell. Lee was right there, taking a shoulder, whispering hello out the side of his mouth, eyes scanning for observers.

Bamber didn't want Laver to know that he'd been knocked out, and so Lee guided the man toward the front door, where he hoped there'd be no security camera. Up the steps, Lee used his right knee to pin Laver against the wall, fingers emptying the only pocket that bulged, drawing out a handful of coins and a set of keys, heaviest among them a leather pendant Audi keyring attached to the standard front door key. Lee held the smaller man with a grip in his armpit, and turned the key even as he looked up and saw the cold lens of a security camera inside the doorway. It was unusual to have the camera facing the door from inside the house, and Lee felt a moment of panic as he looked for an alarm system that might've been tripped. There wasn't one visible, and he wedged the door open with a heel and hefted the now unconscious Laver onto his right shoulder, distributing the weight across his back in a fireman's carry, entering the cool vestibule of the lower floor. The weak light between the drawn curtains revealed an open-plan lounge area with a view of the park across the road and a kitchen with a view of a small courtyard to the rear, containing a lap pool and koi pond.

Lee had a decision to make. Either he put Laver to bed and make his search, removing the video footage of their entry on his departure, possibly triggering Laver to search his prized and illicit possessions, or Lee could continue to play the role he'd begun back at The Rose – that of a young man who'd spun a yarn about being fresh from the mines, but who'd raised suspicions with his willingness to bludge drinks off Laver, heading out early into the carpark to follow the man home, to ambush him and gain entry to his house and belongings.

Lee knew which would be more fun, but he decided on the former. Laver would likely not remember much about the preceding evening when he awoke in about twelve hours, and unless he later questioned the bartender, there was little chance of Lee being identified.

Lee carried the architect up a flight of stairs made from recycled jarrah sleepers, scanning the rooms until he reached the top floor, containing Laver's vast bedroom with a view south to the river and west to the ocean, where the sun glowed like a coal above the seam of sky and water. Lee took in the lay of the fastidiously maintained room: not a sock on the floor or a door or drawer opened in the built-in wardrobes and chests. He pulled back the doona on Laver's bed and dropped him onto his back. He went and drew the curtains, returned to take off Laver's shoes and socks, placing the shoes in the rack inside the largest cupboard, the socks in the dirty washing hamper. He took off Laver's trousers and put his wallet and keys into the bowl beside the door, which contained other sets of keys. He put the trousers and Laver's shirt in the hamper and leaving the man in his pinstriped boxers, rolled him under the doona, tucking the pillow under his head and putting him into the recovery position, to avoid him swallowing his tongue. Lee went back to the bowl by the door and took up the keys again, before heading downstairs. He went straight to the security camera, mounted on the wall, and followed the wiring down a thin conduit concealed behind an exposed steel beam, to a small filing cabinet whose paintwork had been removed. The buffed, plain-steel look blended with the steel beam and the supporting I-bar which ran along the ceiling above. Lee opened the cabinet and found the camera source: a black and white monitor with two live feeds; one from the camera above his head and another showing a darkened room. The feeds were being recorded onto a

VHS player beside which were six tapes marked for every day of the week, for each of the cameras. Lee ejected the current tape and looked at its spine, marked *door/Monday*. Its tabs weren't broken, meaning that the tapes were probably rotated on a weekly cycle, recording over the previous week's footage, which weren't time-stamped. The feed for the darkened room wasn't being recorded, so Lee had nothing to worry about there. He put the cassette back in the player and rewound for a couple of minutes, pressed record and let the footage resume. He took up the keys and began his search where he suspected the darkened room to be – in one of the two subterranean floors.

25

Lee did a final walk-around of the hanging doors, boot and bonnet, and the chassis which sat in the middle of Tony's workshop. Outside the workshop, the easterly was pulsing off the desert, making the tin roof tremble, but inside the hermetically sealed painting room, the air was heavy and still. Lee was stripped to his boots and jeans because of the heat, but even so his torso was slick with sweat, and inside the mask his nose dripped. The banks of lights illuminated the car body from every angle, but he still did a circuit holding a hook light close to the painted surfaces, looking for evidence of sag or unevenness or missed layers between coats. The paintwork looked good, almost too good, and he felt the familiar satisfaction of the proper application of a hard-earned skill. The last few hours had passed quietly inside the painting chamber, with only the hiss of the electric paint-gun and the muffled steaming of his breath within the mask to suggest its passing. White on white on white: the colours of the body parts and the light and the walls of the plastic-curtained chamber – the only exception the deep tan of his bare skin. He felt the strong urge for a cigarette as he left the chamber, turning off the lights and looking back a final time to admire his work, but regretted it immediately. What had seconds ago glowed with light now lurked in the shadows, hung from hooks and mounted on spikes, resembling a butcher's shop or a slaughterhouse floor.

Lee washed himself in the sink beneath the silvered mirror, lathering up his arms and scrubbing at the dried paint on his skin with a slab of abrasive sponge. He dried himself with a threadbare towel, then lit a cigarette, drawing in the sweet hot smoke and exhaling through his nose. It was only now that he picked up his pager and saw the number flashing on the screen. He was expecting a call from Bamber, to confirm the fixer's receipt of the grainy polaroid image retrieved from Laver's basement room, which Lee had put into an envelope and dropped into the letterbox of a Mosman Park flat, as agreed. But Lee didn't recognise the number on the pager, and he was too tired to wonder. As he'd hoped, the concentration and exertion of the past hours had brought him to the point where he might sleep. After what he'd seen at Laver's house, his retreat into task-oriented work had been a relief. The alternative was to let himself into Gerry and Frank Swann's boxing gym and work out his fury on the heavy bag, but the Dodge's doors needed painting, his client was waiting for the finished vehicle, and he was glad that they were done.

Lee went back through to Gerry's workshop. He'd planned on working until dawn, when he might return any calls, but sunrise was a few hours away. He checked Gerry's answering machine one final time. There was no word from Gerry Tracker about his return date from Leonora, which meant that he might be out in the bush with Blake, his son. Lee hoped that they were both alright, and that nothing had happened to them. Like so many in the Aboriginal community that Lee was aware of, Gerry and Blake had seen a staggering amount of death among their kinfolk. Gerry himself had a dodgy heart valve, and last month he'd passed out on the freeway doing a hundred, having the presence of mind to take his foot from the accelerator and brake as he went under, still writing off the client's car. Gerry was like a father to Lee, and Blake like a brother. Leonora was a long drive away, and he thought about calling the community during the afternoon, just to make sure, on the pretence of calling about the vehicles he'd serviced. Gerry would see through the pretence, but that'd be alright.

The suburban streets of Spearwood, Hamilton Hill and Beaconsfield were quiet and empty. The streetlights that illuminated the façades of the houses gave the suburb the air of a film set, complete with painted tree silhouettes and a projected moon. He drove slowly, settling into his weariness, not wanting to wake himself up, aiming for the autopilot drift from his car to his bed, as he'd done so many times.

Lee entered his street and began the routine. Glide to a park. Pull the handbrake. Put her in neutral, turn off the ignition and pull the key. Open the door without letting go of the keys, to isolate his front door key. The rest would take care of itself.

But not this morning. He smelt the cigarette smoke and saw the thickened shadow beside the veranda pillar that framed his front door.

From zero to a hundred in a heartbeat, Lee's mind turned to his recent client Marie and her husband, the man who'd killed before and was cruel enough to put out his cigarettes on her skin. Lee slipped the door key between his fingers to form a jabbing blade, eyes wide and shoulders tensed, taking in the bank of shadow. Alert to movement, his heart jumped when he saw a figure release from the wall, rising from the bentwood chair placed beside the door. It was a woman, standing into the pale moonlight cast between the pillars; the young woman from the nightclub, the rookie cop, her name was Lisa, now seeing the alarm on his face and opening her hands to show their emptiness, amusement in her eyes, reaching a hand toward him to take his own, gently guiding him to her.

26

The phone rang in the hallway and echoed through the house. Lee was dreaming of walking through a city he'd never visited, despite recognising the buildings and shopfronts as familiar, and for a few moments the clarion echo of the phone was a distant police siren, until he opened his eyes. Lisa was getting dressed in the corner of the room, away from the blades of morning light framing the heavy curtains, and he saw from the expression on her face that the telephone had disturbed her making a quiet exit. She smiled at him, belting up the heavy blue work trousers that were part of her uniform. Her chest was bare, and he could see that she wasn't self-conscious, and so he smiled back and rubbed sleep from his eyes.

'You going to get that?'

Lee had tuned out the phone, despite its volume and insistence.

'If it's important, I'll get a page.'

As he said this the phone died, and then the pager still attached to his jeans, kicked off beside the bed, began to buzz.

Lee sighed but didn't move. The gym bag that Lisa had brought in last night was empty on the bed. She clicked on her bra, then reached for the pale blue short-sleeve shirt that was ironed and hanging on the door of Lee's old wardrobe. He noticed now that she'd showered, and had brought her own towel and bag of toiletries. He thought to comment on it, but she was reading him anyway, noticing the things that he noticed, as he noticed them. She smirked, buttoned the top button, ran a hand through her short hair, put her hands on her tactical belt and framed her shoulders back.

'You enjoy that?' she asked.

'You wear it well.'

'Women in uniform, eh? Why is that?'

Lee smiled. 'I don't know.'

'And you don't care either, right?'

'Never thought too much about it. It's just you and me here.'

She glanced at her watch. 'Not any longer. I'm switching shifts, as of midday. Better go.'

She walked the short distance and kissed him, ruffled his hair, turned and walked to the door, picking up her gym bag, knowing that he was watching, still smiling.

He heard the latch on the front door click, then a minute later the engine of her Civic turn over, little scrape of sand against tyres, and then she was away.

Lee turned back into the pillow, but the sleep was gone. She'd told him about the shift change early this morning, just as the sun was rising, as he drifted into sleep, his laboured breathing and hammering heart of a few minutes previous dying away, his legs still shaky, her face in his neck, her calm breath on his ear.

It was only then that she'd admitted she found his home address by logging into the RTA database, matching his car rego to his name, and then his street number. After all, he hadn't called.

He'd thought about calling, he replied. Thought *a lot* about it, but didn't know her shifts, didn't know if she had a partner, didn't know anything about her really. And he'd been working nights, days, nonstop since he'd seen her that first time. She didn't ask on what, and he didn't offer an answer. She was already kissing him again, rising above him.

27

The page was from Frank Swann. Lee dialled Swann's home number but there was no answer, then tried his mobile 'brick' in case Swann was in his car. The mobile was handy enough for Lee to have his eye on buying one, but the cost was prohibitive, and the thing was too large to fit in anything smaller than a briefcase. Swann used his essentially as a car-phone, due to its size and weight, but it was a handy piece of kit, as demonstrated when Swann answered on the third ring, the sound of freeway traffic becoming muffled as Swann wound up the electric windows on his Brougham.

'You calling from home?' Swann asked, and Lee answered in the affirmative. Swann suggested that they meet at his house, and Lee readily agreed – it would be good to get the older man's advice on how he thought the Enright case was tracking.

Lee got there before Swann, who swept the Lincoln-green Holden into his drive, coming to a precise stop beneath the shading arms of the bottlebrush, above the sand-filled tray that was there to catch the Brougham's leaking engine oil. Lee waited on the front porch, in the shade, scratching the coat of the Swanns' dog, as she liked. He could never remember the dog's name, but that didn't matter to the dog, who seemed to favour Lee above everyone, except perhaps Swann. The dog was part kelpie and part staffy, which made it look like she was smiling at Swann as he climbed from his car.

Lee didn't know what case Swann was working on, except that he was working less and less these days. While the coming of the internet had made his job easier in some respects, allowing him to track disreputable corporate types and the companies they worked for, it had also opened up the field he'd made his own – stockmarket scams and scammers – to a broader range of players, many of whom never set foot in Australia. Detection and tracing of said crimes increasingly involved online surveillance that Swann found frustrating and tedious. His strengths lay in knowing everybody, and accommodating a vast array of informants, among people who owed him favours. Swann's old-school way of doing things was becoming increasingly difficult, in an era when serious criminals made sure to keep away from jurisdictions where they could be arrested, and instead were able to operate safely from a distance.

Lee could see the effort it took Swann to raise a smile for the dog, whose tail was thumping the porch decking as it shivered with excitement. Swann rubbed her silky ears and nodded to the front door.

'No,' Lee answered. 'Nobody else home.'

Swann took a seat in one of the old rattan chairs that were bleached by the afternoon sun. Lee sat back against the weather-boards and lit a cigarette whose smoke made the dog abandon him and go to Swann. Lee waited for Swann's words to match the heat in his eyes.

'The first guy you looked at. The town planner. He's gone missing.'

There was an interrogative aspect to the statement in Swann's voice, reading Lee for his reaction, which was to voice the first thought that came into his head.

'I don't know anything about that.'

Swann believed him; that much was clear. 'Leopards and spots, Lee, it's my fault for letting Enright—'

'Nah, he didn't gull you,' Lee interrupted. 'Me either. I'd actually be surprised if he or his man Bamber would be that stupid.'

Lee watched Swann, remembering the dark thoughts he'd been entertaining regarding the deeds of Laver, and before him, the town planner Drew. 'Of course, I don't have any children,' Lee added. 'Bamber's been like a junkyard dog off the leash. All it would take is an order from Enright.'

'What are some other options?' Swann asked.

Lee nodded. He realised he hadn't asked for the circumstances, the background to the disappearance. 'Someone else in the little chain of pedos, removing a weak link? But how would they know? I've been discreet. How did you find out?'

Swann was eyeing Lee's cigarette a little hungrily, Lee realised, and so he stubbed it out and slid the packet toward his pocket.

'An old sergeant I know, at Central. I got him to look into Drew, after you gave me the name. Thought his name sounded familiar. Turns out that his elder brother was murdered, about eighteen months ago. Bludgeoned and bashed, found in a shallow grave up in Gnangara. Coppers put it down to a gay bashing taken to the next level, it looked so frenzied.'

'Why did they assume that he was gay?'

'Depends on the investigating D's. Wore a pink shirt? Had an earring? Don't know, but I'm in the process of getting the files. It's still an open investigation.'

'Drew the younger. How do they know he's missing? I was only there a few days ago.'

'Neighbour called it in. Noticed his front door, wide open at night. Lights off though. Coppers found the place had been trashed, attempt had been made to burn it down, but the bedroom mattress with accelerants had flamed out.'

Lee resisted the urge to light another cigarette. He straightened his back against the boards, stretched out his legs.

'You can smoke around me, Lee. Just don't give me one, even if I ask.'

Lee grinned, lit a cigarette. 'Why would Bamber, if he was taking Drew, trash the place? I already gave him everything he needs. Why make it look like a home invasion?'

Swann shrugged, pushed the dog away a little. She could be a bit demanding when she wanted affection. She waited a beat then went back to nudging Swann's hand. He relented, and began to stroke her ears while she lay her head on his knee, until Lee's pager began to trill, and the dog's ears pricked.

'Look at that,' Swann said. 'She knows that sound. Knows that it's always followed by bad news.'

'Yep,' Lee agreed, looking down at Bamber's number on the illuminated screen.

28

'It's put the whole thing at risk,' Bamber hissed, not waiting until Lee had locked the Fairlane and turned to him. Lee nodded toward the nearby bus stop, whose vandalism-proof glass sides had been smashed in, laying a puzzle of glittering pieces across the footpath. The newly trialled glass surfaces were apparently easier to clean of graffiti, but the claim of being impact-resistant was too much of a challenge to suburban kids – every second bus stop seemed under repair.

Lee and Bamber crunched over the glass. The burnished steel ceiling of the bus stop protected them from the fierce sun, whose rays always seemed more venomous mixed with traffic fumes. Heat radiated off the four-lane highway onto their faces and hands, and Bamber was already sweating. Lee could smell the booze on him. Beads of sweat pushed through the skin on his forearms and just as quickly evaporated. He hadn't shaved, and his hair had been combed with his fingers, which made Lee suspect that the Canning Highway meet had been called because it was close to Bamber's residential address.

Lee tapped out a cigarette and lit it as a bus swooshed past, raising grit into their faces. On Swann's advice, Lee was determined to say as little as possible, sufficient only to make it clear to Bamber that he'd done nothing to Drew. The rest of the time he was tasked with reading the fixer, to ascertain if he'd failed to control himself. If so, according to Swann, should anything come to light, it'd be standard arse-covering practice to try and put the blame for Drew's disappearance on Lee. If Lee's gut told him that Bamber was lying, or being evasive in any way, then he was to walk away, and not look back.

'Can I get one of those?' Bamber asked, his voice throttled with fatigue. He took the cigarette and lit it, his lungs rasping out a cough before the smoke settled. Bamber stared at Lee hard, then smiled weakly, nodded to the floor.

'I told Enright that you weren't the type. Take matters into your own hands and go the full vigilante and whatnot. But I had to look into your eyes and see for myself. Frank told you what's gone down?'

'Yes, although only what you know,' Lee lied. 'Why did you call him, anyway, and not me?'

'Apart from the fact that he's your boss, the same reason as I'm sitting here with you. I needed to hear it in his voice. The surprise. His worry for you. Which I did.'

Bamber hadn't told Swann about Drew's older brother, and his murder a year and a half ago. Lee wondered about that, and Bamber's temper, but for the time being he just wanted to make sure. Bamber had previously threatened Drew with murder, had been visibly traumatised by the material Lee had discovered. But would that anger lead him to break his employer's trust and put the recovery of the photographs in jeopardy?

'I have to ask,' Lee said. 'Did either you, or Enright, perhaps through another channel, have anything to do with trashing Drew's place, his disappearance?'

Bamber looked at Lee, note of frustration there but nothing else. 'No, son, I've fantasised about taking him for the long drive, but no. My question to you is, could you possibly have tipped him to the break-in, made him run, make it look like an abduction? I've got eyes and ears at all the motels, the country servos and campgrounds.'

Lee shrugged, shook his head. He'd been more than careful. The question wasn't worthy. 'Did the coppers search the shed, find the rest of the stuff under the filing cabinet?'

'No, not yet, and maybe never. And how would that help us? At the moment they've got a civilian gone missing, a white man, kind of a big deal. But if they learn he's a pedo, they'll give up, and fair enough too. We *want* them looking for him, at least for now.'

Lee agreed. 'Have you made the second payment for the photos I took from Laver?'

'What makes you think there's a second payment?'

Lee didn't have to think much on that. 'Human nature.'

Bamber laughed, but there was bitterness in it. 'Yeah. Human nature. You think the blackmailer might be cleaning up as he goes along?'

Lee shrugged. 'I would've thought they'd leave that up to us. We're the emotionally invested party here.'

'Yes. Sure enough. Although maybe they see it as a public duty, like we all should.'

Lee ground out his cigarette. A bus poured down the hill from the west. The steep incline was the inspiration for the song 'Highway to Hell', or so the story went, due to the number of smashes, or perhaps the nearby house of heroin dealer Chambers, hung by the Malaysians back in the '80s. The bus slowed, boxed in by a grey Honda driven by a grey-haired old man, before swinging wide and dropping into the deeply shadowed valley. Lee watched the bus slide by. The driver hadn't glanced their way to see if they wanted to get on, making the most of the momentum.

'So what next?' Lee asked. 'Do we wait for Drew to turn up, dead or alive or, assuming there's more contact from the blackmailer, do we continue?

Bamber didn't hesitate. 'We continue. I don't know what happened to Drew, and I genuinely don't care, so long as nothing points our way. If you're sure that you didn't leave anything in Drew's place that might finger you, we're golden.'

'I'm sure. A question. Your mate, or mates in the force. Any of them involved in the investigation into Jessica Enright's kidnapping?'

Bamber gave Lee a sharp look but smiled. 'Fucking dog with a bone.'

Lee reflected Bamber's grin. 'Only one way to learn.'

Bamber nodded. 'That's true enough. But only while we're waiting for our mystery man to contact us again, with another name. And not on the clock, either. Your own time. This bloke's a commander now. Homicide, CIB, Major Crimes – they burned him out. He's back in the uniform. Essentially an administrator. He'll be good on the background, assuming he agrees. Name's Duncan Corbett, in his last few years of service. He's hard to get hold of, but I'll put in a word, and you give him my name – not Enright's.

Lee offered Bamber another cigarette, which he declined. It might be the hangover, or it might be the gentle pressure of time spent together, forming a weld, but Bamber was clearly warming to Lee.

'Thanks,' Lee said. 'Let me know—'

Bamber put up his hands. 'If I hear anything. Course.'

Lee turned up the hill toward his car while Bamber walked deeper into the valley, where the golden arches and their promise of stomach-settling grease were no doubt calling to him.

29

Felicity Enright stood out from the rest of the drinkers at The Left Bank by virtue of being alone, and hidden in the shadows behind a pillar. Her table had been moved from a sunlit corner; Lee could see the drag marks on the cement, away from the swirling groups of midday drinkers, faces reddened by the harsh light, sunglasses shielding their eyes. The river beneath the Stirling Bridge glittered blackly under its strip of shade, whereas everywhere else its surface was beaten silver as the easterly gusted down the limestone canyon studded with mansions and apartment buildings.

Lee went to the bar and ordered himself a pint of Guinness, hoping that the drink would serve as both painkiller and semi-solid lunch. Waiting for the head to settle before the bartender completed the final pour gave him time to watch Felicity Enright in the shelving mirror, away to his left. She wore an expensive pair of sunglasses, large enough to cover much of her face, although her hair was pulled back into a simple ponytail, and she didn't appear to be wearing lipstick, or makeup. She was eerily pale in the soft light beneath the grapevine arbour; her long arms and hands an antique milky white, which in Australia could only mean she never went outside during the day. She sat very still, moving only to raise her cigarette to her lips, often forgetting to ash. She never moved to touch her drink. Her long fingers rested beside a highball glass filled with rapidly melting ice, alongside what looked like a jug of Campari and soda. Lee wondered if she was medicated, or whether her stillness and lack of expressiveness was a form of blending in. At a table nearby, a glass fell and smashed on the concrete. Felicity didn't flinch, or turn to look.

Lee approached with his pint and was readying himself to smile and speak when Felicity looked directly at him. She had clearly been watching him too, and she nodded toward the empty seat opposite her, stubbing out her cigarette and reaching for her packet to take another. When she'd lit up, blowing smoke out of the side of her mouth, she offered Lee the packet of Silk Cut. He took one and accepted the flame, having never heard of the brand before.

'I got a taste for them in London,' she explained. 'Dad imports them for me.'

Her voice was slow and deliberate, her accent a little plummy, as though she kept company with the older members of the Western Suburbs set.

The cigarette was a bit weak for Lee's tastes, and he twisted off half the filter and dropped it into the ashtray, which made Felicity raise her eyebrows and smile. 'Yes, sorry, they're one milligram. My concession to trying to quit, or at least cut back. That's a novel adaptation.'

'Thanks for meeting me,' Lee said. 'And for travelling south of the border.'

Felicity smirked, and lifted off her sunglasses, revealing hazel eyes that glinted green. 'Barely. I can still see my homeland across the river. Just in case I need to, you know, repatriate in a hurry.'

'Hopefully that won't be necessary. I'm not sure what Louise told you about me, and why I wanted to meet …'

Lee let it hang there, hoping that Felicity would take it from him. He had to proceed cautiously, after all. Enright had made it clear that he didn't want Felicity tipped to the photographs, or to the demands for money. If Louise hadn't been a mutual friend, he might pretend at being a journalist, or a writer interested in the kidnapping never resolved.

It was the look in Felicity's eyes, however, mildly amused at Lee's discomfort and yet edged with light, the kind of light created when sunshine passes through tears, that made him understand.

'You know everything. About the photographs. The names. My role in all this.'

Felicity nodded, blinked, resetting her eyes. Clear and determined now, leaning forward, her voice a whisper. 'Yes, that's correct.'

'Bamber,' Lee added. 'He's taking quite a risk.'

'Not really. He's never stopped looking, after all these years. He made a promise, you see.'

'That's good to know. Good to know that everything I tell Bamber will come to you.'

Felicity took another puff, blew the smoke out hard. 'Although not necessarily the other way around. I'm assuming you don't want him to know, about … this.'

'I'm assuming that he knows I'll approach you. I can't talk to your father. I've read the files. Despite the size of the investigation, and the personnel involved, every line of inquiry peters into nothing, not even speculation or unanswered questions, just … nothing.'

'I guess the question is, why do you want to speak to me? Why do you want to attempt more than you've been asked to?'

The question took Lee by surprise, although it shouldn't have – he'd anticipated her asking him. It was the tone in Felicity's voice, and the look in her eyes that told him she already knew the answer. 'At first, to prove to Frank Swann that I can handle something this complex. Then, to learn on the job, about … a major police investigation, about this kind of crime, about the corporate world, and people like your father.'

Felicity's expression hadn't changed, as though she was waiting for what she knew came next.

'But then I saw the photographs. Not just of your sister, but …'

Felicity surprised him by placing her cigarette in the ashtray, taking his hands. Lee watched the blue veins in her wrists that snaked up her forearms into the crook of her elbow. For someone so thin, she had a surprising strength. He looked at the matching strength in her eyes, burning with a clear light that became brighter and fiercer as she began to speak.

30

Lee put the Fairlane into gear and powered up the East Street hill, away from the river. He was caught in school pick-up traffic near the John Curtin Senior High School turn-off when his pager began to vibrate. He'd been anticipating a summons from Bamber related to a third set of photographs, but the call was from Firmin, the Club Summertime owner. Lee ignored the pager and waited to turn past the school, trapped in a line of 4WDs and people-movers as the school siren sounded. As though someone had kicked an ants' nest, hundreds of students began to pour out of the main gates, clogging the paths and slowing the traffic even more. Lee was headed to Frank Swann's house to debrief, after Felicity had talked almost uninterruptedly for an hour, occasionally leaning toward Lee's recorder when she wanted something emphasised, or to repeat herself on the occasions nearby drunks had laughed thunderously or shouted to their friends. Twice, women had seen the recorder and recognised the brand of Felicity's large glasses propped on her head, and approached to ask if she was someone famous. Both times Felicity had ignored them until they went away, swearing at her rudeness.

There was a lot that Lee needed to talk about with Swann, specifically Felicity's frankness about her father's relationship with Jessica, who he refused to talk about, and her worry that some of his financial backers were 'dangerous' men, capable of anything if they thought their investments were in jeopardy. Enright had always been over-protective of Felicity, unsurprising given what had happened to Jessica, but lately he'd become even more obsessive about her movements and friendships, always a sign that he was under greater stress than usual.

The pager vibrated; Firmin calling again. The line in front of Lee wasn't going anywhere, and so he swung the Fairlane out and U-turned under the high limestone walls, headed back to the public phone on the corner of George Street, in the shade of the nearest block of flats.

Firmin's voice was loud enough to make Lee hold the phone away from his ear. Firmin generally awoke at this time, ready to head to his clubs by nightfall. His hearing had deteriorated over the past years, the inevitable product of decades in noisy clubs and band rooms.

'You haven't put your hearing aid in!'

'What? I can't hear you.'

Lee shouted down the line and heard some rummaging as Firmin realised what was amiss. A few seconds later his voice returned at its usual volume, with its radio-host qualities of whisky and smokes.

'I need you to do me a favour.'

Lee reminded Firmin that he was on a job, that he'd sworn off Summertime shifts and other sundry engagements until after he was done, but the old man wouldn't be dissuaded.

'It's a swing by and observe thing, Southern. Something you can do while on your way to more important tasks. There's nobody else I can trust. What's so funny?'

'You say that to everybody, all the time. Even to Rowdy Tim. It's a bit stale, as a management tool.'

'You've just proved my point, Southern. I trust you because you notice shit like that and say shit like that. Nobody else does, or will. Why I need your eyes, and your expertise and discretion.'

'I told you I'm not acting as spotter so you can send some boys to bash the Hastie brothers.'

Firmin snorted. 'I need you to take a look at a bloke living down there in Wattleup and tell me if it's the same bloke who did us over. That's all. He took stuff of mine that isn't insured, and I want it back, before it goes to market. Will you do that for me? You and Rowdy are the only people who got a look at him, and Rowdy, you know I'm not sending Rowdy – he's liable to sit on the front fence in full view with his binoculars turned the wrong way round.'

The image made Lee smile, mainly because of the truth of the statement. He told Firmin that he'd try and get down to Wattleup, which, contrary to what Firmin said, wasn't on the way to any-where, but didn't make any promises. Despite that, instead of heading over to Frank Swann's house to debrief, and knowing that Bamber could page him at any minute, Lee put the Fairlane onto Leach Highway, which would give him access to Stock Road, the quickest route south to many of Perth's most far-flung suburbs.

31

Wattleup was more a rural area than a suburb – an occasional house visible among bush blocks, horse ranches, chicken factories and farms growing cabbage and broccoli. Between the low fences were parched fields teased by the liquid promise of the heat mirage upon the dusty horizon. This was flat country, part of the sand plain that stretched hundreds of kilometres north and south, wedged between the ancient hills to the east, and the Indian Ocean.

Lee killed the Fairlane and cloaked himself in the dense silence. The Kwinana industrial area wasn't too far away, and he could smell the acrid fumes of the aluminium smelter on the breeze, but there was no traffic on the roads, and the only sign that the cement factory to his north was operating was the grey dust coating the spindly banksia and wattle trees beside him. He'd parked down a dirt track away from the small outpost of houses and shops a few hundred metres distant. Parking in front of the shop selling pet meat, or the other selling horse manure, would only call attention to himself, and so he pocketed his keys and jumped the fence of the nearest paddock, which he hoped would bring him behind the row of five houses opposite the shops.

The trampled grey sand nearest the fence raised dust as he slogged through sparse clumps of wild oats and rye grass, flies doing laps of his face. Mosquitoes launched themselves off the silvered jarrah fence posts and competed for airspace with the flies. Lee pushed his sunglasses tighter against his eyes to keep out the flies and the dust, and waved away the mosquitoes until he'd gained a patch of cover behind the row of houses. Their back fences were a single line of unpainted asbestos sheets, some with holes kicked through, others pushed over by a windblown embankment of sand. Lee crouched among a stand of immature melaleuca, colonists from the nearby swamp, looking for signs of a dog in the third yard along the row. The yard was covered in concrete pavers, except for a circle of grey sand where a Hills hoist angled up at the hot sky.

Lee dusted off the Pentax SLR body and removed the distance-lens cap. He put the camera to his eye and zoomed in on the back windows of the third house, shadowed beneath a jerry-rigged pergola made of corrugated-iron sheets, held down with bricks. A few scattered milk crates did for seats beneath the pergola, and there were beer cartons filled with dead soldiers and an ashtray made of a sun-bleached conch shell, but it was hard to tell if the house was currently occupied. If Lee was on Firmin's clock, and not Enright's, he might have made a passable hide among the melaleuca, despite the flies and mosquitoes, and settled in to wait, but there was no way of knowing how long it'd be before someone appeared.

Lee's pager began to vibrate, and he saw Bamber's number. He put down the camera and took up a piece of broken asbestos, threw it overhand so that it clattered over the tiled roof before sliding down into a rusted gutter. Lee took up the camera and concealed himself behind a pale trunk, set the zoom on the back door. He waited a minute, scanning across the rear windows in case someone was watching back at him, but there was nothing, no sign of movement or life. He picked up a chunk of broken orange roof tile and repeated the action, the projectile smashing loudly against the roofline peak before disintegrating. Lee knelt in the dirt and watched through the lens, but there was nothing to see, not even from the neighbouring houses, which at least looked occupied, with pot plants and vehicle resto-jobs under tarps, and a line of blue singlets drying on a wire. Lee put the cap back on the lens and hung the camera around his neck. He stood on sore knees and shook the sand off his ankles. He was about to step away from his hide when he heard a distant chime, like the sound of an alarm clock entering a dream, and dropped to his knees again. He uncapped the camera and put his focus back on the rear window of the nearest house, the image coming together through a blurred canyon of broken asbestos, mottled leaves and harsh light reflected off the Hills-hoist and tin shed. He tweaked the focus on the lens and the slightly increased depth of field took him through the rear window of the property and into the back room, a kitchen of some sort with an ancient titty calendar, and a chipped veneer pantry door.

A shadow moved past the window and then the chiming stopped. Lee adjusted the lens again but the image didn't get any clearer. The only way to cast a shadow on the wall would be to pass across his line of vision, and yet nothing tangible had appeared. All Lee needed was a moment to confirm the presence of the man who'd raided Club Summertime and bashed Firmin. He kept the camera at his eye and tapped out a cigarette, began to smoke, the sun on his back beginning to bite now, his scalp fizzing a little with the prickling rays, and he wished he'd brought a cap.

Lee put his cigarette to the dirt and rolled the ash off it, before sinking the tip into the sand and starving it of oxygen, burying it out of habit. He hadn't taken his eyes off the rear window for near two minutes but nothing else had moved there. He heard a crack, and then a metallic thud, followed by a familiar echo through the trees around him. Out of instinct he dropped and rolled, taking in the car body fifty metres to his left – a sun-bleached EJ Holden without wheels and doors. The crack sounded again and this time he saw the bullet smash through the front panel, no more than a foot from where the last bullet had ended its journey, the hard echo of the high-powered rifle flowing over him and radiating in every direction.

Lee recognised the calibre and knew the damage such a bullet would do. The bullets had passed over his head as he crouched in the sand. Within a second he was up and running, away from the dense grevillea thickets and wattle trees he remembered lined the northern boundary of the block – a perfect sniper's position. Running low and giving his back to the bigger marri and jarrah trees between him and the shooter, he emerged onto a sandy track that led to the nearby wetlands. Instead of heading toward them, he took cover behind a giant pale tuart and glanced behind on either side, making sure to sweep his eyes wide. There was no visible movement for a good half-kilometre, where the low scrub became a solid wall. The rifle could shoot a bullet that far in a microsecond, but there weren't many shooters who could make that shot, not when Lee was moving. He kept to the track but jogged the distance between trees, making sure to skirt the open areas until he'd reached the road, a good kilometre south of the houses and a few hundred metres shy of where he'd parked his car. He put the Ford in gear and his foot on the gas, opting to pass the houses he'd been observing rather than U-turn, slowing when he reached the house opposite the pet-food store. From the front, the house appeared just as empty and silent as its neighbours, the only sound the high whine of a bone saw as he passed the handpainted sign announcing a horse-meat sale, then fifty metres down the road another sign marked by a life-sized red kangaroo, beside the words *roo meet 50c a kilo.*

32

Connor Baird pushed the sleeves of his camo jacket up to his elbows, in deference to the sugo-scented heat in the Stirling Highway pizzeria. Lee and Connor were the only customers, and the owner, a tall man with a ginger goatee not much older than themselves, sat at the till counting out the day's float, priming the register with new paper.

Despite the heat, Connor wasn't sweating, at least not on his paper-white face and hairless forearms. Lee nodded and listened while Connor explained the mechanics behind accessing secretive hacking sites, where information and programs could be bought and sold. Lee had heard of this before, in the classes he sat in on, and yet the hushed tones of his lecturers when they spoke of them reminded him of the voice adults used when discussing drugs with children; sufficient to explain but hopefully neutral enough to resist encouraging exploration. Connor Baird was naturally a visitor to what he described as the id of the web, the places where the kind of performance he despised on most chat sites and discussion boards was unnecessary. Where transactions were done anonymously. He chuckled now as he reached for a slice of Americano, one of the three pizzas he'd ordered to go with his litre cup of Coke.

'I don't know how Enright's business will be billed, but it was pretty funny buying the program using Enright's corporate card.'

'Please tell me he's not paying for this, too?' Lee swept a hand over the steaming trays of thin-crust.

'Nah, that wouldn't be smart. Cameras in here. You're paying for this.'

'Good. Go on. What did you find in the emails?'

Connor finished chewing on a leathery bit of crust and washed it down with Coke, daintily wiping his mouth. 'The program worked perfectly, once I was in. Beautiful coding. Will continue to sit there, invisible, and work for you too, so long as they keep using the same local area network. Most of the bigger corporates have their own intranet systems, or at least have better security. Be that as it may, and before I tell you what was in the emails, I did want to point out one anomaly, which may or may not be relevant. As I was uploading the spyware into the Enright system, there was a glitch. Bad enough for me to go back to the sellers for clarification. They were good enough to take a look, whoever and wherever they are – Ukraine, San Diego, San Paolo, Lagos—'

'The glitch. You were saying.'

'Oh yeah. Basically, we aren't alone in there. There's another actor, alongside us, watching everything Enright says and does. Full access to their accounts, planning, you name it. Which is odd. This bloke have many enemies?'

'Too many to count. Could be a corporate rival? What did they say about the software?'

Connor took a deep slurp of his Coke, degassed himself with a belch behind his hand. 'Yeah, they just said it wasn't theirs. That it looked custom-designed. Sophisticated. Elegant but limited. That it'd been there for some time.'

Lee pondered over that while he tapped out a cigarette. 'Couldn't be something that Enright, or Bamber use to spy on their colleagues? Regular workplace surveillance?'

Connor shook his head. 'Not needed. All workplaces spy on their workers' emails. They don't need this program for that. Either way, I'm on it. I'll let you know what it downloads, what it copies etc.'

'Good. Thanks. Does that mean it'll be watching you, right back?'

'Depends how often it's accessed, monitored. But yes, in theory, it might be alerted to us. But only us in the most abstract sense possible. This program I'm using is routed through multiple servers worldwide. Untraceable.'

'And the other program?'

'Clever boy. I'm on to it. It's going to cost, but Enright's paying, so who cares, right?'

Lee took out his lighter and placed it next to his cigarette. 'The printouts. You read through them?'

'Yeah, nah, yeah. Got bored. Read a few, but only going back a couple weeks. Nothing I could see about the Caymans. A bit about you, but I'll leave you to read that. Pretty clear to me that they're unaware of being monitored. Unusually long emails to one another.'

'Enright and Bamber – they don't like to talk, or even be in the same room.'

'Makes sense. I've printed all their email correspondence going back a year. Can do more if required. The program I'm using, like I say, is a beauty. Using it for the task you've given me is like taking a Ferrari for a drive to the corner deli. Your choice, of course. Can do more and look deeper, at your request.'

Lee stood and gave a Connor a handshake that turned into an awkward hug. The computer genius sat and pushed the three pizzas to the middle of the table. He'd eaten one and a half slices.

At the till, Lee paid the manager and asked for takeaway boxes for the uneaten pizzas, which would fuel the giant brain in Connor's skull for at least a few days.

33

Frank Swann held Lee's gaze, returning it with a sharper emphasis that told Lee the older man was reading his eyes, his face, the tone of his voice and his body language all in the same moment. Lee's nonchalance wasn't fooling the ex-detective, whose silence was both a friendly judgement and an irresistible force.

'Like I say, high-powered rifle,' Lee said, when he couldn't take the silence any longer. 'I'm pretty sure they were aiming above my head. A warning. The two shots that hit the car were neatly clustered.'

Swann sat forward, stared at Lee's cigarette enviously. 'The question is then, how'd they know you were there? You said someone in the house fielded a call a minute earlier?'

'Correct.'

'Who knew you were going to be there, apart from Firmin?'

'Nobody.'

Lee realised that Swann had led him to this point, quietly and expertly. The implications were Lee's to chew upon. Swann sat back in his chair and watched his dog patrolling the front fence, waiting for the postie to arrive, when she and the dogs in the neighbouring houses would do their best to hound him out of the street.

Lee had already explained to Swann how the favour he'd done

for Firmin, agreeing to check in on the house, in no way interfered with his paid employment for Enright. 'Except for nearly getting shot,' Swann added dryly, although there wasn't any judgement in his words. Swann knew that Lee worked the door at Club Summertime, and he knew Firmin from way back – a fellow survivor of the old system where copper, crim, prostitute, drug dealer and Northbridge club owners were all part of the same black economy, managed by a few detectives. Lee didn't need to be told that Firmin had lasted so long because there were layers to his game – public and private, legal and illegal.

Swann's dog walked laps of the front fence, ears pricked for the sound of the creaky bicycle. Lee watched Swann watching the dog, then stubbed out his cigarette and cleared his throat. He was pretty sure that he'd convinced the older man there'd been no harm done. Lee had been shot at before, and he was convinced that whoever was behind the scope of the rifle had merely wanted to warn him off. Considering himself warned, he'd called Firmin from the nearest phone booth, and told him that he wanted nothing more to do with the raid upon Club Summertime, at least until he'd finished his job for Swann.

Lee went over everything with Swann that Connor Baird had told him, and the emails most significant to the blackmail threats. Lee had asked to see whether there was anything in the company finances that might be of interest, especially if linked to Caymans accounts, but it was too early to tell.

Swann nodded, reached under his rattan chair and lifted up a manila folder, bound with a shoelace.

'Thought I'd save you some time,' Swann said. 'I thought about having you trawl through the records at Companies House, for everything related to the Enright corporates, but one phone call and a carton of Cullen's cabernet sauvignon, vintage nineteen eighty-two, to be paid by you – got a friend called Brian on the job. Take these away and have a read through – any questions I'll be happy to answer. It's the few legitimate pieces in the jigsaw that is the Enright corporate group of companies, historical and current, but only those required by statute.'

Lee sat forward, took the heavy bundle. 'Did you take a look?'

Swann grinned. 'Couldn't help myself. I know that Enright's financials may have nothing to do with anything, considering the task he's set you, but for my own sake I also thought it'd be good to examine the Caymans angle he mentioned at meeting one.'

'And?'

'There's nothing there. Not sure why he mentioned it, either. He's doing what all the big corporates are doing – setting up a head office in Singapore, routing all profits through there so that he doesn't have to pay Australian income tax. In his case, he's then using the money he didn't have to pay in tax to invest in more developments here, and the profits from that go overseas again and the whole cycle repeats. It's the genius of modern capitalism – where we citizens are accountable to the laws of our little nation-states, corporate entities have all the freedom and entitlements of the traditional buccaneer. More, actually. Some of those buccaneers occasionally got caught. Enright hasn't paid more than a few hundred bucks tax in the past five years.'

'So why were you grinning when you gave me the folder?'

Swann smiled. 'It's the shell companies he's using. Never seen anything like it. Most Enright-types use a few, to distance their investors from scrutiny, to hide assets or to avoid tax, but across the suite of Enright companies, he's using dozens. Directors listed on stock exchanges in Bulgaria, mostly, as well as Albania, Montenegro, Slovenia, a few others.'

'Which tells us?'

'That he's *owned*. Could be organised crime, could be new Eastern bloc entrepreneurs willing to back a long shot. Hard to say without contacts over there, of which I have a few, but ...'

'None of this might be relevant to Jessica's kidnapping. The photographs. The blackmail.'

'Correct.'

'And untangling the web of shell companies, and what they might mean to Enright, is the work of months, if not years.'

'Correct,' Swann repeated. 'We can go there if needs be, but let's hope we don't. Even scanning through the corporate structure gave me a headache, precisely as it's designed to do.'

Lee stood to leave, hefting the file. 'I'll have a look tonight, and if I've got any questions ...'

'Keep your head down,' Swann said, a sly smile on his face, in reference to the shooting incident earlier. 'Here we go ...'

Swann's dog began whining and running the low picket fence-line. Up the hill from Swann's house, other dogs had begun barking, howling and scratching to get at the postie, whose heavy red bike pulled into view, weighed down with panniers of letters. He was an older man who took no notice of the dogs, pulling his bike along the cracked footpath with his legs, as though he were running on water. At the sight of him, Swann's dog went from frustrated and excited to outright attack mode, smashing into the fence and snapping her jaws, barking all the while.

'Jesus,' Lee said.

'I know. Other than a walk, this is the high point of her day. But watch this.'

Lee and Swann were hidden from the postie by the flower-heavy branches of a frangipani. The postie slowed his walking-riding and stopped in front of the gate. The dog speared toward him snarling and barking but then stopped obediently and sat. The postie reached through the gate and patted her head, slipped a biscuit out of one of the panniers and fed it to her, talking to her the while. But as soon as he looked away from her and put his feet on the pedals she stopped wagging her tail and began again to snarl and then growl, escorting him to the other edge of the gate with vicious barks that echoed around the fences. As soon as the postie was out of her sight she looked back toward the porch, where Lee and Swann were watching. She panted and smiled at them, game over.

'There's a lesson to be learned in that game, somewhere, about something,' said Lee.

'I agree,' said Swann. 'Let me know if you figure it out.'

34

Lisa found a park close enough to the post office that she wouldn't need to use her binoculars. She tilted the rear-vision mirror and caught the hard flashes of windscreen glare behind her. Whoever went to the post-office box wouldn't be able to see her in the same glare from the windscreen of her transit van, unless she moved, which she wouldn't be doing. Even so, Lisa unclipped her seatbelt and climbed between the front seats and into the rear, where she took a seat on a milk-crate.

The time on the dashboard clock read two pm, which Lisa correlated with her wristwatch. She had tuned her watch to the one o'clock news, however, and so knew that it was correct. She took up her camera with the long-distance lens and removed the dust-cap. She blew on the front of the lens and caught her reflection in the bluish distortion of the glass – truckies cap to conceal her hair, and dark wraparound sunglasses. She squared the milk-crate between the seats and dialled in the focus on her camera, then began to follow the few pedestrians that passed behind the post office to the McDonalds and service station: a thin Islander woman with a child in tow; a scrawny white boy with neck and face tattoos, still wearing his prison-issue KT26s, too large for his feet. An older couple supported one another along the footpath that was lumpy with tree roots, presumably from the stand of rivergums that fronted busy Armadale Road. They walked with the bow-legged shuffle of those with bad hips, both of them framing their outer feet with walking sticks, hands holding one another by the waist, by the belt, moving as the one emotion-linked creature. Lisa was so preoccupied watching the old couple that she nearly failed to see the Mercedes sedan enter the carpark from her left. A new-model Mercedes in an Armadale carpark stood out like a diamond on a plate of gravel, and so it wasn't hard to track, circling behind Lisa's transit van before finding a park twenty metres to the left of the post office.

The woman who exited the Merc looked confident, didn't glance around, despite the purse in her hand. She was tall and her spine was straight, her chin at a perfect right-angle to her long neck. Poised, and trained, Lisa thought, admiring her simple, understated yet obviously expensive slate-grey suit, her black Nike trainers the only odd note. The woman locked her car with the press of a button and looked toward her destination – the bank of post-office boxes that faced the carpark – moving sinuously through the cars between them, a playful little hop over a kerb. By the time she reached the PO boxes, avoiding the flattened cardboard and litter left by a rough sleeper, the expression on her face unchanged from the moment she'd left her car, the key had appeared in her hand. Without needing to locate the relevant box from the two hundred or so in the wall, she opened the PO box and took out a stuffed brown envelope from her purse, put it inside, turned the key in the lock and swung away from Lisa, back toward her car. It was now that Lisa pulled focus on the lens and scanned the middle and further distances to either side of the post office. She heard the Mercedes purr into life and saw its shadow pass across the post office wall, moving out of her line of sight and presumably back onto Armadale Road.

It is movement that catches the eye, her trainers had taught her, whatever the camouflage. Lisa swung the lens through a full arc, looking for the slightest agitation of a branch or grade-shift within a shadow. There was nothing on the hill behind the carpark or in the fruit-coloured playground of the McDonalds, the two places with the best vantage points.

Lisa checked her watch. Five minutes past. She heard the metallic yammering of the big diesel before she saw the Landcruiser, entering the carpark via the McDonald's drive-thru exit, two men in the front seats talking animatedly while rearranging white paper bags and cups. The men were familiar to Lisa but, even so, she began to take photographs, keeping her thumb on the semi-automatic trigger while adjusting the focus with her other hand, the camera sitting on the shoulder of the front passenger seat. The Landcruiser passed her but neither of the men looked her way, both of them ducking down to look at the PO boxes. Lisa had hoped that the men would park, as the woman had parked, but instead the Landcruiser veered toward the wall of PO boxes and pulled to the curb, cutting her view. She heard a car door open and began to panic. The only way she would make the shot would be to exit the van, but then she would be visible to the men.

It happened fast, and she didn't see. Presumably the man had taken the envelope left for him, but if he had put something inside the PO box, in exchange, then she'd missed the moment. The Landcruiser accelerated wildly over the root-humped bitumen before swinging back toward her, one of the men cursing the other as he wiped thickshake off his face with a napkin, the other man laughing and pounding the steering wheel as he drove.

35

Lee smoked a cigarette and walked laps of the Dodge. He'd reassembled it, making sure not to scratch the fresh paint of the front and rear panels, the four doors. After that he'd spent two hours polishing the clear-coat with an orbital sander, using a lambs-wool plate then a chamois block and rag inside the panels and pillars. He'd then refitted the dashboard, seats and carpet, and connected all the electrics. He was still waiting on the chrome-work from a nearby fabricator, but jacked up on its imported air-cushion absorbers, and with its headlights on, the vintage car looked showroom quality. The engine was already tuned and the custom carbie and extractors he'd fitted weeks ago meant that it was ready for the road. He desperately wanted to take it for a test drive but didn't want any dust or pollen on the new skin.

A drive would also help clear his head. As he'd worked the wrenches, sockets and screwdrivers through the night, waiting for another page from Bamber, sending him on his next mission into the next sick man's desires, Lee had run through his memory of the case files, and the emails Bamber and Enright had exchanged since the first appearance of the demand letter. What was surprising was the lack of surprise in each man's first encounter with the letter, almost as though they'd been expecting it, and what the letter meant for the détente between them. Even before the appearance of the letter, there was an element of malice in their communications, although more from Enright's side than Bamber's. The threat was often explicit, of the 'if you fuck this up again' kind, experienced by the employees of arseholes the world over, often relating to intelligence gathering tasks on rivals, and potential targets for business deals. But when further complaints were made, of which there were many, no action ever seemed to eventuate. This was, Lee assumed, because Bamber knew too much about Enright's former life, and yet if this were true, it didn't explain the one-sidedness of the exchanges, with Bamber rarely, if ever, standing his ground. For all his faults, Bamber didn't seem to Lee the passive-aggressive kind, nor the kind to hold his tongue in the face of humiliation. Perhaps, like an old married couple who hate each other but depend upon the predictability of their company, the exchanges had become habitual to the point of ritual. And yet there was something in Bamber's silence, beyond the fact that it clearly infuriated Enright.

A good example was an exchange between the two men following Lee's hiring to do the burglaries. Enright had railed against Swann, for not taking the work himself, and then against Bamber, for not taking a harder line against Lee. This much was predictable, perhaps even understandable, from a distraught father who wanted the best personnel available. Bamber's response, however, was as sly as it was mysterious to Lee – rather than defending himself, or pointing out that Swann was Enright's first choice, and so his employees should therefore be equally trusted, Bamber had given Enright what amounted to a list of Lee's best attributes. Foremost among these was Lee's dispensability, in the context of a necessary plausible deniability, as might be expected, before delivering a profile of Lee that was clearly well researched, and conducted before Lee's introduction to Enright, almost as though he'd known in advance that in asking for Swann, he'd get Lee. To support his argument Bamber had testimonies taken from Lee's teachers, and a social worker from Lee's childhood that Lee didn't even know existed. During the months when Lee's father was on the run, and while Lee was himself hiding out with his mother down in Pemberton, numerous witness statements had been taken by investigating officers sourced from people close to Lee's father, who had in every case praised Lee for his loyalty, his smarts and his toughness. From this, Bamber had built up a profile on Lee, sold to Enright as demonstrating Lee's 'worldliness beyond his years', his 'combat training that any soldier would envy' and his 'trustworthiness'. It wasn't possible to know whether Bamber's talking-up of Lee was part of some other strategy, but if Lee didn't know any better, he might suspect that the sad old bastard had developed a grudging respect for him.

The most recent emails from Enright to Bamber were entirely task-oriented, outlining the transferring of money to the Caymans account or inquiring as to the state of play. This was surprising, in the context of the new threat to his daughters' wellbeing, and the evidence of abuse against Jessica. This was the time for a normal father to become angry and frustrated, potentially murderous, rather than calm and clear, unless this was itself an aspect of Enright's ruthlessness. Lee didn't know, but he was curious to find out.

One thing Lee had looked for, but hadn't been able to find, was communication between Enright and the Cayman's bank, based on his prior dealings with them, inquiring about the owner of the account he was sending money to, although perhaps that kind of relationship demanded that such inquiries were kept to telephone calls, or couldn't be made at all, and so Enright hadn't bothered. Lee decided that he'd ask Bamber at their next meeting whether such a call had been made, if only to make it appear that he didn't know, as cover for the knowledge that he'd gained from Connor Baird's electronic surveillance.

The radio alarm clock in the corner by the sink went off, set in case Lee had fallen asleep. He roused himself off the flattened cardboard box where he'd been sitting and smoking, watching sunlight seep into the valley. True to their promise, Lee heard the heavy diesel thrumming of the chrome fabricator's Bedford Truck pull into the alley, beginning its negotiation of the potholes and ridges of the old driveway. Lee turned off the alarm and scrolled up the garage doors, excited at the prospect of seeing the bumpers and trims, decals and light fittings all shiny and new.

36

Commander Duncan Corbett sat behind his desk in the corner office on the eighth floor of the Police Headquarters building in East Perth. As though he couldn't help admiring the view, every few seconds Corbett glanced over Lee's shoulder at the suburbs that stretched south-east along the ridgeline of the ancient range that disappeared into the southern horizon. Lee knew this because he'd taken the lift up from the aggravation and noise of the first-floor police station, until he'd emerged to the view from the air-conditioned top floor of the building where the Commissioner and his deputies, and the various operational commanders, were housed.

Lee had done his research, courtesy of a brief meeting with Frank Swann, and so made sure to dress appropriately in black jeans and a collared shirt and suit-jacket borrowed from his employer. Corbett was, according to Swann, old-school in every way, and he looked it too. His broad face was as worn and furrowed as an old track, and his Brylcreemed hair was combed into a precise side part. His eyes were clever and judgemental, used to finding fault and being obeyed, taking his measure of Lee from across the vast wooden desk.

Corbett belonged to the same generation as Swann but had taken a different path. He'd avoided the attentions of the detectives who'd tried to kill Swann and who ran things in the city by staying in uniform for most of his career, working his way up from frontline constable to sergeant, then senior sergeant in charge of the Kalgoorlie Station for near a decade, before burning out as a plain-clothes after a decade in sex crimes and homicide. He'd then returned to the uniform and to rapid promotion through the ranks of inspector and superintendent to his current position. He looked comfortable in his elevated environment, his jacket bearing the insignia of his rank, and his officer's hat hung from a rack. With his large and scarred hands on the desk-blotter, and his eyes now fixed firmly on Lee, he was an intimidating presence – the man had clearly cracked some heads.

Corbett glanced over Lee's shoulder at the clock high on the wall, whose ticking was audible in the stillness. Lee needed to proceed with delicacy and haste – Corbett gave the impression of being a busy man, who didn't suffer fools.

'Thanks for meeting with me, Commander,' Lee began, following Bamber's strategy now, getting straight down to business by giving Corbett something that he didn't already know, describing the photocopied image of Jessica Enright, naked in the bunker where she was ultimately found. This was a risk in that, according to Bamber, Corbett had been one of the senior detectives in charge of the Enright kidnapping case, and apparently viewed the paying of the ransom as both a betrayal on Enright's part and the main reason why the kidnappers were never brought to justice. Corbett's eyes narrowed as Lee proceeded, leaving from his story the two recent payments Enright had made, and the two break-ins

Lee had conducted to retrieve the images. He presented himself as someone working for Bamber, Corbett's ex-colleague, both of them trying to ascertain whether the image of Jessica Enright was in fact genuine. Knowing that he would ask to see it, Lee took out a photocopy of the image and passed it over to Corbett, minus the cut-and-pasted words of demand.

'This isn't the original. This is a photocopy.'

'The original sent to Enright was a photocopy. Bamber sent it away for analysis, what kind of copy paper or machine it was done on et cetera, somewhere over east. There were no prints on it.'

Corbett held it up to the light, raised his eyebrows. 'There wasn't any accompanying note? Just the photocopy of the photo here?'

'Correct. Mr Enright has identified the person as Jessica, due to the presence of the bangle on her arm.'

Corbett gave Lee a hard look, held it, the sound of the ticking clock becoming louder by the second. Lee knew the look – Corbett was reading Lee for a lie that he'd identified, although the lie wasn't yet clear.

Lee needed to break the silence. 'What Mr Enright and Mr Bamber want to know, is whether there were any images circulating at the time of the kidnapping, or after Jessica's return. They don't remember there being any in the record of crime reports, and in the absence of any kind of demand, they're worried—'

Corbett slid the photocopy onto the blotter. 'What do you mean, circulating?'

Lee understood the implication. 'A bad choice of words. My apology. Existence. The existence of any photographs.'

'No, there were not. Nothing of the kind.'

Lee sat forward, nodded to the picture. 'Which tells us that the kidnappers must be back, even if we don't yet know their demands.'

Corbett settled into his cushioned, high-backed chair, steepled his fingers. 'Based on their form, I take it that Mr Enright and Mr Bamber haven't yet made this a police matter? Do they intend to?'

Lee was ready with his prepared answer. 'Yes, as soon as a demand is made, or there's any further contact. You have Mr Bamber's word on that ...'

Corbett snorted. 'You're very wet behind the ears, Mr Southern, despite the notoriety of your father. Bamber's word isn't worth anything to me, and shouldn't be to you, either. Now, if you don't mind ...'

Lee stood, but put his hands on the desk, which made Corbett stand too, not wanting to be stood over. Lee put out his hand, and Corbett looked at it, reluctantly pressing a large hand into Lee's own.

'Please, Commander, if anything comes to you, anything at all, do call Mr Bamber on this number.'

Lee handed over Bamber's card and nodded, left the office. Before he'd walked a step he heard the punch-dial of Corbett's phone, beeping through the numbers. Lee pretended to search for something in his jacket while Corbett's secretary looked at him, until he heard the sound he'd hoped to hear, Corbett beginning in on Bamber, who'd certainly been expecting the call.

37

When Lee found Bamber, sitting out on South Mole again, the ocean silky in every direction and a Korean-flagged ship approaching the port, the fixer didn't want to talk about Corbett. Instead, Bamber reached for Lee's cigarettes and tapped himself out a Stuyvie, pressed the dash lighter, which popped out and rolled on the floor.

'Fuck.'

Lee put his lighter to Bamber's cigarette, rolled down his window, watched the giant white ship enter the harbour mouth with the slow gravity of a planet being pulled into orbit.

'What're you so worked up about?' Lee asked.

'I know this one. I *know* him. Met him, anyway.'

Lee waited while Bamber drew the cigarette into a fierce glowing point, taking in a lungful before exhaling an angry cloud out the window, billowing toward the hovering seagulls. He took up a new manila envelope and slapped it on Lee's lap.

'This pervert is a photographer. Professional. Did my wedding, paid for by Enright. Works out of a Claremont studio. Makes a living taking family photos of the western-suburbs types. You know the kind – cheesy sets and bad jumpers, white teeth and lots of hairspray. Went into his studio once, that's what gets me. The guy somehow manages to make ordinary people look like born-agains. Didn't do a bad job on the wedding video, discreet enough to edit out the dirty dancing and vomiting bridesmaids, but afterward I went into the fucker's studio, collected the prints and shook his hand.'

Bamber's recollections, delivered in breathless bursts, gave Lee the impression that he was about to blow a fuse in his head. Lee didn't ask the questions piling up behind Bamber's agitation, instead opened the mouth of the envelope and slid out its contents: an A4 flyer containing a photo of a shaven-headed middle-aged man in a black polo-neck jumper, black French bulldog on his lap; some newspaper cut-outs advertising Chloe Photographic Services; Main Roads maps of a house and street in Mosman Park; and blueprints of a council-approved second-storey extension to the same property – five bedrooms, plus kids treehouse in the backyard.

'He has kids, this one?'

'Yes, two boys. Five and seven.'

'Chemicals,' Lee said. 'Jessica said that the tall thin man in the bunker smelled of chemicals. You ever set up a darkroom?'

'Yes, as a matter of fact. You come out stinking like bromide and hydrochloric acid. And Mr Suburban there is tall and thin too.'

'But if he's the one, why use a polaroid camera?'

Bamber's breathing had settled. A terrible sadness came over his face, just as Lee understood. 'The polaroids were to show Jessica, at the time.'

'Yes,' said Bamber. 'To show her what they could share—'

'If she ever spoke about it. Or gave the police anything useful,' Lee added. 'Meaning that there might be other film, photos, of what happened.'

'Let's hope not. Be careful of this one. Unlike the other two, Pusey's got a bit of history. Before his current career, he was a soldier. Dishonourable discharge, for drinking on duty, and agg assault against a new recruit. Kind of crime that if done to a civilian would mean jail-time, but the army just kicked him to the kerb. The prick fell on his feet though – married into money, sufficient to get him started as a snapper.'

'That's good background. He'll likely be more cautious than the others. I wonder if the progression of names is significant. I mean, why this one now, and not at the beginning?'

'That I can't tell you,' Bamber said, 'What I can tell you, is that when all this is done, and the last photo has been retrieved, and pervert identified, there's going to some serious fucking arson in this place. I will burn these fuckers out if I have to torch the whole fucking city.'

Lee didn't doubt the sincerity of Bamber's words, delivered with the icy calm of someone gone well beyond rage.

38

Lee straightened his jacket and pushed open the swinging gate that led onto a bricked path snaking between raised gardens and toys scattered across sections of neatly cut grass. He was checking Alan Pusey's house first, because the photographic studio would be open now, and because he wanted to remove the house as a possible location – although he doubted that a man with young children would keep compromising material at home. And then there was the matter of wanting to approach Pusey's wife, Christina, whose silhouette Lee could see inside the kitchen, hands pressing a rattling smoothie-maker with the concentration of a sapper defusing a landmine. The noise stopped just as Lee reached the front door, replaced by the blaring of a television somewhere deeper in the house, The Wiggles playing 'Hot Potato' to the accompaniment of a child's tentative voice.

The doorbell rang loud and long. Lee watched the silhouette in the kitchen dry her hands on a tea towel before straightening her hair, picking up a smoothie cup in a performance of nonchalance, padding to the door.

Christina Pusey pulled the door wide open. She was dressed in yoga pants and a pink singlet, the smoothie cup held tightly to her chest, its contents the colour of algae.

Lee held up the clipboard, showed the badge on the lanyard – *Michael Styles, Datatronics.*

Lee introduced himself, smiling, projecting interest in Christina, holding her eyes between little glances of faux admiration at the hallway furniture. Just a few moments of her time. Survey can be done on the doorstep, no need to invite him in.

But she did invite Lee in, and he followed her down the hallway that smelt of flooring wax, through the kitchen that smelt of disinfectant and into the sunken lounge, where the bank of expensive white leather lounges smelt of leather dew, and the tinted windows that gave a view on to a swimming pool smelt of Windex.

Christina Pusey had had a busy day, or perhaps the family home was always kept this clean, although it was more than clean – the room feel hostile to not only germs, but all forms of life.

Lee sat himself on the end section of the L-shaped couch, watched Christina Pusey's eyes track his boot-steps on the white carpet, which were fortunately clear of dirt.

She sat across from him, crossed her legs and took a sip from her health-shake, grimaced a little. Her eyes were a little unfocussed, and her blinks were slower than the usual, as though it took an effort to open her eyes. Exhausted? Medicated? Lee didn't know, launching into his list of fabricated questions on behalf of the local council – what did Mrs Pusey think of the local government schooling available, how accessible were places of recreation from her house, could the council be doing more to maintain the street trees, questions that Lee arrived at following a quick scan of the letters to the editor in the latest *Fremantle Herald*, before typing and printing out the fake questionnaire. As Lee had anticipated, Christina Pusey had plenty to say on each matter, which gave him time to glance around the house and yard. The television upstairs was now playing the *Bananas in Pyjamas* theme song, although the child was no longer singing, but was clearly jumping or dancing. There was a single corner of the yard that was invisible to Lee. He could come back later, at night, but instead finished up his questions. As he stood, he pointed toward the tree nearest the blank place in his view.

'Is that a silver princess?' he asked, moving around the couch to look deeper into the yard. 'I've been thinking of planting one, but I was told that they shed a lot of leaves.'

'I don't think so. Alan, my husband, wouldn't stand for that. It doesn't give much shade, but it does attract the native birds.'

There was no shed in the corner of the yard, as he'd anticipated there might be. Instead, a mulch pit and swing set, and grass that didn't get enough sun. Lee thanked Christina for her time, glanced at his watch. It would be dark in an hour, and so he needed to get ready.

39

The building that housed Chloe Photography wasn't what Lee expected – not a shopfront on the Claremont high street, or even a backstreet, but a grand Federation house away from the mercantile district and adjacent to the river. Pusey and his wife owned the land, according to the LandCorp documents, whose value without the building would be enough for him to retire on. Lee assumed that it was part of Pusey's marrying into money, mentioned by Bamber, a nest-egg inheritance functioning in the meantime as a vast set for his photographic enterprise. On the tuck-pointed brick walls either side of the main entrance, creeper vines had been planted above park benches, and on the front porch were love seats and a wrought-iron picnic table and chairs. Out in the garden with views over the river were both a small and a large gazebo, and a stand of melaleuca whose tightly packed branches and ancient boughs curled over one another to give the impression of a darkened forest grove.

Lee sat in the carpark of a bowling club whose grounds were supernaturally green, despite the dry heat – evidence of the attentions of a full-time greenkeeper. Lee scanned the grounds for the greenkeeper, but the carpark was mostly empty, except for a Ford LTD and a couple of Mercedes coupes. The club patrons were inside the deco-styled clubhouse, likely nursing cold ones, plotting success in the next pennant fixture.

Lee turned his attention back to Pusey's building. What concerned him was the security camera fixed above the front entrance, the kind that usually came with alarmed windows and doors. He took out his binoculars and looked more closely at the model, which he recognised. There in the front window behind the wraparound veranda was the name of the security company. Lee reached into the glovebox and extracted a stack of instalment manuals, sifting until he found the make and model that matched the camera. He was familiar with the electrics but needed to be sure, studying the wiring diagram until he was certain.

Darkness fell quickly once the sun dipped beneath the limestone bluff, rising vertically over the river to the west. Lee put the alarm system manual into the knapsack which contained his tools. There were no lights on inside Chloe Photographics. The nearest buildings were a series of small structures beneath a concrete frame, housing generators that belonged to Bethesda Hospital, which were also dark and quiet. Lee looked again at the grounds of the bowling club, then waited for the street to empty of traffic. He locked the Ford and hitched his knapsack and crossed the street, looking for all the world like a man headed to the Claremont Jetty to wet a line.

Lee entered the driveway on the hospital side of the shared wall. He went to the back of the block and used the corner to lever himself up and over the bricks, where a wattle tree provided cover from any camera mounted in the rear of the photographic business. In case there was, he pulled down his balaclava to cover his face, zipped up his jacket and put his hands in his pockets. He emerged from the bushes quietly, scanning as he went. There was no camera and so he went to the rear veranda, mounting the steps and triggering the security light. He waited until the light died and knelt at the back door, protected by a locked security screen. He took out his crowbar and levered it into the gap between lock and frame, careful to avoid splintering the frame or scratching the paintwork. He gently levered until the lock popped loose. It was the interior door that would be alarmed. Lee took out his wire snips and placed them in his jacket pocket. With his set of picks he worked on the familiar old Lockwood until it was disabled. He put the picks back in his bag, put the torch in his mouth and with the crowbar ready, opened the door.

He had thirty seconds. Lee had established that, like all old houses, the fuse box was on the front veranda. In such cases, because it was easiest for the installer; the alarm system control was nearly always inside the house but directly behind the fuse box. Lee skidded down the long hallway and into the front room. The alarm system wasn't locked, and ignoring the punch-pad by the door, he unclipped the alarm face and roughly pulled out the mechanism. He reached the count of twenty seconds as he untwisted the wiring and with the wire snips cut the brown ground wire, then the red wire as per the instalment instructions. He counted down the last ten seconds, ready to strip and reconnect the wire if the alarm sounded, or the blue light outside began to flash. If the security company or police arrived, he didn't want them to see his work.

No alarm sounded, or blue light flashed. Lee stripped the wires ready for reconnection and laid out four rows of blue electrical tape on the wires for when he returned.

He was in a showroom for the various picture frames Pusey had custom-made for his clients. The shadowed tables covered in frames gave the room the air of a funeral parlour, except that to illustrate his wares, and his work, Pusey had framed photographs in various sizes and styles of a single family – his own – dozens of them on the walls. Lee recognised Christina from her absent look and ballerina's posture, Pusey's arms around her neck and holding the hands of his two boys, who looked like wax figurines with painted smiles – Lee could see what Bamber meant about a born-again look.

Lee shone the torch on one frame, looked like hand-carved wood, and according to the tag went at eight hundred dollars a metre. He had a quick scout around the room, looking mostly at the floorboards and ceiling, to see if there was a cache-space, but doubted Pusey would keep anything in a room open to the public.

It was the same in the other front rooms of the building, which would have once been the lounge room and dining room, given over now to photographic sets, incorporating portable lighting and interchangeable backdrops. The kitchen still existed but was laid out with expensive tea sets and doilies – more props, Lee assumed. Lee found the darkroom in the back corner of the building, in what would have once been a bedroom. The windows were painted black, and an interlaced curtain of black plastic sheeting protected the door, which locked from the inside. Lee shut and locked the door, turned off the torch and flicked on the one of the two overhead lights, whose red globe cast a blood-bright pall over the cabinets and shelves and tables where Pusey developed his prints. Lee killed the red light and turned on the standard globe.

Pusey's was an old-school set-up, with the mounted Zeiss enlarger an impressive machine – big and antique-looking, with a green enamel skin. Pusey's customers paid handsomely for the product of an expert craftsman, and so there was nothing modern in the room – even the timing clocks and cutting tables looked vintage. Not for Pusey the machines that printed photos inside the hour, as advertised in chemists around the country – feed the film in one end, collect the photos out the other.

There were no prints strung on the clotheslines that ran above the tables, whose trays were stacked ready for use. The chemicals used to draw out and fix the image in the paper were kept in a fire-safe beneath the tables, which wasn't locked. Lee took out the chemicals and shone his torch into the safe, looking for false walls or anything that didn't belong. He replaced the chemicals in the safe and turned to the bank of cupboards and cabinets that filled a corner of the room. A whole filing cabinet was given over to receipts and customer orders, each neatly stamped and dated. Lee looked through the alphabetically ordered names but nothing appeared familiar. He took out each of the trays and rapped his knuckles on the sides, then pulled the cabinet away from the wall, not finding anything unusual. He did the same with another cabinet that stored lenses and photographic paper. Opening the new packets of paper would expose the film and potentially raise Pusey's suspicions, and so Lee switched out the clear light for the red light and opened each of the packets, looking for hidden prints or images, of which there were nothing. This wasn't too surprising.

Pusey was a photographer with a professional darkroom – he would likely store illicit material, long-term, as negatives, creating prints at will, and yet there weren't any negative rolls in the cupboards. Lee was thinking about the best way to take a look at the top floor of Pusey's suburban home when he opened the final cupboard, empty but for a laptop computer and a large number of cameras, and lenses – thousands of dollars-worth of equipment – each in their padded bags. They were all SLR cameras with the exception of a smaller padded bag containing a digital camera. Lee opened the bag and took out the camera. He was familiar with the model, as one he'd been thinking of buying, a high-end stills and video Ricoh camera that was just within his price range.

It was then that Lee understood. He turned the camera on and switched to review, but the card on the camera was blank. Lee took out the computer from its bag. It was a new-model Mac laptop. He opened the case and turned the computer on, waited the twenty seconds it took for the machine to warm up, presenting him with the login screen. Lee didn't even bother. He shut the laptop and put it back in its case, looking at his watch. One good thing about Pusey's studio being in Claremont was the nearby presence of Connor Baird, no doubt awake now and staring at a screen, who'd know what to do. Lee took up the laptop and the digital camera, killed the lights in the darkroom, and left the house through the back door. Outside, the moon was hidden behind a single cloud, illuminating its edges so that it looked like a neon sign, putting a silver skin on the river that sat quiet and still beneath the pale limestone cliffs.

40

Lee had to tread softly with Bamber. He'd handed over the cloned hard drive in the carpark of Captain Munchies, the lights of the port casting a sulphurous halo over the container ship moored alongside them, beyond the levee built to support the train lines. No trains were running at that hour, and even Captain Munchies was closed until dawn, when the morning port workers and those finishing the night shift would arrive for their breakfast burgers. Bamber looked longingly at the sprawl of skip bins and chip-smelling oil drums edging the building, whose fridge lights glowed through the front door. Seagulls waited in small huddles on the fractured tarmac and on the nearest fence-line.

It hadn't been possible to hack into Pusey's laptop immediately. While Lee watched, Connor Baird had removed the hard drive and connected it to his Mac desktop. He'd then used a de-encryption algorithm to release, then copy the data onto a portable hard drive. The operation had taken Connor less than four hours, during which time Lee sat and smoked, watching the hacker at work. He came away with a sore throat, while learning more than in a semester of computing studies class.

'There was no sign of any photographs, or prints, anywhere in Pusey's building. This guy's moved with the times, and likely made, and kept digital copies, assuming that the picture of Jessica is in there.'

'Must've been useful to this bunch of sick fucks, having a photographic studio available to them. Just as useful, I suppose, to have a sick fuck who can digitise their stuff, make it easier to hide.'

'That's what I was thinking. We opened the first few images, but there are thousands on there,' Lee said. 'Videos too. You're paying me by the hour, and that's days of work.'

Bamber grunted. 'I understand, son, really I do. You don't want to infect that pure mind of yours by swimming in the oceans of filth. But what you're telling me is that you're unsure whether the picture of Jessica is in this ... little black box?'

'That's correct. It might not be. The laptop wasn't locked away, which is odd. There was no safe in the building. I didn't want to open the files in front of my friend.'

'Fair enough. But the few files you opened?'

Lee nodded. 'Not obviously illegal. Photos of children taken somewhere in South-East Asia. Street scenes. Kids wheeling their bikes. Selling fruit at a roadside stall. But not ... artful. Not the work of a professional photographer.'

'Considering the others you've found, that doesn't sound so innocent. And the laptop is back in the darkroom? No sign that you were in and out?'

'Correct.'

Bamber tossed the hard drive in his hand. 'Soon enough, I suppose, we'll be able to download our brains to one of these. Fit the whole of human wisdom into a grain of sand, which seems about right.'

Bamber was playing a kind of game, gauged by his wistful words. 'What is it?' Lee asked.

Bamber gave Lee the full force of his copper's stare. 'The other pervert. The one you drugged and tucked into bed. He's gone missing too.'

Lee allowed Bamber to read him a full few seconds before the older man looked away, reached again for Lee's cigarettes. 'Was due to fly to Singapore yesterday, to give an address at a conference. Didn't make the plane.'

'How do you know he's missing? Maybe he—'

Bamber shook his head. 'Scum like that, you'd figure he's all alone in the world, but no, two sisters, one's in care. Dying of motor neurone. He called the other one, the healthy one, from a phone box outside the chemist where he picks up his scripts. He's reliable, this pervert. Never misses a day without visiting his sister, with his other sister. She went round to pick him up. Lights on in the house, car there, but nobody home. She let herself in, nothing packed. He wasn't at The Rose, either. She waited a few days then called it in. It's officially a matter of concern.'

Lee considered the news, watched Bamber closely, but gave up because he couldn't tell whether Bamber was involved. Now that the fixer's outrage at dealing with the likes of Pusey and Laver had burned away, leaving him with a cold disgust that matched Lee's own, Lee could see the harder, more determined investigator underneath.

Lee decided to make it easy for him. 'No, Bamber, I didn't have anything to do with it, and no, I didn't leave any trace of my ... visit to Laver's house. Like I told you, I wiped the security footage. You said Laver's sister had a key, well, I doubt she has a key for his locked basement. House of horrors. He wouldn't want her looking in there.'

Bamber nodded. 'The cops either, I suppose, if they take the missing person's report seriously. Might he be down there? Could've had a heart attack while whacking off, putting himself up in the sling, something like that?'

Lee pursed his lips. 'It's possible. He'd want to lock the door behind him when he's down there, in case of visitors, knowing his sister has a key to the front door. You want me to take a look?'

Bamber thought about it. 'Nah. If he's in there, dead, amongst all his filth, that's a win. Let him rot. Rather that than the coppers getting wind, at this stage, of his secret life.'

'His sister might get the same idea though. Locked basement room. Missing brother. Though I guess the same applies – if it's natural causes nothing can come back on us. But just in case – that Corbett copper I visited – the commander. What kind of juice do you have with him? He didn't speak too highly of you.'

Bamber laughed. 'The prick hates my guts. But that's no issue. It's safer like that, makes him more predictable. We're from the old school. We've got stuff on each other.'

'Is he on the hook? I mean, if needed?'

'Not exactly. And no more on the subject. Corbett's got nothing to do with this. You spoke to him, he's a company man now. He was no real help back when Jess went missing, and he's no further use to us here.'

A Ford Transit van entered the carpark, swung its headlights onto the Captain Munchies shopfront, killed them.

Bamber looked at his watch, at the van, at the seagulls, as though they might divine the identity of the driver. The gulls stood silently, feathers ruffled by the cold easterly wind, watching as the driver exited the van, lifting a long string of keys from his pocket, moving wearily toward the locked doors while the seagulls crept up behind him.

41

Lee rolled into McLeery Street, eyes burning with fatigue, hints of an orange-cordial sunrise in the branches of the Norfolk pines at the end of the road. He slid the Ford into an empty bay a few houses from his own, as was his habit, killing the engine, and then with easy, automatic movements, pulled the keys, popped the boot, took out his tools.

The bag seemed heavier in his weariness, but the dawn chorus of honeyeaters and magpies lifted his mood. Lee looked for the Honda Civic that belonged to Lisa, the cop, who'd be off shift now, and was glad that it wasn't there. All he wanted was a hot shower and a glass of water, and then five or six hours in the sack. If the photograph of Jessica Enright was in the cloned hard drive given to Bamber, that meant there were two remaining photographs, out in the wild. He doubted that the kidnap crew who took Jessica Enright consisted of more than a handful of men, and Drew and Laver didn't seem like kidnappers to Lee, on first impressions at least. Lee assumed that the role they'd played had been secondary, hiding or transporting the child. They were roughly the same age, white-collar types, and so were either childhood friends or met at university or something similar. Pusey on the other hand had been a soldier with a history of violence, despite now living a respectable life in the burbs. Lee didn't know about the other

Drew brother, the one who'd been murdered, and would have to ask Swann to make inquiries. If he had a history, like Pusey, then they were potentially the kidnapping team. Either way, judgement was coming for the men, as soon as all of the photographs were recovered, of that there was little doubt. Lee didn't want to know the details of how that went down. If he was building a case, it'd be different, but in the absence of doing a proper investigation, knowing too much about the men in advance of their punishment was also potentially dangerous. Not knowing beyond the surface of things would nag at him for a while, but he'd get over it.

Lee opened the front door and left his tools where they fell. He went into the curry-smelling kitchen and drank a glass of water, then another. Still in robot-mode, he snagged the towel on the hook outside the shower and laid it on the sink in the bathroom. While waiting for the running water to heat, he checked himself in the mirror. He looked beat-down and twice his age, the only consolation his understanding that a lack of sleep, dehydration and two packs of Stuyvies in twenty-four hours will do that. He watched the fog on the mirror rise until his chest was silvered over, and then his face.

Lee got under the hot blast and ducked his head, felt the scalding water on his scalp. He soaped himself automatically and brushed his teeth, then turned off the spigots, extra hard so that they didn't drip. He reached for the towel with his eyes closed, and at that moment heard the whump, and then the bang, whose force made the bones of the house shudder and the windows rattle.

Lee recognised the sound. He climbed into his jeans and ran barefoot to the front door, then out onto the street. Lee's neighbour, an old Burmese man named George, was already running his garden hose through his front fence onto the street while his wife, Bennu, still in her pyjamas, fed it to him until the length was gone. Lee took up the hose just as Bennu turned on the tap, running the length of the fence until he reached the Ford, putting the weak stream of water onto the nearest trees and the gutter filled with leaves, and then the tyres of the car, whose insides were pulsing a bright orange flame out of its windows, entwining in a flaming dance on the car's roof and bonnet. Lee walked onto the street and kept the stream on the tyres and then directed the water inside the car where it did little more than make the car hiss. The fire was contained, at least, and Lee was glad that he'd taken his tools out of Gerry's Ford, even as the people of his street emerged from their houses and stood at their front fences holding mugs of tea, like they did when there were firework shows down at the port, watching the car burn while waiting for the fireys and the police to arrive.

42

Swann arrived at the scene before the Fremantle cops, for whom torched cars weren't a priority, as well as before the fire department, who were battling a blaze in the hills near Mundijong.

Lee and Swann walked around the Ford, whose tyres had melted into black puddles, Swann pointing out the absence of a popped petrol cap, or darker streaks of burnt paint on the car's bonnet, boot and roof, where accelerant might have been poured. There was nothing of the burnt Ford which suggested a random attack. Lee helped Swann lift the creaking bonnet, looking for the origin of the explosion, but apart from melted high-tension leads and distributor cap, the engine was blackened, but undamaged. It was then that Lee looked at George, his neighbour, looking up at his security camera, mounted on the corner of his front porch, hooded with a plastic shopping bag. George looked at Lee, and shrugged.

'This was deliberate, and it wasn't done by kids,' said Swann. 'The way the inside of the car is opened up, I bet if I get under the chassis, I'm going to find evidence of an ignition point, somewhere under the door frame. A little package of Semtex or C4, would be my guess. If the shrapnel didn't kill you, or the flames, the shock wave would've turned your organs to liquid.'

Lee felt a shiver. 'Connected to the ignition, or set after I arrived home? I was only away from the car for a few minutes.'

Swann nodded toward the hooded security camera. 'The latter. Not rigged to kill you, necessarily, although we can't be sure. It might've gone off early. We don't want forensics looking at this, but if they did, I bet they'd find evidence of some kind of timing device in the mess. Those things aren't always reliable.'

Lee nodded, ran it through his mind, could only come up with one answer.

'Warning shots fired at you yesterday,' said Swann. 'Car blown up today. But you don't think it's related to the Enright matter?'

Lee tapped out a cigarette and put it to his lips but didn't fire up – the stench of burnt rubber and melted plastic was too strong. 'I've been pretty careful. Straight-up burgs. Certain as I can be that I haven't been filmed, or followed. There's only me, Bamber and Enright involved as far as I know, so little chance of a leak.'

'What about the daughter? Louise's friend.'

'Felicity? She knows what I'm doing, vaguely, but only because Bamber is telling her. I don't see why she'd want to warn me off, and she didn't seem the type to blow up my car, or know anyone who might do it for her.'

Swann gave him the look, the one that said 'how can you be so sure?'

'I guess there's the question, I suppose,' Lee said, 'as to why Bamber is feeding her details behind Enright's back.'

'You have any ideas on that?'

'No. But I've been meaning to speak to her again. I think I need to find her sister, whatever Enright thinks. I think there were more people involved in her kidnapping than her statement in the police report suggests. Knowing how many will give me a better idea, I think, of where this is going to end, or who might be behind the letters.'

Swann nodded. 'Which leaves this mess here.'

'Yeah,' Lee agreed. 'The people Firmin sent me to photograph. The Hastie brothers, and the man who robbed his safe. They must have followed me. I'm pretty sure that they didn't, but I can't see any other angle.'

'You've been duly warned, twice.'

'I'll need to speak to Firmin. Make a few things clear.'

Swann gave Lee a hard look, catching the tone in his voice. 'Firmin is a useful guy to have onside,' Swann said. 'In our line of work especially, unless there's no other option.'

'There's no other option. I've told him repeatedly to leave me out of it, whatever his beef with the Hastie boys. But here we are.'

'Unless you were followed by them, as you say, from the Wattleup subdivision.'

'Fair point. That would be on me. You're right – no need to go burning bridges. Firmin's been good to me, apart from dragging me into this shit.'

Swann patted Lee on the shoulder, his regular fatherly gesture, then turned down the street. He lived a five-minute walk away, across Hampton Road. Lee smiled at the older man's shuffling off in thongs, jeans and a suit-jacket with no shirt – an outfit hastily assembled so that he could get to Lee quickly.

Lee watched Swann turn the corner, was about to turn away himself when he saw a blue Honda Civic entering McLeery off the main road. There were plenty of blue Civics on the city streets, but assuming that it was Lisa, he waited beside the burnt-out Ford. The Civic hit the intersection where Lee became visible, raising a hand in greeting, but the Honda's windscreen sparkled with reflected light, concealing its driver, before turning sharply down Martha Street. The behaviour was odd enough to make Lee trot to the corner, where Swann heard his footsteps and turned, put a hand to his ear as if to say, what? But the Civic was turning south onto Hampton Road, and Lee shrugged, headed back toward his home. The police had finally arrived, a paddy wagon double-parked on the street, as two uniformed officers knocked on his front door. If the Civic driver had been Lisa, did she avoid stopping because of the sight of Lee next to the burnt-out Ford, or the arrival of two of her peers?

43

Lee smoked his cigarette and waited on the grassy slope over-looking Cottesloe Beach, crowded with kids wagging school and nut-brown retirees, sprawled on camp chairs and gaudy towels, rising only to cross the baking sands before dousing themselves in the clear blue waters. The afternoon sun had extra venom, reflecting off the ocean onto the bright surfaces of the surf club to his left, radiating from the tarmac where his Ford F350 truck was parked, its tray jutting into the turnaround that led to the exit.

Lee preferred not to use his own vehicle when working for a client, instead borrowing from Gerry Tracker's two or three customer vehicles, but with the Fairlane blown up and his meeting with Felicity organised, he didn't have time to get to Gerry's shop and take another vehicle.

The two police who'd knocked on Lee's door had been easily distracted once Lee hailed them from the street, calling them to the burnt-out Ford. Lee had called it in, but he didn't want the two coppers inviting themselves in to his house, where his tools were in the Gladstone bag just inside the doorway, and his firearm hidden beneath the floorboards.

Lee's neighbour, George, had given him a funny look when he'd denied knowing who the Fairlane belonged to, the two coppers taking his answer at face value before writing down the plate numbers and heading off to another call. George had seen Lee driving the Ford, but either way he said nothing as Lee helped him wind in his garden hose, hand over elbow. George was a Holden driver, his immaculate silver Torana parked inside the safety of his sheltered carport, and he only muttered, 'Wouldn't admit to owning a Ford either,' in his thick accent before retreating inside the cool darkness of his limestone cottage.

Lee watched Felicity Enright climb out of her taxi, dressed in cotton trousers and sandals, a peach-coloured long-sleeve shirt and a wide-brimmed hat. The ensemble made sense in the heat and light, coupled with her sunglasses that obscured much of her face, the blush of heat on her cheekbones only emphasising the paleness of her skin.

Lee stood from the park bench and shook her hand. 'Let's get into the shade, shall we?'

He gestured to the pavilion tearooms above the clubhouse, and she nodded. 'I can't stand summer,' she said. 'I get migraines, and this light ...'

Lee followed Felicity to a table at the back of the room, furthest from the windows that gave onto the ocean. They ordered coffees and only now did Felicity remove her sunglasses.

'Thanks for meeting with me,' Lee said. 'Short notice and all that.'

Felicity waved at a fly, which settled on the table between them, cleaning its face with its front legs.

'No worries,' she replied, although the words sounded odd in her mouth. Lee wondered what an Ocker bloke like Enright made of his delicate and cultured daughter, whose quietly intelligent eyes were fixed on Lee's own, a look of faint amusement growing there, as though she were privy to Lee's thoughts.

'I'd like to speak to your sister,' Lee said. 'Or at least try. The people that your father and Bamber have sent me to look at, they're involved somehow with Jessica's kidnapping.'

'What makes you think that?'

It was a fair question, although asked with a degree of knowingness that took Lee by surprise. 'They're all linked with one another, in a way I haven't had time to establish. They're the same age, ethnicity, north-of-the-river, similar educational, socio-economic—'

'I believe you, and yes, I'll try and help you. Anticipating your question, I brought this.'

Felicity reached into her handbag and withdrew a single bank statement, which she smoothed out and put between them. It was a Westpac credit card transaction record, dated to earlier that month. Lee scanned down the purchases: shoes in Collins Street, clothing stores and liquor shops across Melbourne. Thousands of dollars worth of purchases, and there, at the end of the month, a single payment of ten thousand dollars to cover the interest and capital.

'This is great, but I was hoping that you might have a more ... direct way to contact her?'

Lee let the question hang there, but Felicity didn't look away. She leant forward, pushed the bank statement toward Lee. 'If I had her number, I'd give it to you, even though I don't see the point in contacting her. What makes you think she'll have anything to add to what she knew back then?'

'You're right, she mightn't have anything to add. But she was a child then. A frightened child, shunted, so far as I can tell, from interview to interview. Did she ever get any counselling, see—?'

Felicity's laugh was bitter. 'Jessica, even as a child, wasn't the kind of person who could be counselled, advised, unlocked or guided. And after the kidnapping, she became even more … riotous.'

Lee didn't answer, was a bit stunned by the ice in Felicity's voice, who hadn't finished. 'It was a travesty, how everything was handled, looking back on it. I don't blame her one bit. I'm trying to be protective, even if it doesn't sound like that. My dad had the power to shut everything down – the newspapers, the journos and writers who sniffed around, looking for the story. My dad wouldn't have let a psychologist poke around in Jessica's head, even if she'd wanted that, begged for it.'

'He said to me that Jessica received counselling, afterwards.'

Felicity looked away, fixed her eyes on a mother and child, walking down to the beach, towels draped around their necks. 'Did he? I suppose, I was just a child. But I don't remember that.'

Lee nodded. 'It must have been hard for you. The worry, the fear, then after her return, some little relief before the breakdown of your father's relationship with Jessica. And then the silence. More than a decade now of absence.'

Felicity's eyes filled with tears, before reaching for a serviette and dabbing at her eyelids. When she opened her eyes, they were full of cold fury. She laughed again, pointed at the bank statement. 'At least my sister hasn't lost her taste for the good things in life. Her taste in shoes, clothes is impeccable. What are you doing?'

Lee stood and took up the bank statement. 'I've got to make a quick call.'

'Good,' said Jessica. 'I need a drink. Will you join me?'

Lee didn't even bother trying to make an excuse. 'Back in a minute. I could go a cold beer, and a whisky chaser.'

Lee turned to the door as Felicity raised her hand. Right away the nearest waiter was at her side. Lee exited the air-conditioned vestibule of the café into the hot breath of the easterly wind gusting off the distant desert. He tapped out a cigarette and headed for the small bank of payphones by the ice-cream kiosk, the smell of saltwater and disinfectant wafting from the men's change room that echoed with the sound of a lone voice, singing 'Your Cheatin' Heart'.

44

Lee watched Paul Enright step lightly on his small feet across the mooring ropes and rubber barge-floats on the timber walkway that led from the clubhouse to the *Current-Sea*. He wore a grey sharkskin suit with his tie loosened and one of the flaps of his shirt hanging over his belly. He saw the three of them waiting – Lee, Bamber and Frank Swann – and gritted his teeth. A squall of wind and dust from the summer roads rounded into the marina and tore at his hair, which he held on to, stepping aboard his launch – the biggest in the row of superyachts and powerboats which began to bob and sway as the wind caught the choppy river.

'This better be fucking—'

Lee looked at Bamber and Swann, whose grim expressions mirrored his own. Enright took his cue from them, and bit down on the abuse he'd no doubt been fermenting on his drive from the Premier's office, where he'd been in a meeting about a new Mandurah development, trying to get more land released.

Lee didn't waste any time. 'Bad news, Mr Enright. You're going to want to sit down.'

Enright looked to Bamber and Swann, who nodded in agreement. Bamber stood and gave his seat to his master. Enright sat beside Swann, the plastic cushion wheezing under his weight.

He was sweating heavily, a sheen on his face and scalp. Lee could smell his sourness, but Enright didn't remove his jacket.

Lee put his hands up in admission. 'I know you told me not to do it, to just focus on the recovery of the pictures, but something was bugging me about the three men I've looked at. I went looking for Jessica … had an investigator friend of Swann's look for her, in Melbourne—'

Enright looked immediately frightened. 'But she'll run. She told me she'll run.'

Lee held Enright's stare. 'Too late for that. She's not the one spending your money, Mr Enright. Hasn't been, for a long time.'

Enright laughed, but there was no humour in it. 'What the fuck's that supposed to mean. Bamber?'

Bamber nodded his chin toward Lee, who resumed. 'The investigator went to a clothes shop in Melbourne. Expensive clothes shop. Multiple purchases made there every month, as well as at boutique shoe shops in the same area. There was something off about the description of the purchasee of the clothes. Same as at the shoe shops, those that remembered her. One of the boutiques had sold a dress that required adjustments. A call was made once the adjustments were complete. The investigator tracked the phone number. It didn't take long. He ended up in a flat in St Kilda. The occupant was a female, aged around forty. He convinced her to let him in. She's been the one buying the clothes, the shoes, the perfume and the rest. Her front room was basically a shop. She's a former prostitute. Makes a living now flogging the stuff she's been buying on your credit card. She doesn't have a pin number for the ATMs or the bank, so she can't get cash advances. So she buys and sells designer labels.'

Enright's eyes were on his hands, which were wrung together. His face had lost colour. 'Jess must've lost her card,' he said, but he didn't sound convinced.

'I'm afraid not. The woman said that one day she opened her letterbox, and the card was in there.'

'Did she know who left the card? Was it Jess?'

'It seems like that. Jessica was her next-door neighbour for a month or so. They never talked beyond hellos. The description matches. She only remembers that her name was Jessica and that she was from Perth. She never saw her again after she found the card and started using it. She doesn't know if Jess left the card, or someone else.'

'A year and a half ago?'

'Correct.'

Enright looked again at Bamber, who shrugged, had nothing to add. Now the colour returned to Enright's face. 'You speak to me, you grim cunt. I pay for your advice. What does what I just heard, mean?'

Bamber looked down at Enright's hand, which had wrenched into his forearm, bunching his shirt. He looked until Enright removed his grip.

'Could mean a number of things. She might have started a new life, one that doesn't require your financial help. Giving the prossie the card might be her sense of humour ...'

'Or?'

'Or, she might not have left the card at all. Someone who wanted it to look like Jess was still buying, spending, living in that area might have planted it. Jess might have ... y'know. Gone missing, again. Been taken. The notes we've been getting. It might be related. Someone from the beginning, covering their tracks.'

There was a malice in Bamber's voice that was hurtful even to Lee. He interrupted. 'Those are the two extremes.'

'But why would someone take her again?' Enright asked.

Lee didn't answer, and when Bamber didn't speak, Frank Swann cleared his throat. 'The original investigation. I've taken a look at it. Was piss-weak. Your daughter ... Jessica. She might've seen things, or people, that she didn't admit to at the time. She was just a kid, not her fault. But the investigating coppers, they didn't follow some pretty obvious leads. Either because they were angry with you, for paying the ransom, considered the matter over, not worth their time, or ...'

'What?'

'Or, lots of things. They were shit at their job. They were told not to look too hard. They had a full plate. The boys at the top, they were wary of you.'

'Ok, enough. What are you saying, we need to go back and do a better investigation? That was a long time ago.'

'But the letters,' Lee said, 'the men I've looked at. Jessica's disappearance. Something's brought it all back up.'

'I don't give a fuck about the letters,' Enright snarled. 'Young fella, you need to get your arse over to Melbourne, and find my Jess.'

Swann shook his head. 'Lee's staying here. My man in Melbourne, he'll do a better job. He knows the lay of the land there.'

Bamber chimed in. 'I agree. I'll organise to pay him, starting today.'

Bamber wouldn't meet Lee's eye. None of them wanted to say what they were all thinking. Eighteen months was a long time for someone to disappear.

45

Because Lee was already north of the river, he headed alongside the wide brown waters out of the suburbs and into the city. It was getting to peak-hour traffic on the freeways, and parking bays were opening up in Northbridge as the after-work crowd emptied out of the bars, replaced by the nightclubbers and street-people. Lee found a bay on the edge of Russell Square that faced Club Summertime, whose heavy doors were propped open. The faint sounds of Mudhoney's 'Blinding Sun' could be heard as he approached the club, greeted by the yeasty tang of beery carpet.

The club wasn't open for another couple of hours, and there was nobody on the door. Lee waved at Michelle, who was restocking the fridges, ripping into cartons of bottled beer and cruisers. Now Lee smelt grenadine and bitters, freshly cut lemon and lime, and Michelle's familiar perfume, sprayed on extra-thick to get her through another long, sweaty night. She stood from her stool and waved Lee over. She tilted her head away from the camera mounted over the stairs, and under the guise of mixing Lee a lemon, lime and bitters, leaned toward him.

'Firmin's in a foul mood. Never seen him this bad, even when that liquor and gaming D tried to game him.'

'*That* bad eh?'

Last year, a rogue detective had tried to bludge even more money out of Firmin, who already paid the man's superiors. The detective was aware of this, but it was tied to the opening of a new Firmin club, down south in Albany, and the simultaneous rejection of a rival's application for a liquor licence, and so apparently called for a new arrangement. A new arrangement was made, but Firmin hadn't been happy, barely leaving his office for weeks.

'Thanks for the tip.' Lee necked his drink and reached over and put the empty in the sink, before heading to the security lock by the doors, punching in 0000, hearing the door click open.

Firmin was seated at attention, his hands wrapped around a tumbler of whiskey, the bottle of Tullamore Dew near empty on the desk strewn with invoices and receipts. His eyes were so red-rimmed that he looked like the monster in a silent movie. The impression was aided by his famous head of hair, dented where he'd slept on the cot beside his desk. A cigarette burned in the ashtray on the corner of the table, and Lee could tell from the finger of ash that it'd been lit, but not smoked.

Firmin smiled at Lee, and waved at the chair opposite him, but there was no warmth in his eyes. 'Can I do you for?'

Lee sat, and sat forward. 'You look a little rough, mate.'

Firmin laughed, a congested laugh that sounded like the V8s he so adored. He stopped himself abruptly when he began to wheeze, reached for an inhaler under a sheaf of receipts, took a good four hits.

'Yeah, true enough. You're a reader. Feel like that book about the painting, the young guy poncing about town while his painting gets old and dirty with all the bad deeds.'

'*The Picture of Dorian Grey*.'

'Yeah, that's the one. Your job finished? You back to work the door?'

Lee shrugged. 'No, I'm not. You've got Rowdy Tim, the others.'

Firmin grunted. 'They're straight-up foreskins. Disappear when things get hard. They don't like violence, the way you do.'

'I don't like violence.'

'Maybe not. But if you can't defuse a situation by using your words, at least you know how to handle it. Unlike the others. I've got two aggravated assault charges pending on Rowdy, and that's just from last week. But if you're not here for your old job back, what do you want?'

Lee tried to make his voice even. He knew that Firmin would read his assertiveness as aggression. Lee had no problem with losing Firmin's friendship, or his job, but he needed the older man to listen.

'That house you had me sit on. The one that ended up with me getting shot at. I think they got a reading on me. My friend's car that I'd borrowed, got blown up outside my home. Can't think of anyone else who'd do that.'

'How'd you know it's not the job you're working for Frank Swann? He's got more holes in him than a Swiss cheese.'

'I thought of that, of course, but I can't see it. What's the latest with the Hastie brothers, the other bloke who robbed you? You still watching their place?'

'They shot through, 'scuse the pun, after pot-shotting at you.'

'It was a warning shot, I'm pretty sure. But that makes it odder. If you've lost them, why are they coming at me?'

Firmin emptied his tumbler, refilled it with a steady hand. 'That I can't tell you. If I get a bead on them, 'scuse the pun, perhaps you'd like to ask them yourself?'

Lee had hoped Firmin wasn't going to say that. 'I've told you, it's not my business. With the greatest of respect, you need to sort it out.'

Firmin's eyes flamed; Lee had crossed the line. The old man grinned, but it was a grin of disappointment, and the pleasure of suspicions confirmed. 'I've been sorting out pricks like the Hasties since I was a doorman myself. There's a reason I've lasted longer in this business than anyone else. It isn't because of being smart, or ruthless, or well connected. It isn't because of hard work. It's because I can read people, and I can read you right now. You know as well as me the only way the Hastie problem goes away, is if *you're* part of the solution. My advice is to quit whatever you're doing for Swann and help me sort the brothers out. I'm happy to pay you for your time. I mean, I can see the pride in you. They shot at you and blew up your car. What more fucking motivation do you need? They're not going to stop. They live for that shit. It's what gets them out of bed in the morning.'

'I'm not going to quit my work for Swann. I guess this is where we part ways.'

Firmin sighed, reached into his desk. 'What kind of car?'

'What?'

'What kind of car, what year, the one they blew up?'

'Ford Fairlane. Nineteen eighty-five.'

'The ZL?'

'Yes.'

Firmin wrote a number in his chequebook, ripped out the cheque and passed it to Lee. The number was generous. Lee folded the paper and slid it in his pocket, stood, and put out his hand. Firmin didn't stand, or reach out.

'If that's a sayonara handshake, I'm not doing it. Just think about what I said. You've always got a job here.'

Lee nodded, turned and went down the stairs. Rowdy Tim, the doorman, was just arriving, carrying his lunchbox with him.

'Vegemite and lettuce?' Lee asked.

Rowdy stood aside. 'Of course. Vegemite's made from beer.'

Lee patted the big man on the arm, the smell of Lynx filling out the air. He moved to leave but Rowdy coughed, cleared his throat. He looked reluctant, wouldn't meet Lee's eye.

'What is it?' Lee asked. 'I'm running late for something.'

Rowdy nodded up the stairs, leaned closer. 'You sort it out, with the boss?'

'What do you mean, Rowdy? We spoke, but—'

'Boss told me you got shot at, that's all. Just take care, brother.'

Lee gave Rowdy a quizzical look, but the big man was smiling, or trying to smile, a gesture made sinister due to the number of missing teeth and the stark redness of his exposed gums.

'Will do,' Lee replied, turning from the sight of the big man, lunchbox held tightly to his chest.

46

From her position inside the van, long-distance lens at her eye, she watched the two men prepare. The pet-meat shop next to her had closed its storefront but she could hear the sound of bandsaws cutting through bone in the adjacent tin sheds. Every now and then a man in a plastic apron and white gumboots left the shed and carried garbage bags full of flesh and bones into the refrigerated shipping container to the rear of the shed. The man never looked at the van parked by the road, but she took photographs of him nonetheless.

The two brothers in the front room of the Wattleup semi-detached that was her focus were dressed now in black jeans and black boots. The older man with greying hair wore a dark-coloured donkey jacket and the other a black leather jacket, despite the heat. The greyhair was rifling through a sports bag while the other watched. When he was satisfied, the greyhair swung the bag onto his shoulder, taking its weight. The other checked the magazine of a small pistol that he slipped into the inside pocket of his leather jacket. The two men disappeared from view as the curtains were pulled and a porch light turned on, despite the fact that the sun was an hour from setting.

She put down her camera and placed it into its padded bag. From there she climbed into the van's cabin and took her seat behind the wheel. Glancing behind in the rear-vision, she saw that the men hadn't left their home. She pulled the van off the hard shoulder and drove five hundred metres down the bush-lined road until she came to a cutaway that led into a shaded area, beneath a stand of large marri trees. She nosed into the cutaway and killed the engine. She didn't have long to wait. Two minutes later the two men drove past in their Landcruiser, neither of them looking into the shadows. They were always talking, these two men, despite being brothers, living together and working together. She didn't bother wondering what they might be talking about, but did consider how oddly capable they were at their jobs, considering they were hardly observant. She supposed it was because they looked a little dangerous, despite their easy laughter. As far as she could tell, this was so normal that most people took them for granted. They didn't stand out until it was too late, when they'd done what they intended to do.

She backed the van onto the road, slid the stick into drive and began to follow them through the deepening shadows of the banksia woodland. Even over the sound of the van's engine she could hear the trilling of thousands of cicadas, their calls rising in pitch as if in warning.

47

Lee sat on the tray of his F350 and smoked a cigarette, watching the light drain from the valley outside Gerry Tracker's mechanics workshop. After what had happened to the Ford Fairlane parked outside his home, he didn't want his truck to be exposed. He peered inside the back window of the truck and saw that it had gone seven o'clock. Soon it would be dark, but there was nothing for it except to wait. He'd just called Felicity Enright and told her about the meeting with her father. Bamber would have passed the news to her already, but Lee had promised to call her. It seemed like days ago that they had sat at the Cottesloe pavilion tearooms while she drank gin and Lee drank beer and whisky, while the Melbourne investigator had worked quickly to locate the user of Enright's credit card. He had called Lee on the tea-house number and broken the news that Jessica Enright was in the wind. It wasn't the news that Lee expected, and he'd been nervous about telling Felicity, who'd watched him come unsteadily across the crowded rooms with that bemused smile on her face until she read Lee's own, and the panic began to set in. Her face coloured and tears returned to her eyes as he told her, leaving nothing out, while watching her to see if she already knew. If Felicity had been acting, she was very good, but he didn't think so – her tears were real and a tremble had come over her hands that brought the glass of gin to her mouth and emptied it in a gulp. She mightn't be close to her sister, but the news that she'd once again disappeared made the recent events with the letters, and the photographs, and the knowledge that her sister had suffered abuse at the hands of her kidnappers, all the more real. Jessica wasn't living the high life in Melbourne, perhaps wasn't living at all. Lee had tried to calm Felicity but all of the scenarios he'd imagined were already there in her eyes. He'd gone away to call Bamber with the news, and when he'd returned she'd paid the bill and was waiting for him with his cigarettes and keys. He'd promised to call her, and left.

Lee heard tyres over the grate at the head of the alley and slipped off the Ford's tray. Domenic's dark hair and large-frame black glasses peered over the steering wheel of a tan Holden Commodore, which in the last light looked in good nick. Domenic smiled and revved the engine, pulled up alongside. He had a wrecker's yard in Bibra Lake with a sideline in fixing up totalled cars and selling them on. Lee knew without having to pop the bonnet that the engine and other vitals would be sound, and that the inside would be neat, as requested, for the purpose of providing a tidy and serviceable car to Gerry's clients while their vehicles were being repaired. Lee walked around the car and could barely see the dent in the rear panel that Domenic had beaten out. Insurance companies were prone to write off perfectly good cars, if the repair bill exceeded the value of the car itself, and Dom was the beneficiary.

Lee counted out the two thousand dollars he'd taken from the bank to cover Firmin's cheque, and signed the transfer papers that Dom smoothed on the bonnet. The extra thousand that Firmin had paid to replace the torched Fairlane would go into Gerry's kitty, for Lee's use of the workshop. Because he was away in the bush, Gerry hadn't made any money in the time since he'd left, and the grand would cover his rent for two months.

'That's for the Holden.' Lee peeled off another two hundred. 'And this is for picking up the Fairlane. There much rubber left on the road?'

Domenic grinned. 'We cleaned that up for ya, young fella. No sign the Ford was ever there.'

Domenic was a short stocky man who walked with a limp due to a motorcycle accident. The years of hard work and fierce sun had knotted his muscles and made the skin of his arms grained like old wood. Lee shook Domenic's hand and saw the headlights down on the street, where Dom's son, Domenic junior, was waiting to take his father home. Domenic folded the bills and stuffed them inside the front pocket of his King Gee work-shirt. He was usually keen for a cup of coffee and a chat, but it was dinnertime and Lee could tell that he was eager to leave. Lee waved him off and got inside his F350, drove it inside the workshop and parked it alongside the Dodge Phoenix he'd restored. The Dodge looked beautiful in the fading light, its mirror-finish paintjob reflecting the dents, dings and patches of Lee's battered truck.

The phone in Gerry's office began to ring. Lee assumed it was Gerry, pocketed the Ford keys and hurried across the darkening space into the office, framed out with treated pine and chipboard. He pushed aside a chair whose castors squealed, and lifted the receiver.

It was Swann. 'Lee, thought I'd catch you there. Nobody picked up at your place. You working on the Dodge?'

'Finished that last week. Was here picking up a replacement for the Fairlane from old Domenic. What's up?'

'I think you should come over.'

Lee was silent for a bit. 'No worries. Be there in twenty.'

'You got something on? You with someone?'

'No, but I'm stuffed. Haven't slept much the last few nights. Was hoping to get an early one.'

Now it was Swann's turn to be silent. 'Fair enough. It's about today's meeting with Enright. I've been thinking about it all day. The missing men. Now the daughter. I think you should take your earnings and walk away. I'm happy to contact Enright and make the call.'

Lee didn't know what to say. It wasn't what he expected to hear.

'You been doing background? Have you heard something, or what is it? You got that feeling?'

Swann had often described to Lee the feeling he got when a case began to go south – anxiety hovering above a mounting sense of dread. In the short term it sharpened the instincts, but if it didn't dissipate it needed to be taken seriously. From what Lee knew of Swann, however, he always pushed through it.

'Yeah, I got that feeling. And I've been taking a look. The case files, the company profiles.'

'I don't know what to say, Frank. I'm learning a lot. The Enright stuff isn't causing me any trouble – it's the Firmin problem with those Hastie dickheads that's giving me grief. I've talked to Firmin and we're clear. I'll keep my eyes open, I promise.'

'The task Enright and Bamber set you. The break-ins. That's all fine, part of the job, but—'

Lee understood. 'Someone's cleaning up as they go along or tipped the targets to what's going on. Which could leave me exposed. I get it, but I think it's all coming to an end. There are supposed to be two more photographs, but there hasn't been any further contact or letters about another photograph to retrieve. There may not be another.'

'That's my point, though. Because you're curious, because you're learning on the job, you didn't stick to the break-ins. So you know a fair bit. Depending on how this thing plays out, *you* could be considered a loose end.'

Lee thought about the other entity, quietly and unobtrusively watching the Enright company comms, monitoring the emails and reading the files and reports. He hadn't checked in with Connor Baird, his hacker mate, something he'd been meaning to do.

It was true that he was tired, and perhaps losing his awareness of what was happening at the periphery, where according to Swann things often mattered more than what was right in front of you.

'I'm not sure, Frank. Why would knowing about photographs of Jessica Enright, and a little bit about the kidnapping, put me in danger?'

'That I can't tell you. But you've got to watch out for a set-up, and you've got to watch out for … I don't know.'

'I will. Just need a good night's sleep.'

Swann was silent for a long time. Silent, Lee supposed, because he was Swann's employee, but he wasn't listening.

'If you want me to walk away, I will. But give me tomorrow to think about it. Take another reading of things, when my head is clear.'

'Fair enough. One of the detectives who investigated the Enright girl's kidnapping, he'll talk to you. I spoke with him today. It was on the phone so he didn't go into detail, but reading between the lines, there's something off. You can trust him. He's left the job, isn't part of the machine. Never was, so far as I can tell. Promise me that after you've talked to him, if something feels wrong, you'll take your earnings and walk away. You've done well. A town like this, so many secrets, so many sharks in suits, you'll never be out of work. But you've got to stay a few steps ahead, learn to trust the—'

'Feeling. I will. Talk to the copper. I promise.'

Lee wrote down the details, the cordless phone wedged in the crook of shoulder and ear, the sound of a freight train rumbling through the valley below.

'Meanwhile,' said Swann. 'I'm going to look closer at those Enright companies, the overseas-based ones. Their directors. Ask around a bit. How they got to own so much of Enright. What they want. What he owes. What it might have to do, if anything, with the photographs.'

Lee thanked Swann and hung up. The shadow companies that Swann had just spoken of, that constituted a majority of Enright's holdings, shell companies based in the Balkans, Singapore, whose directors were unknown, Swann would get to the bottom of it – it was his bread and butter. Lee dialled the number for Connor Baird, who picked up on the third ring. He sounded exhausted and wired at the same time. He wasn't one for small talk and so Lee got down to it. The sound of rustling paper as Baird retrieved his logbook, began to read through the Enright company emails pertaining to Lee. There was one from earlier in the day, Enright authorising the payment to the Melbourne PI, to track down Jessica Enright. A few in the previous days with Enright demanding status reports, but nothing extensive, nothing revealing.

'The other person, persons, inside the Enright company, spying alongside you. Did you trace them?'

Baird laughed. 'I tried, but no chance. The software they're using is older than mine, but encrypted, like mine. I'll never find an IP address, but I might be able to find out a server address. The chances are high, though, if they're as smart as they seem, that they'll be routing everything through several servers, perhaps dozens.'

'Yeah, could you keep trying? Just in case?'

Connor agreed and Lee hung up, slumped into the chair, cracked his neck, felt the world heave and spin as he closed his eyes, knowing it for a mistake. He opened his eyes and stood, supporting himself on the table.

The blue Honda Civic was parked outside his home. Lee drove further along the street, thought about driving to the beach and sleeping in his car. She couldn't have seen him in his new ride, the Holden that ran smoothly but smelled faintly of wet dog and burnt engine oil. Lee pulled to the kerb outside his neighbour George's place, saw that Domenic had done a good job removing the wreckage and burnt rubber off the road and gutter. He looked further down McLeery, tried to engage the Spidey-sense that his father had trained into him, the awareness of others' eyes upon him, but he was too tired. If anyone had seen him arrive in the Holden, then they were very well hidden.

Lisa was still in uniform, reclined on his old couch, her chunky boots up on the veranda railing, the insignia on her pale blue shirt catching the light from the single bulb above her. Lee smiled at her, but she didn't return the smile as she watched him come, reading him true. She stood and waited, a cheeky concern in her eyes, her hands on her hips until he was within her reach, when she took his hand, placed it upon her cheek, leaned up into his kiss.

She smelled of rum-scented tobacco and breath mints, and old sweat. Reading his mind, she said, 'I need a shower. You look like you need a shower.'

'I surely do.'

'Then maybe … later … we can eat?'

Lee hadn't thought about food in a long while. Even longer since he ate. 'We could walk down the hill, to Ruocco's?'

She took the keys from his hand, kissed him again. 'I'm bushed. Let's order takeaway.'

Lee could go for that. He followed her into the house, Lisa finding her way into the kitchen without the lights, then into the shower, holding out her hand for him to join her.

They lay in bed beneath the ceiling fan, Lisa's head on his shoulder. The cool air blew over their skin. They had showered, eaten, made love and lain there, never more than a fingertip from one another. Lisa was on another shift change, returning to mornings, and she was nearly as tired as Lee. On their previous meetings she'd been talkative and playful, but also watchful, almost wary. Now she was neither. He couldn't see her face, and didn't know whether she had her eyes open, or was asleep. He wanted to ask her why she'd driven away earlier, when she'd seen the two coppers at his door, but the moment never seemed right. It certainly wasn't right now. Lee swung his spare arm over and killed the lamplight. Lisa groaned, burrowed closer into his side.

48

Ex–Major Crimes detective Bill Moreland didn't appear to be thriving in retirement. His red-brick strata in Dianella was the most forlorn looking of the three units, even in the clear light of a hot Perth morning, the front yard all dead weeds and grey sand, a cane blind askew in the front window. He'd taken compo, he said, for a buggered back after falling down some stairs while carrying file boxes, twenty years into his career. He'd been glad to take the money because he'd expected his back to improve, at least enough to take a deskbound security job somewhere, monitoring CCTV or running background checks, except that his pain hadn't dissipated with the home rest.

'Nobody to complain to, that's my problem. Live alone and the telly doesn't give much sympathy. Bit hard on the dating circuit for a bloke who winces every time he picks up a fork. Dosing myself instead on the morphine, dribbling into my napkin isn't a good look either.'

Moreland's eyes were pinned, and Lee wondered if the morphine comment betrayed a deeper relationship with the drug. Lee felt a twinge of jealousy, but then remembered the time he'd come off, which always healed him of the desire.

Lee sat with his hands around his mug of tea. It was lukewarm and too milky, and he wasn't going to drink it, but it stopped him from reaching for his notebook and pen. He was there to listen, and nothing else, but Moreland was a lonely man and was eking out the preliminary small talk. Lee focussed on the sallow skin around his sunken eyes which betrayed a little irony, an awareness of what he was doing as he observed Lee in turn, something Lee expected from the ex-detective.

Finally, Moreland reached for his mug, took a sip and gave a sigh of mock satisfaction, a little shrug to indicate that he was ready.

Lee nodded. 'I know it's a while ago, Mr Moreland, but—'

The ex-detective didn't look pleased, reared back at the unintended insult. 'It's my back's stuffed, not my brain. I remember all my cases, some more than others. My dad was a pug – champion bantamweight stunted by malnutrition, but that's a different story. He had lots of wins, but always said that it's the losses that stay with you. He was right. That Enright girl kidnapping, especially. That was a bad one. I never had children, can't imagine what that must feel like, let alone what it was like for her.'

'Why was it a bad one, beyond the obvious? They got her back.'

Moreland grunted. 'Took a long while though. I wasn't lead detective, but I felt it. Followed on from a couple of other kids that went missing. Didn't get *them* back. One image I'll never forget – little Brian Oliver's body, found at the tip. Tossed away like garbage. The fucker, or fuckers, actually drove into the local tip, dumped him with a load of construction rubble and household junk, rolled up in a tarp. Only discovered by luck, when a citizen waded in and tried to retrieve himself a discarded fishing rod. They didn't CCTV the entrance, those days, didn't take down regos or give receipts. No record of the driver. Then there was little Annalisa Malone, you're probably too young to remember this shit, shallow grave in the Gnangara pine plantation, in the ground for two months before she was found, again by accident. I was on both cases, still unsolved. They were before the Enright girl, but fresh in mind as they say. We didn't know whether the ransom letters were some dickhead Joe Public joke or the real deal. Enright wasn't exactly forthcoming.'

Lee put down his cup of tea, cold now. Moreland wasn't joking about the cases staying with him. The fingers of his left hand trembled and his eyes were shining.

'I don't know how much Frank told you,' Lee said, 'about what I'm doing.'

'Nothing. But that's Swann. Knew him back in the day. Good copper. The way he was treated. Fucking disgrace.'

Lee had to keep gently pushing forward. 'He said I should speak to you about the kidnapping. That you said there was something off.'

Moreland's hand stopped shaking. His eyes became steely, then softened the longer he looked at Lee. 'Yeah, off, but only in the sense that there was nothing really *on*. Nothing suspicious. Not like some cases I worked. But considering what we'd just worked on, two dead children, one aged eight, the other nine, after the initial scramble and setting up of a team, the logistics, going back to the sex offenders, working our fizzes, I don't know …'

'You felt like you weren't supported?'

'Nah, not that. It was an Enright kid. This was before the WA Inc scandal stuff, before the dirt all came out. Guys like the Conlans, Bond, Enright – they were lords of the fucking town.'

'My understanding is that Enright was more an accountant, a financial advisor to the big boys.'

Moreland laughed. 'Glad I put down my tea already. What you say is a crack-up. Enright was all that, but a lot more. He got a cut on all the deals, especially the ones brokered for the government. We're talking tens of millions. He had the ear of everyone who was anyone, is what I'm saying, and when his kid went missing, you can imagine. No stone unturned and all that. And we worked it hard. All of us. No worries about overtime. Uniformed out there doorknocking, or door-kicking, you get the idea. Personally, I couldn't give a fuck about Enright and his money, his power – I was working for his missing daughter. It was the same for my colleagues. We had pictures of her, and the two dead kids on the wall above the tea urn.'

Moreland paused, gave Lee a sceptical look.

'But then Enright paid the ransom,' Lee said, 'after three weeks. Don't worry, Mr Moreland, I'm working for Swann.'

'But Enright is your client.'

'His daughter Jessica has gone missing again, in Melbourne. The reason I'm here. So you worked it hard, until the ransom was paid. What happened after that to give you concern?'

'The girl getting released was a good result. Of course it was. A great deal of relief, I can fucking tell you. The ransom letters weren't a joke, and there was no need to visit another set of parents, break the news. The girl was brought in for a statement. The team was cut back to me and two others. We took her statement and Scene of Crime went over the Baldivis place, fine-tooth comb. Nothing forthcoming.'

'I've read the statement, and your reports. The Baldivis block, where the container was buried. Where Jessica was held. Who owned the block?'

'That not in the report?'

'No.'

Moreland had asked a question he knew the answer to, smiled wryly down at his hands. 'Well, that was embarrassing. The block was owned by the state. It was a drug profits asset seizure. Used to be owned by the Junkyard Dogs. Your boss was involved with the crushing of that particular one-percenter outfit, no?'

'Before my time. No chance an existing bikie, knowing the place was empty, might've—'

'We looked at that. Of course. They were all either iced, or put on ice. None of the fuckers left. We looked at the neighbours. People in the relevant government department. Nothing.'

'Were you able to establish when the shipping container was buried there?'

'Yes, we were. The container was last registered to a lot in North Fremantle. Post the seizure of the block itself. Looked like it was purposely built to house little Jessica Enright.'

'Neighbours didn't see or notice anything?'

'You've looked at the crime scene pics. People live in woop woop for a reason. No neighbours saw anything.'

'Bit of a risk, though. Building on land that isn't your own?'

'I guess so. But the kid was underground. The house was empty. The kidnappers came once a day, for a few minutes.'

'Mind if I smoke?'

Moreland reached for an ashtray on the sink behind him,

passed it over – an antique Bakelite ashtray with the Swan Lager logo stamped into it. Lee took out a cigarette and offered it to Moreland, who shook his head.

'Is there anything else not in the Jessica Enright statement? Anything you wanted to know more about, but couldn't get from her?'

Moreland laughed again, shook his head. 'Where do I fucking start? The first interviews, the kid was in shock. We trod softly. Vague on the details of how the kidnapping went down, how many men etc. She knew she was taken off the street outside the Claremont Hungry Jacks, one minute cutting through the alley leading to Bayview Terrace, next she's got a bag over her head, immediately sedated. Woke up in the hellhole they made for her. Daily visits for three weeks. Then one day, she was blindfolded and released, a park in the city. Later interviews, my impression was that the kid had been told, counselled, whatever, to give us nothing else than the jack shit we already had.'

'That's important, isn't it? Was she afraid? Her demeanour, state of mind, doesn't come across in the interview records.'

'I reread my notes this morning, knowing you were coming, to confirm my memory of the whole thing. Memory is usually a bad record, but this time it was reliable. The first interviews, like I say, she was in shock. As you'd expect. Afraid? Yes, to the point of paralysis. The last two interviews, I can't say. They were done at the Enright mansion, I wasn't there.'

'Who conducted those?'

'The big fella upstairs – Commander Corbett. Then head of

Major Crimes. Came out from behind his desk, due to pressure from above, is what I heard.'

'And in those interviews, was a woman ever present? A female detective, counsellor, lawyer, family member?'

'Not to my knowledge. We'd do things differently now, of course. Enright was present for the Corbett interviews.'

'And going on the interview transcripts, you get the feeling that in those Corbett interviews, Jessica had been coached to say as little as possible?'

Moreland cast a grave eye over the wall behind Lee. 'To the point where she couldn't even confirm what she'd said earlier. I think Enright wanted the whole thing wrapped up. Corbett was happy to oblige, for political reasons, or to save the daughter and Enright further trauma, or both. We weren't happy about it, the idea that there were men out there, snatch a child and put her in a hole, free as larks, spending their earnings – those kind of scum won't stop at one. Believe me, letting kidnappers roam free isn't good for anyone. It's not a common crime in this country because we go hard on it. Other parts of the world, its common as shit. But we could only follow the evidence, and that didn't go anywhere. I continued with some of the stuff that came on the tip-line, but that didn't go anywhere either.'

The older man was shifting in his seat. They'd been at the kitchen table for a half-hour, and his back was clearly signalling its distress.

'You said before, that Enright wasn't forthcoming. What exactly did you mean by that?'

'Just that he wasn't interested in us holding his hand during or after the kidnapping. He never told us how the ransom was paid. We couldn't force him to either.'

'One last question, Mr Moreland. Were there any answers that Jessica gave, seemed evasive, not right, or contradictory?'

Moreland stood, put his hands on his hips, stretched his back and grimaced at the pain. He spoke through gritted teeth. 'That's a helluva question, son. What are you getting at?'

Lee stood, picked up his cup, made ready to take it to the sink. 'We're trying to establish how many people might've been involved. They were, or some of them were, clearly professional. It's related to Jessica's situation now.'

Moreland looked at the cup in Lee's hands. 'You're well brought up, mate, I'll give you that. You going to wash it too? But your question. Hard to say. Outfit like that, you'd want it to be small as possible. That's basic fucking logic. Then again, we're dealing with crims. Now go on, before you leave, ask the question you really want to ask. The one I asked Jessica, indelicate man that I am.'

'You asked her whether she was abused during her captivity.'

'Asked her. Had to ask her. Standard question. Her answer was no, but there was a moment, she looked directly at me, it was like she was back in the container, in the dark.'

'Terror?'

'Hatred. Rage. Disgust. But mostly hatred.'

Moreland followed Lee's eyes down to his hand, which had resumed trembling.

49

Lee got off the Kwinana Freeway south of the river, turned onto a small road that circled the golf club, came out in front of the zoo. There were no payphones before the entrance, and so he headed south again, looking for a deli. He found one just before Canning Highway, small and rundown, like every other deli he knew, no money going into maintenance, unable to compete with the corporates. The phone box was missing its door and smelt of piss, but when Lee dropped in two twenty cent pieces and punched in the numbers he heard the ringtone break as Moreland's phone connected. The phone rang out until the ex-detective's answering machine kicked in. Lee gave his name, hung up and immediately dialled again. This time Moreland picked up.

'That was quick,' he said. 'What did you forget?'

It hadn't been until he left Moreland's place that the feeling of disgust and anger at what he'd heard began to peak. Frank Swann had asked him to meet the detective and then examine his position. The meeting hadn't changed anything, or advanced anything, or tweaked his instincts enough for him to walk away. And yet, in the image of Jessica Enright, in a formal interview, enraged and vulnerable, staring back at the detectives, he'd felt the proximity of something, at one remove, or several removes, but there all the same. The kidnapping had been professionally done – the child taken, hidden and returned in exchange for money – a transaction like any other, to those who feel nothing for others. But there was something else too, beyond the ruthlessness and efficiency, in Jessica Enright's response to Moreland's question – the proximity of something darker, crueller and colder that she had suffered. Some would call it evil, others not, but whatever it was called, Lee felt it in his heart.

'I'm going to run a list of names by you,' Lee said. 'If you recognise one of them, just tell me.'

Swann had told Lee not to give Moreland anything from the Enright case, to not involve him, to not ignite that need in the ex-detective for involvement, for understanding, or closure.

'Sure, go ahead.'

Lee worked backwards. 'Alan Pusey.'

'Nup.'

'Donald Laver.'

'Negative.'

'Gavin Drew.'

Silence from Moreland, until the ex-detective whispered, 'Say that again.'

'Gavin Drew.'

'I don't know that name.'

'But?'

Moreland sighed. 'It's here in my notes. We looked at a guy called Tim Drew, had prior sex offences, dating back to his school years. But he was into boys. We put a line through him. He was murdered last year, the year before. I did raise a glass when I heard that.'

'Do you know much about his murder, beyond what was in the papers?'

'Matter of fact, yes. I called a mate. The bastard was bashed, this much is known, but whoever it was, didn't know what they were doing. He had a severe subdural haematoma, head injury, likely sustained during his ... even as I say the words ... things are falling into place.'

'He was snatched. Where from?'

'His home, they think. Food left on the table. Smoke alarms alerted the neighbours, coffee pot left on the stove.'

'If they were going to kill him, make an example, why not do it at his home?'

'Crueller for a person, and their family, to never be found. And we don't know that the purpose was murder. He'd been badly bruised, battered, had defensive wounds, even bloody knuckles. Wherever they took him, tortured him, his hands and feet were too tightly bound with cable ties, completely cut off the circulation, and he had bleeding on the brain. He died of a stroke in whatever chair he was tied to. Whether they tortured him for fun, or information, we'll never know. And if it was for the latter, we don't know if he gave it up. Never know.'

It could be a coincidence, Gavin Drew and Tim Drew, the one a murdered paedophile, the other a paedophile now missing, but Lee didn't think so.

'Thanks,' Lee said. 'That's very useful.'

'But you're not going to tell me why? I can help ...'

Lee heard the desperation, the need in Moreland's voice, the very thing that Swann had warned him against. 'I'm not sure yet.

I'll need to call you back, run some things by you, if that's ok?'

Whether Moreland heard the lie in Lee's voice, or whether he was used to it, Lee didn't know. Moreland hung up the phone without saying goodbye. Lee put back the receiver and turned to his ride, before remembering the deli. He hadn't eaten since last night, and the sign outside the deli said fresh sandwiches, made to order. He couldn't stomach food right now, but he needed fuel – a chocolate bar and an iced coffee would keep him going.

50

The men are late this morning. It isn't the normal day of the week for them to meet, and perhaps this has something to do with it. The beach is just as empty as during their usual dawn rendezvous, although the morning sun is now headed toward its zenith, the sun beating hard on the van roof from where she watches them. Even the seagulls, tramping the dune line or otherwise sitting in the shade of the clubhouse wall, look wearied by the heat, the fierce points of light that fire off the water, the white sand, the silos and buildings around them. The air is clear to the oceanic horizon, boiling with a heat mirage, a couple of container ships moored in Gage Roads, the low crumbly moonscape of Rottnest Island behind them. She takes another mouthful of water, watches the sweat ooze from the pores on the backs of her hands.

There are only three of them today. She knew that this would be the case, having read the email sent by the youngest one, to the oldest one, telling him that 'P' needed to be present tomorrow, or there was little point meeting. He had news to share. He wasn't going to use the phone any more. It was too risky. Please make sure you delete this email, then delete it from your trash.

The oldest one is pale, lean and tall, submerged to his neck while the youngest one, equally thin and tall, treads water, a bucket hat protecting his thinning scalp from the burning rays. The other man, who would be 'P', stands with his back to her, and he must be talking, because the other two haven't spoken in a while. Just to be sure, she checks the focus on her long-distance zoom, making sure that the image before her and the identities of the men can be captured without question, and that no claims can be made against the depth of field to suggest that the men aren't tightly huddled together, communicating with one another.

She doesn't know where the other two men have gone, and she doesn't care. Her work is to follow, document and preserve, and nothing more.

The men have been in the water for thirty minutes. That is longer than the length of time that they usually meet for, perhaps because the dawn air is colder, even though the water temperature doesn't change. She should know, having swum at the same beach her entire life.

When the man called 'P' turns his head to the beach, for the third time in a minute, while each time she captures his face, his thick eyebrows and neatly combed hair, still dry, it occurs to her that the men are waiting for something, or someone.

As she thinks it, she sees him. His familiar silhouette, and walk, despite the camouflage – a poncho-towel and bucket hat, large sunglasses, none of which he'd ordinarily wear. Seeing him chills her, makes her burn at the same time, stepping daintily across the baking sand, his thongs overlarge, careful lest any sand collect beneath his feet. He doesn't strip off the costume when he reaches the shoreline, the crystalline foam churning at his ankles, but walks right in, his hands smoothing the water, wading deeper into the cool blue shallows, the men turning as one. She clicks off a few shots, then takes the camera from her eye, clips on the lens cap, places it back inside its padded bag. There is no point documenting anything from here – the tears in her eyes are hot and painful. She can't see, and sobbing, plunges her face into her hands.

51

Lee's pager began to vibrate as he drove over the traffic bridge into Fremantle. One hand on the wheel, he unclipped the pager and recognised Bamber's number, before swinging the Holden into the glare reflected off the harbour waters, driving beside the train embankment until he reached the Australia Hotel. He ordered a middy of draught from the old manager, who was still wearing his flesh-coloured hernia-corset after moving barrels in the cellar. Lee asked for phone change and went into the corridor leading to the bathrooms, dropped the twenty cent pieces.

Bamber answered on the first ring. 'Lee, I gotta ask,' he opened with. 'Pusey's photographic studio, heritage listed, a big deal, got burned down last night.'

'You know it wasn't me.'

'Yeah, maybe, but I have to ask. The alternative is even worse. Means Pusey is onto us. Twigged, somehow.'

Lee thought about it. 'No chance of that. I left it the same as before I went in. Unless his laptop has played up, making him suspicious. But burning down a million-dollar building to remove evidence, that's a bit over the top.'

Bamber sniffed. 'Not if he's thinking of fleeing. All his money is tied up in a heritage building, and in his home – now he'll be able to claim insurance, take the cash and disappear, like Laver and Drew have disappeared.'

'But if he's destroyed any evidence, he has no need to disappear. It can't be the coppers, or an investigation that he's afraid of. It's got to be you. He knows if he can be tied to Jessica Enright's kidnapping, he won't be breathing for long.'

Lee imagined the pictures in Bamber's head, the memories of the knees he'd smashed and the heads he'd cracked in the search for information, at the time of Jessica's disappearance. If Pusey and the others were involved, they would know the stories, and they would run.

'You might be right. They mightn't be onto you. Guilty minds and all that. But something's alerted them. I'm asking you to be extra careful.'

Lee told Bamber what Moreland had told him, about Gavin Drew's brother, Tim Drew, tied to a chair and beaten until a fuse blew in his head and he stroked out. If the others were part of the kidnapping, that would put the fear into them.

'That was how long ago?' Bamber asked.

'Eighteen months ago.'

'Why wait until now to disappear?

Lee couldn't answer that question. Bamber was right, it was a long time to take to get your affairs in order. Something recent had scared them.

'On Pusey's hard drive, the facsimile. Was the photo there?'

'My oath it was. And so much more. Enough poison to kill the bloody oceans.'

On the drive back from Moreland's, Lee had decided not to contact Swann. There was more he needed to understand about the Jessica Enright kidnapping. Meeting Moreland hadn't convinced him otherwise, as Swann had hoped, and yet now, standing in the hotel corridor, sepia photographs of dockworkers crawling over a merchant steamboat, gantry crane swinging a laden net, lumpers carrying jarrah sleepers up a narrow gangplank, he saw acutely that he was no longer needed, no longer useful. There hadn't been another demand to retrieve a photograph. Jessica Enright's kidnapping was personal to Bamber, personal to her father and sister. Lee was merely hired help, and it was vanity and self-interest for him to continue on.

'I guess that's me then,' Lee said, hiding the reluctance in his voice. 'I've done what you asked. If you pay Swann, he'll see to the rest.'

'Fuck off, son,' Bamber said quietly. 'It was you who went looking for Jessica in Melbourne. Against orders, to be sure, and heartbreaking for her father, but it was the right call.'

'No sign of her?'

'Nope. But I'd like you to—'

'If there's another photograph, another burg needed, call me. Otherwise, I'm checking out.'

'So be it,' the older man said, a surprising calmness in his voice. 'But remember. You breathe a word of this, to anyone. I ever hear a bar-room story about photos of Jessica Enright, the tycoon's daughter, I'm going to visit you. You understand?'

It didn't need to be said, but Lee could hear the finality, the cutting of ties in Bamber's casual malevolence. Lee hung up, took a deep breath, was surprised to find that rather than feeling regret, or shame welling up in him, he felt instead a surge of relief, a physical and emotional release that made his skin tingle. Rather than heading outside into the heat of the day, Lee ordered another beer and a side shot of Jameson. He took the drinks into the beer garden and lit a cigarette.

Lee planned to head home, and sleep. The sun was hot in the beer garden courtyard but his bedroom would be cool and dark. Nothing had been said, but he assumed that Lisa would visit him once her shift was over. Lee had no interest in a serious relationship, but at the same time he liked Lisa's company, appreciated her confidence and sense of humour, something that spilled over into her lovemaking. Assuming she wasn't too tired after the eight-hour shift, he planned to take her out to dinner somewhere, and ask all the questions he'd been meaning to ask, the kind of questions that normally get answered before people hook up, such as where she was from, what she did in her spare time, how she came to be a copper. He knew that the questions would amuse her, as much as the asking of the questions would amuse her, and he looked forward to seeing her smile, the way her front lip lifted over her incisors, which were prominent, the knowing sparkle in her eyes.

But first Lee had to make some calls. He finished his beer and necked his whiskey, enjoyed the sweet burn, a match for the sunlight on his forearms. Back at the phone in the corridor, he dialled Swann first of all, leaving a message on his answering machine that said simply, 'I took your advice.' Lee then called Connor Baird, who he knew would be sleeping. On Connor's answering machine he told his hacker friend that the job was over, and so not to worry about the stuff they'd been talking about. Lee hung up and was two steps toward the main bar when his pager vibrated. It was Firmin. Lee sighed, thought about ignoring the call, but dug out twenty cents and heard the metallic beats as he dialled the nightclub. Lee had just walked away from a job, without knowing when Swann would find something else for him. He planned to give some money to his mother for her birthday, and put the rest on his rent, in advance. The chances were good that in the coming weeks he'd end up needing to work the door at Club Summertime.

Firmin's gravelly drawl was exaggerated, and Lee knew that he'd been drinking, most likely hadn't slept.

'What was that again?' Lee asked.

'I said, I've got an address for you. The bozo who robbed my safe. As promised.'

Lee knew that Firmin had promised no such thing, in keeping with his traditional MO, because very few people were likely to correct him.

'You didn't promise me anything, Firmin. I told you I wanted nothing to do with him, or the Hastie brothers either. Get one of your regular crew to pay him a visit.'

Firmin was ready for him, as Lee expected. 'Yes, but…like I said last time, my boys are good at going the bash, but they lack…finesse. I don't want you to send him a message, or hurt him. I just want you to break in and get back what's mine. Some of the stuff they took is uninsurable, for reasons of sentimentality. The insurable stuff – I'm going to have to pay ten grand in excess alone. I told them to fuck off. I'm offering to pay it to you instead.

You go in, nice and quiet, steal back what's mine, assuming there's anything left, I give you ten K. Do I have your attention, young man?'

Firmin had Lee's attention. He could live a few months on ten grand. He could pay off a chunk of his mother's mortgage with ten grand.

'Just a burg? No heavy stuff?'

'It's up to you to make sure nobody's home. In and out. There's nobody else I can trust with this.'

Lee rolled his eyes. 'That line again. But first, tell me how you got the address? You already spilt blood over this? I don't want any part in more dramas—'

'Listen to you, like a fucken choirboy. But no, no blood spilt, yet. I got a tip-off, for a reward, something Michelle put on the street. Rowdy Tim did a drive-by and saw the Landcruiser, clocked that somebody was home.

'The place in Wattleup, that I got shot at over?'

'No, he was there. That was him. This is a house in Yangebup, near you. You won't even have to drive fifteen minutes.'

'What's the address?'

Firmin spoke the words, and Lee wrote the address into his notebook. He could feel the alcohol spongy in his legs, knew that it'd been a factor in how quickly he'd accepted Firmin's offer. He would be looking for a Gladstone bag taken from Firmin's safe, and if the robbers had emptied the bag, some velvet sacks containing opals, rubies and sapphires, a tin shaker containing gold nuggets, a S&W antique pistol, some floppy disks containing his ledgers, his 'true books' and not those submitted to the tax department, fifty odd sets of keys belonging to his vintage car collection housed in a Malaga warehouse, and other miscellaneous bric-a-brac from Firmin's mother's estate.

The smarter decision would be to wait until nightfall to visit the Yangebup home, but Lee was set on meeting Lisa. He decided to drink a coffee at the bar and head south into the suburbs.

52

The Yangebup house was newly built. You could see the yellow builder's sand through the cracks in the bricked drive and between the rows of turf rolled across the front yard. Plastic scrim was still attached to some of the window frames, and the tin roof had boot marks where the roofing plumbers had knelt to drill. The housing estate streets looked like they'd been built by the same firm, cookie-cutter rendered brick homes with the same size blocks and the same flat profile where the dozers had come in, torn out the bush and levelled the land. The bush behind the houses was scattered with building rubble, plastic waste and tea-tree and banksia trunks and boughs pushed into piles. Further up the street, a house was half-complete. Green treated-pine roofing joists glittered with steel framing, and the naked front yard was crammed full of parked utes and trucks. Lee could hear the commercial radio turned to full volume. The street was empty and there was no chance of someone complaining.

Lee did a couple of drive-bys and wondered at the stick-up merchant's choice of hideout. Perhaps it wasn't a hideout, having done his time in the Wattleup semidetached. Perhaps he'd bought the place with his earnings from the rob.

Lee scoped the bush behind the house for a point of entry but saw that the workers at the building site up the street were clustered mostly in the backyard, which hadn't yet been enclosed. If Lee entered the house over the back fence, he would be visible.

The Landcruiser wasn't parked in the drive. There were no security cameras visible. Lee drove back down the street and parked on a well-used dirt track that led into the bush. He left the car and walked slowly round the corner and into the street.

Pedestrians stood out in new suburbs, where everybody drove to the shops, the oval, the schools. An unfamiliar young man walking the streets would catch the eye, but Lee's glances right and left told him that the houses were empty – no cars in the drive, no prams on the porch, no toys or swing-sets in the yard. Lee pulled down his cap and focussed on the building site up the rise, but nobody was on the scaffolding that clad the nearest wall, and the bricklayers were all in the back.

Lee went straight to the front door of number twelve. From his pocket he removed the set of picks that his father had trained him to use when he was a child. The lock was a standard steel knob security arrangement, and he had it open within a minute. He hadn't made a sound, and before he entered he tried the doorbell, which rang out the familiar Westminster Chime sequence. Lee waited thirty seconds before he slipped on his gloves and entered the house, which still smelt of fresh paint and plasterboard dust. The slate tiles that led through the house toward the kitchen were quiet underfoot. In the kitchen, the sliding back door was built into a larger floor-to-ceiling window frame that covered the rear wall, giving a view onto an empty backyard and the bush behind. Lee tried the door, which was key-locked. He retraced his steps and started in the front room, darkened by a heavy blind. The room smelt of stale cooking oil and socks. Despite the three bedrooms with double beds in each, two of which still wore the manufacturer's plastic wrapping, someone had been sleeping on the fabric couch beneath the front window. Lee cracked the blind and saw that it gave a clear view down the drive and along the street. A go-bag containing a few pairs of jocks, socks, t-shirts and a toothbrush, as well as a small Browning pistol with an extra magazine, was tucked under the pillow and blanket laid over the couch. He put the gun back in its bag and zipped it up, placed it carefully on the floor next to the couch. He wasn't armed with anything except a tyre iron, useful for prising floorboards or smashing in plasterboard.

The room was empty apart from the bedding and bag. Lee took up the bedding and rolled it, slung it onto the floor. The house was large and it'd be a big job to search it thoroughly. He would need to get up in the roof-space and take a look in the yard, to see if there had been fresh digging. The house was built onto a concrete slab and so there wasn't anything beneath his feet. The bedrooms had been empty, which just left the kitchen and the laundry, both useful places to hide material. Before Lee headed out of the front room he knelt and began to work on the heavy couch, pressing the cushions and running his hands down the seams, looking for incisions or lumps. When this turned up nothing Lee put his fingers under the base of the couch and with a bit of grunt turned it on its side. There was the cut in the elastic upholstery that he'd been looking for, a clean cut beneath one of the couch's wings, which had been crudely re-stapled. Lee stabbed the sharpened end of his tyre iron into the elastic and ripped a hole, then got his fingers into it, tearing away the black cloth until he could see the bag, wedged up into the wing, supported with a stuffed towel and a pillow.

Lee had to laugh. It was no Gladstone bag, as Firmin had described it, but a vintage Louis Vuitton carry bag, now scratched and scuffed, a little golden ornament still attached to the handle and the zipper-stitching pulled away in a few places along the seam. Lee pulled the zipper and tipped the contents onto the floor. Four blue velvet bags and a tin canister, which landed with a thud. Lee opened the lid and saw the nuggets, looked alluvial, smooth and shiny, a good ten ounces by weight. Lee put the canister back in the bag as well as the velvet sacks, which he presumed contained the jewels described by Firmin. Three green floppy disks that weren't named held together with an elastic band were underneath the jewels. Lee tipped those into the bag and picked up the largest container – a steel strongbox whose lock had been forced. Inside the box were dozens of keys, whose fobs held the steel, enamel and bronze logos of vintage Ford, Chrysler, Buick, Chevrolet, Dodge, Cadillac, Jeep and other American companies that Firmin collected. Losing these keys alone would cost Firmin thousands of dollars. They had the used look of primary keys, rather than spares. Lee pulled the latch on the box and set it inside the bag. A manila sheaf of papers bound with twine and a plastic folder that looked like it contained receipts went in with the rest. Lee started collecting up a small pile of silver, brass and pewter cast animals, and what looked like collectable silver and gold coins, each in a hard plastic case. He recognised an American gold eagle, a very rare nineteenth-century coin, and was turning it over in his hands when he saw a shadow cross the edge of the blind. Adrenalin surged into his limbs, his mind became clear. He dropped the coin into the bag and took up the tyre iron. He assumed it was the man, returned, although he hadn't heard the rocks-in-a-tumble-dryer sound of the Landcruiser in the drive. He stood and peeked through the blind, felt his guts tumble at the sight of a black Tactical Response Group vehicle, built like a tank, and two divvy vans parked across the street. A dozen of the police commandos were piling out of the rear of the truck, loading shotguns and checking each other's Kevlar, dropping visors over helmets. The sight was dreamlike, slightly unreal – the TRG only called to incidents involving armed offenders, where it was customary to shoot on sight, and to shoot to kill. Anybody who'd seen Lee enter the house would have called triple zero, or the local cop shop, who would have sent uniformed coppers. Whoever had fingered him might have mistaken his tyre iron for a gun, possible at distance, or … Lee didn't have time to think. He remembered the shadow on the blind, understood that he might be surrounded, thought about giving himself up. But the TRG's reputation dissuaded him – there was a good chance he'd be gunned down, armed or unarmed, and there were no witnesses in the street.

Lee took the bag and moved through the house. The kitchen sliding door was locked and so he cut left, into the laundry. It was then that he saw the man who'd robbed Firmin's safe, bound hand and foot, mouth gagged, sightless eyes, a bullet hole in the perfect centre of his forehead, blood puddled beneath him where he'd been stabbed. The blood was still fresh, hadn't congealed, ran in a clean gutter toward the drain in the centre of the tiled room.

Lee stepped over it, turned the doorknob, felt fresh air on his face, heard the boot-steps on the drive, the front door crunch open. Lee hefted the bag and tossed the tyre iron over the neighbour's fence, not wanting to be armed, not wanting to give them a reason to shoot him down. He glanced along the side of the house, nothing yet, leapt to the steel-blue Colorbond fence in front of him and hefted himself over, the bag still on his shoulder. For a moment his back was a naked target for a police shooter, then he hit the dirt on the other side of the fence, which rang out down its length. Lee heard the crackle of miked comms as he sprinted toward the back fence, turning and seeing that the builders up the street were stopped in their labours, one of them cheering him on, a couple clapping as he leapt, landed and cleared the back fence, down in the cool grey sand and invisible to his pursuers, but only for a moment, a helmeted head peering over the fence from the block he'd escaped from, not seeing him as he backed along its length, hidden in shadow until he broke for the cover of the banksia scrub, a shout behind him, the thudding of a heavily armoured man trying to climb a fence – Lee a hundred metres clear now, then two hundred metres, well out of shotgun range, sprinting and jumping logs with sand spurting from his heels and the balga and zamia palms whipping his knees. He made what he hoped was the dirt track where he'd left his car, and turned left, downhill toward the suburban streets. There was the Holden, parked nose-out. Lee increased his pace until he reached the Commodore, whipped out his keys, his nerves jangling just like the keys in his hand, shaking, fumbling, finally getting the key in the door lock and then going through the same process before getting the key in the ignition, turning it over, surfing more than driving down the sandy track toward the cul-de-sac entrance where he got the driver's door shut, his seatbelt on, his cap and sunglasses removed, hitting one hundred clicks on the quiet streets until he made the tributary road, then slowed and turned into the flow of traffic headed north.

53

Lee needed to get home and take a shower, scrub his skin and put fire to his clothes and boots, but instead he drove into the Spearwood valley that was on his way home, up the broken bitumen drive that led to Gerry Tracker's mechanics workshop. The sun was low behind him, but heat continued to radiate off the blacktop and the tin fence that lined the alley. Lee got out and unlocked the roller door, thought about driving in the Holden but decided against it, instead clattered down the door behind him, embracing the dark coolness of the workshop that smelt of oil and degreaser. He didn't plan on being there long, just time enough to swap out the shortwave radio from his F350 truck into the Holden. The high-frequency radio was set to the local police channel, and he wanted to be sure that nobody had seen him flee the scene. The TRG didn't communicate on the open channels, and so he hoped for reports from the two uniformed vehicles that were at the house, and any detectives who would be converging on the street.

Lee turned on the shortwave, expecting the channel to be empty as it usually was, until an order needed to be given or a position described, a traffic incident reported or an arrest made. The regular cool voice of the day-shift dispatch operator, who Lee had nicknamed Barry White, was instead raised an octave or two, stress bleeding out into the updated report he was reading from, indicating that the death in the Yangebup home was now considered a homicide; the man found tortured and murdered still a John Doe.

Barry White spoke directly to a senior constable at the site, reporting that a forensic team had been dispatched and that their ETA was fifteen minutes. Further uniformed police from the Murdoch station were *en route* to secure the perimeter.

The bandwidth returned to its regular low static hum as the operator and senior constable signed off. Lee didn't waste any time. From the Holden he retrieved his go-bag, containing a change of clothes and a pair of sandshoes. Lee stripped by the sink and scrubbed himself with an abrasive pad, scouring the skin exposed at the Yangebup home, and in the pursuit through the bushland, his mind running the scenarios and cursing himself for not taking better precautions. If he'd shed a single hair at the crime scene, then they'd have his DNA. When Lee was satisfied that there wasn't anything on his skin, no dust or traces of fibre, or spores or seeds from the bush, he scrubbed his scalp with a diluted cup of ammonia, ignoring the faint burn as he let the mixture fizz against his scalp, before dunking his head into the sink and washing it all out.

He dressed in his spare clothes, picking up his clothes and boots with a length of reo bar, dropping them into the fire drum out in the alley. Lee doused the drum with a few litres of petrol, then dropped in a lit scroll of newspaper, felt the whump of heat against his face as the drum sent up a shimmering column of blue and orange flame, Lee waiting for the fire to subside before tossing in anything flammable nearby – a jarrah wheel-chock, some pine two-by-fours and a smashed-up frame of particle board. The fire was good and roaring, and he left it and returned to the Holden, pulled out the driver's floor pan matting, put that in the fire, tore off the front-seat cover, gave that to the fire as well.

Lee wheeled out the high-pressure cleaner and turned the tap, felt the pressure in the hose build until he opened the nozzle, walked the length of the car blasting out any dust or sand that might have collected from parking in the dirt track behind the Yangebup house, getting down on his back and cleaning out the undercarriage in particular, the treads of the tyres, the wheel arches and bumpers.

When he was finished, he lit a cigarette and watched the water drain, carrying any evidence that he'd been near the murdered man down the alley and into the nearest culvert.

It was only now that he allowed himself to dwell upon the image of the body, something he'd glimpsed at the time, but which remained startlingly clear in his memory – the eerie calm on his face, the clean, round entry wound in his forehead, little halo of powder burn around the bullet hole indicating the proximity of the weapon. Most shocking was that intimacy, the work of a small-calibre weapon, a .22 most likely, favoured by hitmen the world over for its accuracy, the fact that the bullet was small enough to pinball inside a skull or body, and therefore do more damage.

Lee stubbed out his cigarette and lit another, shaking his head, the memory of what happened at the house clear enough, but the associated feelings somehow unreal – a sense of numbness associated with shock. The adrenalin was still present in his body, his mind, except for the clarity of the image of the dead man. Lee had seen him at the entrance of Club Summertime on the evening he robbed Firmin, and not since. Had he been the one to blow up Lee's car, right outside his home? Lee didn't know, it seemed ancient history standing there in the fading light of day, the sun moving down to the quicksilver horizon, the hiss and swoosh of peak-hour traffic in the streets below him.

Whoever killed the man had been professional. The scene of death was relatively clean. The blood that leaked out him was trained to run into a drain, and the man had gone quietly, had submitted to his fate, had kept his eyes open while the barrel was placed against his skin. Professional, or known to the man, trusted enough to get inside the house and take him by surprise, bind and torture him, deliver him to oblivion without alerting neighbours, or the builders up the street.

The blood that'd soaked into his shirt, his jeans, draining across the tiles, had been fresh. The laundry door hadn't been locked. The killer, or killers, must have left the house shortly before Lee arrived. Did this explain the presence of the TRG? Had they been called to the house because of the sighting of the killer, or killers, rather than because of Lee?

Lee had to assume that the killers were the Hastie brothers. The dead man had worked with the Hasties to rob Firmin, but the nightclub owner's bag hadn't been recovered by them. Had the man refused to share the spoils with the Hasties? Had he moved from Wattleup to Yangebup to hide from the brothers? The brothers were violent enough to do the deed, but something wasn't quite right. The man had been tortured, then executed.

If the purpose of the torture was to locate Firmin's bag, why hadn't the man talked? The contents of the bag were valuable, but not worth dying over. Either the man had known that he was doomed anyway, or the opposite – he didn't believe that the killer would pull the trigger.

Lee stared at Firmin's bag, sitting innocently on the bonnet of the Holden. He felt a pang of hatred for Firmin, for getting him involved, for refusing to take no for an answer, for sitting ensconced in his pokey office, while sending Lee out to do his bidding. Worse still was the feeling of self-loathing that came over Lee at the recognition that he had nobody to blame but himself. He could have said no, but had allowed the older man to gull him into doing him a favour.

The safest course was to replace the Holden back in Gerry's workshop, and to take Lee's truck. Now that he was no longer working for Enright, he didn't need a vehicle that blended in. Just in case the Holden had been spotted near the Yangebup home, it was smart to park it up, now that it'd been cleaned and wiped. Lee drove the Holden inside the workshop, wiped his prints and killed the ignition, took up Firmin's bag off the bonnet and put the canvas tarp back over the car. He didn't know what he was going to do with Firmin's property, perhaps leave it somewhere for Firmin to collect, but that was a task for tomorrow. Lee placed the Louis Vuitton bag on the bench seat of the old Ford just as the shortwave crackled to life. The radio had been silent for the past half hour. Lee assumed that this was because the police would know that the media were now listening, having reported the homicide on the open channel, and had turned instead to using telephones to call in subsequent details. Barry White, the dispatch operator, had calmed since taking in the report of the murder, his voice back to its regular deep and velvety tones, announcing that 'based on an identification made at the crime scene, attended and confirmed by Commander Duncan Corbett, where a hidden security camera was located by Forensics, that on the authorisation of Commander Corbett he was calling a KALOF for the following suspect: a young male identified as Lee Southern, age twenty-three, last known address twenty-nine McLeery Street in South Fremantle, registered vehicle a white Ford F350 truck, registration 6GB457, considered armed and dangerous, his current whereabouts unknown.'

54

Lee dropped the coin and watched a cray boat enter the sulphur-lit corridor at the mouth of Fishing Boat Harbour, followed by a raucous entourage of seagulls, hovering and rolling in the wind that clanked and whistled through the sails and nets of the moored commercial craft. Lee waited the ten dials on Swann's number and hung up, looked at his watch and counted down the two minutes it took Swann to walk to the Seaview Hotel, at the corner of his street. The brightly lit cray-boat pulled into its mooring, flying the red-and-white Bulldogs flag, its crew scurrying to land ropes and drop rubber fenders, each of them sunburned and grinning, glad to be back in port for the night.

Even though Lee was expecting the phone to ring, it still made him jump. The payphone was attached to the wall between a fish-cleaning station and a waste-oil collection shed, and despite the strong westerly breeze, still stank bad enough that nobody ever used it. Lee took up the phone. 'You heard.'

It was a statement not a question, and Swann got straight to the point. 'You got somewhere to go?'

'A few ideas. My pager can't be tracked, can it?'

'It's a one-way pager, so no, it can't be tracked. What the fuck happened? How'd they get your name so fast?'

Lee didn't know, but talked Swann through the afternoon's

events, the near-escape and the good fortune of going to Gerry's workshop instead of home, where he might have been arrested.

'The TRG. The hidden camera. The quick identification. It stinks of a set-up. Firmin the only one who knew you were there?'

'Yes. But the bag I got for him – why'd he want me fingered?'

'It doesn't rule him out. He might get the bag once you're arrested.'

'But you're right about the set-up,' Lee said. 'If there was a camera there, as they're claiming, it would've picked up the killer, or killers, not just me. It had to be them who set the camera, unless they wiped it, reset it, which means they knew it was there. That must be the Hastie brothers.'

'Might be. If the Hasties think you're after them, they might want you off. Those bastards, it'd be a joke to them to kill someone and then call in the TRG. Either way, you need to get somewhere safe.'

Lee turned to the stinking wall as a security patrol car entered the harbour road, angling its spotlight over the darkened piers, slowing as it passed Lee, the spotlight skimming over the inky waters and white hulls, the vehicle continuing to the turnaround at the head of the harbour mouth.

'I'm thinking of handing myself in.'

Swann laughed. 'That's never a good idea. Not if there's some kind of fix in. You just need to keep away from the TRG. Lie low while I make some inquiries. Good thing you walked away from the Enright matter. Bamber would hand you in, drop of a hat, if he thought you'd make the company look bad.'

Lee watched the security vehicle turn back toward him. 'Have they been to yours yet?' he asked Swann.

'No, but they will. I've filled the kettle. Will head there now.'

Lee imagined Swann standing in the front bar of the Seaview Hotel, old Tom the bartender wiping dirty glasses with a dirty towel. Lee said goodbye and hung up, just as his pager began to vibrate. He recognised Connor Baird's number. He fished around in his jeans and snagged more coins.

Connor answered on the first ring, interrupted Lee as he attempted to put Connor at ease, reassure him that the work he'd been doing for Lee had nothing to do with Lee's situation.

'I don't care about that,' Connor said. 'My parents are away for the week. Come over. The law would never expect a stone-cold killer such as yourself to be hiding out in a Claremont townhouse.'

Lee laughed, thanked Connor and said that he'd be there within the hour. He had a few more calls to make – to his mother, his father, to the number Lisa had given him. He would tell them that he was innocent. His mother and father would believe him, but he wasn't sure about Lisa, who he'd be saying goodbye to, thought he owed her that. Then he'd hide Firmin's bag in one of the rock ledges on the sheltering seawall, on the ocean side where it'd never be found. He would call Firmin last of all, to try to convince the old man to tell the police why Lee had been present at the scene of the murder, why he had nothing to do with it. Firmin had a lot of juice with the copper hierarchy, who'd all come up together in the same streets, through the same years and the same rackets. His word would count for a lot and, in the meantime, it was crucial that Firmin tracked down the Hastie brothers, who'd be headed for the border.

55

Lee sat behind the wheel in the carpark of Captain Munchies, watching the hundreds of gulls career around the streetlights that lined the port, feeding on the moths that were black as the shadows from which they emerged. A CSIRO Antarctic research vessel was docked at the port, newly arrived, an onboard gantry crane lifting webbed boxes and crates. Lee checked his watch again and muttered to himself, lit another cigarette and swore that he'd give Firmin five more minutes, and no more. He was well concealed behind the ramshackle takeaway buildings, parked close enough to suggest that his was a staff-member's vehicle, although every uniformed prowl car in the city had been issued the KALOF, and it was asking for trouble sitting there.

Firmin had told him that Commander Corbett himself, no less, had been on the late news relating how he'd identified Lee, based on the footage he'd viewed at the murder scene, and the coincidental meeting he'd had with Lee the previous week, over an unrelated matter. Corbett was certain of the identification, naming Lee as an employee of Frank Swann, leaving the implications of that statement hanging there.

Firmin dearly wanted his bag before Lee went under the radar. He didn't believe for a moment that Lee was responsible for the murder, and offered Lee a place to hide out, at his Malaga warehouse where he stored his vintage cars. Lee passed on the offer, feeling more comfortable in the company of Connor Baird. He demanded, however, that Firmin call Corbett directly, and set him straight on why Lee was there. Without mincing his words, Lee made it clear to Firmin that if he didn't do that, Lee would do it instead, by way of the media.

Lee hadn't been able to get hold of either his mother or his father. If his mother had heard the news, she'd be on her way to Perth. His father was almost certainly out of pager range, in the Gascoyne somewhere, tending to his crops. Lee had left a message on Lisa's phone, grateful that she hadn't picked up, not sure what to say, almost didn't say anything, then finally mumbled the fact that he hadn't done what he'd been accused of, and that he was sorry.

It all felt like a bad dream. Lee was a bit player in the Enright case and a reluctant participant in Firmin's scheme to recover his valuables, and yet there he was carrying the can, with no obvious way of clearing his name. He'd been at the scene of the crime. A man was murdered there. Lee'd been identified. That might be as far as the investigation went. That might be enough for the police, the prosecutor, the jury and judge.

He was eerily calm because it didn't feel quite real. He knew that he wasn't the first man or woman in this position, imagined how that must feel over the longer process. He would display no remorse, because he hadn't done anything wrong. This too would be held against him, as well as his lack of cooperation, his denial of what appeared obvious to everyone else.

Firmin's time was up. Lee climbed out of the Holden, took up the flashy leather bag, heavy with loot. Making sure that nobody was looking, Lee walked the few steps to the side wall of Captain Munchies, out of view of the carpark and docks. He climbed onto a barrel containing used chip-oil, then looked over the flat cement roof, saw that the bag would be invisible to all but the seagulls. Lee wedged it close to the concrete lip that circled the wall, dropped to the barrel and then to the ground. He emerged from the shadows and made for the Holden, had the keys in the door when he heard the unmistakable sound of a round being chambered into a pistol, then felt the cold press of a barrel against the back of his neck.

56

Lee awoke to the taste of vinyl in his mouth. His head burned where he'd been struck, a mixture of blood and saliva pasted to his cheek, on the surface of the hood over his head. He heard the sound of moaning and understood that he was the source of the sound, his head spinning every time he moved his neck, the moans and the spinning finally coming into sync as he settled his breathing.

He was in the boot of a car, head crammed against one of the wheel arches, the hissing, sucking sound of the rear tyres beneath him, but the smell not right, not the boot of a car but the rear bay of a station wagon. The smells coming to him now in the darkness weren't the musty acrid odour of bad carpet and imprisoned, overheated air, but the smell of men. His thoughts weren't clear yet, with multicoloured lights in fluid shapes playing across his eyes, the darkness inside the hood absolute, and the men in the car not speaking. He could smell sweat and spray-can Brut, and something more floral, either coming from outside the car or from one of the others, a cloying, earthy-sweet smell like jasmine or sandalwood. Then Lee heard the hiss of a lighter before ignition, and a voice he didn't recognise say clearly, 'Please don't smoke.' The smoker didn't reply, but neither did they put out their cigarette, a cheap brand like Holiday or Longbeach, the harsh burnt-dust smoke filling up the car, until the driver's window went down, an electric window, and fresh air began to circulate.

Lee tried to move his hands, but the binding was rigid, suggesting cable ties. His hands were bound behind his back, and he'd lost the circulation in one of his feet. He tried to move his ankles, to get his blood circulating, but his legs were drawn up behind him, and he realised he'd been hogtied.

The panic began to set in. Only moments had passed since he'd regained consciousness, and his senses were becoming clear, but his mind was still lost, somewhere in the blackout. Only now did he realise that he hadn't been arrested. He remembered the last words he heard before he passed out, was struck down from behind, most likely with the butt of a gun. 'Lee Southern, I'm arresting you on the charges of …'

The reason he hadn't resisted, until it was too late.

But if he hadn't been arrested, who had taken him?

The men were still silent. He couldn't see. Lee listened to the sound of the engine, the muffled exhaust beneath his face, pressed into the wheel arch. The car was a four-cylinder, of that he was certain. An automatic, too, by the lag in revs when the engine was put under strain. A four-cylinder, automatic station wagon with electric windows – there were too many on the market.

He had no idea how long he'd been unconscious. He had no idea where he was in the city. He listened for sounds outside the car, now that the window was down. He couldn't hear anything industrial, no airport sounds or the particular silence that accompanied empty parks and bushland. There was very little traffic on the roads, and in the minute or so since he'd come to, the car hadn't slowed or stopped for a change of lights, which meant that he was either on a highway or that the pre-dawn traffic was light enough so that the signals stayed green. The car drove, the men didn't speak, the city didn't reveal itself.

The dread in the pit of his stomach that he'd tried to smother with his series of observations began to swell – the thought that he was headed to the forests on the edges of the city, headed for a hole in the ground, to be covered over with grey sand or bauxite gravel or limestone dust, then a layer of leaves, no sign that he was there, no word to his mother or father, just an empty silence that would enrage his father and break his mother's heart.

He spoke before he knew that he was speaking, words slathered with the drool of blood and spit that he swallowed, but became no clearer to his ears, words pushed out between panicked gasps, until he felt the seat in front of him lurch as a large shape shifted and he knew what that meant and then he was silent, but it didn't matter, he felt the seat lurch again and a sharp light broke in his eyes and then there were no more questions and no more words because everything was dark again.

57

Lee's eyes burned with light, his closed eyelids neon-red with a corona of orange tracing the edges of his vision. His eyes were closed and he was made of light, and he wondered if he was dead, until he heard the sounds of boot-steps, and smelled that same brand of cigarette smoke, began to feel once again the throb at the back of his head, the pain at his wrists and ankles where he'd been restrained.

He was laid out, flat on his back. He started with his fingers, moving them singly and in tandem, then did the same with his toes. When he was sure that he was all there, he opened his eyes, understood that he was blindfolded, gagged, began to panic and twist his neck, sending bolts of pain into his head and filling his eyes again with light.

A hand on his shoulder, but not a gentle hand, not the hand of a friend. The hand moved to his throat, fingers digging for his carotid, his pulse being taken. Lee could feel it, hammering. The hand released, and he felt a cuff circle his bicep, dull pressure growing and growing, and he understood that his blood pressure was being read.

Lee tried to speak through the gag but his words were a blur of vowels, a long ragged string that made no sense, even to him.

The person who took his pulse and blood-pressure moved away, scrapes of leather-soled shoes on concrete.

'He's ready. Pulse has dropped below one forty. Blood pressure high, but stable.'

Now someone heavier approached, meatier, wearing boots. It was the smoker who'd knocked him out in the car, removing the bag over Lee's head and delivering the heel of his hand to Lee's chin. The single percussive blow had made everything disappear, even the face that framed Lee's view of the interior of the station-wagon, red C-columns, looked like a Subaru, a car he recognised even if he didn't recognise the face that had delivered him to darkness.

He had seen a face. Frozen in that moment, and so with him forever.

Lee knew what that meant, began to struggle against his restraints, his left arm completely immobile, the rest of him barely moving – straps across his forehead, neck, chest, waist, hips and legs.

The meaty boot-steps arrived beside him, the whiff of stale sweat and smoke. Lee felt his blindfold tug, heard scissors cutting at cloth, then blinding light, wincing and staring up into a bright halogen bulb, industrial light, his eyes already watering, burning even when he blinked.

The same man's face, coming into focus. Big and brick-shaped, jaw stubbled with ginger, red-rimmed brown eyes, bright even in the shadow cast by his head, thin pale lips, teeth hidden, no expression on his face bar gentle curiosity.

He opened his lips, and his teeth remained hidden. 'You ready for some pain, son? I hope so.'

Lee could hear breathing from the edge of the room, but he couldn't turn his head, although his eyes had adjusted to the angry light. He was in an industrial building of some kind, factory ceiling of open steel joists, new-looking Zincalume roof, a single air vent, whirlybird turning slowly, creaking a little.

He heard an asthma inhaler puff, a sharp intake of air, the big man at Lee's side muttering, 'Jesus Christ,' before leaving his field of vision, then the trundle of something on wheels being dragged to the table. The man's face reappeared again, in his hands the nozzle of an oxyacetylene torch, making sure to show Lee clearly, now his teeth showing in his smile, blunt yellow teeth, crooked as an old fence.

Lee heard cylinder taps open, the man clacking the ignitor, the acetylene burning a dirty yellow flame, baggy and dancing, then the oxygen coming into the mix, the flame sharpening to a pure blue point, hot enough to cut through steel.

Lee felt himself convulse, wondered if he'd wet himself, becoming dizzy, red pinpricks in his vision.

The man grinned, turned the ball valve, killed the flame, dying in a puff of black smoke, like a magician's trick.

The man returned with a hand mirror, held it above Lee's face, the fear in Lee's eyes large and clear, pupils dilated, little snail-trails of tears leaking from the sides. The man angled the mirror and showed Lee his body, held down with haulage straps to a steel workbench, his left arm gaffer-taped to the bench, bar the pale valley that fronted his elbow.

'You're going to die on this table, son. In about fifteen minutes, at my guess. How much I burn you is completely up to you. So is the way you go out. You help a bloke, I put hammer in your arm, take away your pain and send you over to the other side unconscious and unaware, floating like a babe in a basket. You make things hard for me, don't tell me what I want to know, I'm gonna burn you all over like a fucken marshmallow, and if you don't die of that, I'm gonna put a big blast of goey into your arm, you're gonna be wide awake as you begin to stroke-out, as your heart bursts in your chest, as your nerves set fire to your eyes, your hair, your fucken soul. You with me so far, son? Nod if you understand.'

The man's voice was gentle, soothing, like a dentist describing a minor procedure. Lee nodded like a child in the chair, despite himself.

The man smiled again, reached over and with scissors cut the gag off Lee's mouth, dragged it from beneath his head. Lee closed his mouth and swallowed, felt the relief in the hinges of his jaw, but only for a moment, the man taking up the oxy nozzle and the same hiss of a tap as the hose filled with acetylene, as he clacked the ignitor again, the same pillowy orange flame, then oxygen added to the mix, the flame turning into a blue blade, clean on its edges. Lee couldn't take his eyes off it, though he felt his body squirm, then begin to thrash involuntarily.

The hissing of the torch was loud, the man averting his eyes from the flame, then a second set of steps approaching, lighter, leather-soled and more tentative. A pale hand, thin at the wrist, the forearm lined with fine black hairs standing proud on goosebump flesh, holding a photograph before Lee's face. The photograph was of Laver, the architect. Lee tried to hide the recognition in his eyes but failed.

The man who held the photograph, whose face Lee couldn't see, asked in a quiet voice that Lee didn't recognise, 'Where is this man? Where did you take him?'

The question didn't make sense. Lee had expected to be asked about Firmin's bag, about why he'd been following the Hastie brothers, about why he'd been at the murder scene.

'Who are you?' Lee asked but got no reply. The larger man merely increased the gas in the flame, which burned even brighter and louder.

'Wrong thing to say, son. You've been asked a simple question. Last chance.'

The big man nodded to the quiet man who Lee couldn't see. Another photograph appeared in front of Lee's face, this time of Gavin Drew, the town planner.

'Same question. Where is he? What have you done with him?'

'I don't know,' Lee spat, angry despite himself, but on the verge of tears. 'Or the other guy. I broke into his place, their places, that's all. Who the fuck *are* you? Are you police?'

The man laughed, nodded. 'Once I was, yes. No longer. Quietly retired I've been, enjoying my peace and quiet. No longer. Because of you. You might call me a specialist, called out of retirement, to clean up the mess you've made.'

Lee remembered the station wagon that'd transported him. He took a guess, having seen a station wagon at Pusey's Mosman Park home. 'Where's Pusey?' He tried to turn his head to the man beside him, who he couldn't see. 'Is that you, Pusey? I broke into your place, found nothing. I don't know where the others are. I didn't light the fire, burn your place down.'

The man who Lee couldn't see, who must be Pusey, leaned close to Lee's ear, warm enough that Lee could feel the warmth of his breath. 'Where's the Enright girl? I know that you know. Where is she?'

Again, the question threw Lee, he had no answer. He began to mouth the words, but no sound came out. The man beside Lee looked to the invisible Pusey, nodded him away. Quiet footsteps withdrew toward the wall, then crossed the room toward the door, which opened, swung shut. When a few seconds had passed, the square-jawed man closed his eyes, gritted his teeth.

'I believe you, son, for what it's worth. I told them as much. You're too green, and murder ain't Swann's style. So if it isn't you, then it's that prick Bamber, who for various reasons is untouchable. So if I can't touch him, I have to do you. As a message. Not that he'll care.'

Lee wanted to beg for his life, to get past the grim finality of the man's words, the calmness in his eyes, but he couldn't speak. Seeing his struggle, the man turned off the ball valve, cutting the flame. 'I ain't a sadist, whatever others might say. Perhaps I'm getting sentimental in my old age. I'll knock you with the heroin, then burn you after. Nobody will know the difference, except me and you, and then just me.'

The man hung the nozzle on the canisters, walked to the wall, returned with a diabetic syringe, showed it to Lee, flicked off the orange cap. The fit was already primed with a clear liquid. The man held it up to the light, pressed the plunger a little, a fine mist falling over Lee's face. 'Goodnight, son. And good luck.'

There was a noise outside the room, the crashing of steel. Lee felt a sting in his arm, then more crashing. Then came a flooding warmth, the familiar darkness in his limbs, a rapid slowing of everything. He closed his eyes and waited for the end, heard instead another crash, then the door leaving its hinges, the sharp deafening barks of a pistol at close range, sounded like popcorn as he faded out, which made him smile, except for the gunpowder smell, as a weight came across his chest, buffeting him, moving the benchtop, but not holding him back, not holding him down as he floated away, only the answer to the man's question, where is the Enright girl? The answer coming to him now, too late, but not in words, instead in an image, familiar and warm, and it made him laugh now in recognition, and he should be dead by now, and perhaps he was, floating and sinking and floating further away, carrying with him the image of her reflected in the secret smile on his face.

58

The sound of iron, deep in his dreams. A sound Lee knew so well that it roused him, the filmy images of his unremembered dream clearing like mist under his need to get away from the sound of iron. The sound of guns in a bag was a charged memory that demanded alertness, and the deep stillness in his body began to glitch, his mouth cottony, eyes burning, his body vibrating now with something other than the deep-time thrumming of heroin, his eyes opening to the expected image of his father loading sawn-offs and pistols and revolvers into a sports bag, that always sat on the bench seat between them, driving out into the desert, and god help any copper that pulled him over.

But there was no father and no bag of guns in the small room, sunshine coming through an open window, an old cane blind hanging from its cord, bumping slightly in the hot wind that passed over his skin. The sound of flies, batting against his head, forced him to roll out of the recovery position, and as if by some remembered intelligence of his body, he found himself seated on the edge of the bed, his bare feet on the speckled lino marked with dusty boot-prints.

Beside the bed was a bottle of water, and a towel that smelled of vomit. Lee touched his face. Beneath the numbness he discovered a pleasure at the touch of his nails on his skin as he began to scratch at his neck, rising from the bed and staggering out into a narrow hallway, whose ceiling felt unnaturally low, and so he continued into the kitchen that he recognised. He felt no fear at the recognition that he was in the Wattleup house that a week ago he'd been surveilling for Firmin, until two rifle-shots had forced him to move deeper into the banksia scrub.

Lee put his head under the kitchen tap and ran the cold water until he thought he might drown, the water blocking his nostrils and filling his mouth as he drank greedily. When he couldn't drink any more, he pulled his head free of the torrent and began to look himself over, his disjointed perceptions moving from limb to limb, registering the raw abraded bands on his wrists where he'd been shackled, the bruises on his biceps and thighs where he'd been bent to fit the shape of the Subaru boot.

Lee staggered back down the hall, bouncing from wall to wall but moving forward, until he reached the darkened front room of the shack that smelt of grease and ashtrays, where at the base of every wall were piled beer cartons loaded with empties, and fish and chip wrappers, and the odd drained bottle of Bundaberg rum. The couch beneath the front window and the coffee table were the only clean surfaces. He flicked the light switch despite the brightness that framed the cane blinds, and then he saw the copper's uniform, complete with the peaked cap of a WAPOL constable, and the black boots and the duty belt with handcuff pouch, thigh rig carrier and radio. Lee went to the uniform and saw the ID clipped to the front pocket. He saw the face of a young man he didn't recognise, but who looked familiar, until he realised that it was him who the young man resembled. The young man's name was Constable Michael O'Mahony. Lee picked up the uniform shirt and saw beneath it the regulation Glock. He put down the shirt and backed away from the couch, almost tripping where his legs caught the coffee table. He turned and saw the letter, the same photocopied jumble of newspaper headline letters used in the ransom demands made to Paul Enright. Lee snatched at the A4 page and became unbalanced, fell back onto the couch. He held the letter up to the light and tried to focus his eyes. The letter contained more information than the ones he'd seen previously, and this time, the letter was addressed specifically to him. It told him that there were two more photographs of Jessica Enright to retrieve. It told him where the next photograph could be found and what he needed to do to retrieve it. It told him that the safe containing the photograph also contained the video footage taken of the murdered man, at the house in Yangebup – the same video footage that would clear him of the murder charge.

Lee let the paper slip from his fingers, drift to the floor. He put his head back on the couch and closed his eyes, felt the world begin to spin, opened them again and levered himself out of the inviting cushions and onto his feet. He picked up the letter, folded it and put it into his jeans, couldn't help but laugh when he thought of the demand that the letter made of him. It had come down to this – all of the previous weeks work, although the foundations had clearly been laid years in advance. He had to admire the strategy, even if it had nearly cost him his life. But admiration for the people behind the recovery of the Enright photographs wouldn't get the job done. Lee focussed instead on the man who'd tried to kill him, who'd been killed in the act of taking Lee's life. Lee sifted through the memories of the moments just prior to him going under, for what he thought was the last time. The sound of gunshots that seemed so far away. The man's body, slumped across his chest, crushing him. Looking down at the man's head, so strangely relaxed, the neck oddly lengthened, hanging over the workbench, red blooms seeping across the shirt at his back.

Then nothing as Lee went under, coming to in flashes in the backseat of a car, propped upright behind a seatbelt, the man in the passenger seat turning to slap Lee on the face a few times, gentle slaps that Lee couldn't feel, and that didn't work to keep him awake. The memory of being carried from a car on a strong man's shoulder, making Lee feel like a child again, like it was his father carrying him from the car to his bed after a night with his father's friends, down at the shooting-range clubhouse.

Lee looked around at the room where the Hastie brothers had been living the past weeks since they participated in the robbery of Club Summertime, and most likely in the weeks before. He didn't know how the Hastie brothers fitted in with the Enright story, and at the moment didn't care. He was reminded of the sound that had woken him from his opiate dreams, of weapons being piled into a bag. He didn't know where they had gone, waking him as they left, but suspected that he would see them again. He turned to the window and looked out into the street, saw his Holden parked in the drive. He found the keys in the trouser pocket of the copper's uniform, as well as some cash. Lee laid the uniform out carefully, turned toward the bathroom. If he was going to impersonate a copper, he needed to get his body clean, and his head clear. In the bathroom, he stripped and walked into the cold jets, felt his breath leave him for a moment, returning in small gasps that settled as the sting eased and he began to see things clearly.

59

Lee knew where to go, from his previous visit to Central, although this time he was a wanted man, his image on the bulletin board inside the lobby vestibule, alongside a sad array of missing people posters, as well as on the incident boards behind the safety-glass front desk. The front desk at Central had previously been bombed, as well as attacked with a shotgun – both times the attacker had been gunned down in the lobby, or in the carpark. Lee passed the ground floor room where the TRG waited, on call like firemen, their vests, rams, shotguns and tactical gear stacked and hung on the walls ready to be grabbed. Lee pulled his cap lower on his face, discreetly pulling his trousers higher than he'd normally wear them, didn't know how coppers could run and climb and give chase weighted with so much gear.

He looked the part, however, had made sure of that before he left the Hastie's banged-up semidetached in Wattleup, the pale blue uniformed shirt fitting him perfectly, as did the trousers and boots. Despite the foolishness of what he was about to attempt, he felt comfortable in uniform, had been brought up in various camo uniforms by his militia-minded father, although neither of them was temperamentally suited to following orders, or working in an institution. As the letter had suggested, Lee hadn't been able to get hold of Bamber, who'd been bypassed by the letter-writer, it appeared, for reasons that Lee didn't understand. Lee had nevertheless tried to contact him, to let him know that another letter had been given to him, providing the location of another Jessica Enright photograph. Lee was no longer on the Enright company clock, meaning that if it weren't for the alleged presence of a video that might exonerate him, he wouldn't be where he was now, walking nonchalantly down a central police HQ corridor, hitching up his trousers when nobody was looking, his nonchalance just a pretence to hide the hammering of his heart and the sweat on his palms. He was grateful for his dark complexion, because he was flushed, taking deep belly-breaths to calm himself as he approached the stairwell at the end of the corridor. There was obviously some kind of campaign underway to get desk-bound coppers moving, because there was a badly printed poster outside the stairwell saying *Stay fit – take the stairs*, although the campaign didn't appear to be working, or perhaps it was the change of shifts, because the stairs leading higher into the building echoed to Lee's boots alone.

Lee clutched the case file as he climbed, the file that was his pretext for getting past the front-door security, the task he'd been given of hand-delivering the file to Commander Corbett's personal secretary unremarkable enough to secure his entry to the building. The desk sergeant had looked at him twice, then at Lee's ID, then had been distracted by a call, talking down the receiver as he scribbled Lee's ID number and name, checking in Lee's weapon, pressing the button to unlock the heavy security door.

Lee felt his nerves settle as he climbed higher, enjoying the burn in his thighs and the tightness across his chest. He didn't know how long he'd been asleep in the Hasties' car, and house, but the hammer in his blood had dissipated to the extent that he felt it now as a coldness on his skin, a tiredness behind his eyes and an automatic quality to his movements and thoughts. He was nervous but moving forward, no question that his anxiety would prevail over his desire to bring an end to being blamed for a murder.

Lee knew the feeling well – he'd robbed banks while on heroin. The adrenalin and the fear were always there, but the icy calmness and automatic choreography carried him through. It was what allowed him to do what he was doing now, although it was also what would get him caught – doing without thinking. Lee put the thoughts out of his head as he neared the eighth-floor exit door, slipped the file into his armpit and reached for the door handle.

He twisted, but it was locked. He couldn't believe it – everything had gone so smoothly. The plan he'd been following, robotically, trustingly, hadn't mentioned the locked door. The shifts had been changing as he'd entered the building, the sun setting over the river, and he'd presumed that the senior management worked nine to five, with a few working later, as required. He'd timed his entry to central to coincide with the arrival of the night shift, when he assumed senior management would be at home, and he'd clearly assumed correctly, although he hadn't anticipated the locking down of the higher floors. The locked door meant that the lift would likely be locked to the management floors as well. To attempt to enter the lift would mean passing the desk sergeant again, who would certainly notice him, and remember his errand.

Why hadn't the desk sergeant mentioned that Corbett's floor would be locked? Lee didn't know, couldn't risk the sergeant's or others' scrutiny, not when his face was on the board behind the duty staff desks, not when the TRG were waiting metres away.

Lee knew that the clarity and decisiveness of his movements were influenced by the opiate in his blood, but there seemed little point in worrying about that. He looked down the eight flights of stairs, listened for boot steps, the cracking of a door, heard nothing but his ragged breathing. There was nothing on the landing to suppress the sound, except for a steel garbage bin, with an ashtray cover filled with butts. Lee saw that the bin was crammed with iced-coffee cartons, and coffee cups, takeaway plastic sandwich cases and assorted chocolate wrappers and crushed paper bags. Lee took out his lighter and set fire to the rubbish, which began to smoulder, and then to burn. Lee went higher up the landing and held the garbage bin toward the smoke alarm and fire-retardant sprinkler above his head. The smoke alarm began to trill. Lee raised his eyes at the fire sprinkler above his head, prayed that it would engage, then felt a moment of shock as it began to hiss, as the alarm began to howl down the stairs, in the rooms across the door. Lee listened once more at the stairs, then stepped back and delivered a fierce front-kick to the plate beside the lock-barrel. The noise was horrific, only partially tamped by wailing alarm. The small fire was burning out, the stench of melting plastic strong in the pale grey smoke that wafted until it was hit by the water now emerging in stuttering sprays, becoming stronger. Lee kicked at the door again, which gave, swung open. He took the bin, soaked through now, and slipped it inside the door, took it with him to hide elsewhere, somewhere it wouldn't be noticed. He shut the door behind him, turning to the offices that were dark and cool, no lights or signs of life. Lee didn't waste any time. He needed to get to the contents of Corbett's safe. Anything that happened after that, including being identified, leading to a stand-off, a siege, his arrest – none of that would matter if he could get to the materials in Corbett's safe. Corbett, he assumed, was safely out of the picture for now, at home in his slippers, wouldn't be called up for an errant fire alarm, at least until the damaged door lock was noticed, when it would all rain down.

Lee didn't have a lot of tools, gambling on the security of the building itself, moving through the thickening air of the corridors, dark wood panelling and worn blue carpet, his way illuminated by the reflected light of the city to his west – Bond Tower the tallest among them, a jigsaw puzzle of office lights surrounded by darkness running up its face. Lee went straight to Corbett's secretary's desk, placed the bin beside it, began to rummage through the drawers, nothing locked, found a ring of keys in the stationary drawer, went from there to Corbett's office, locked the door behind him, moved a filing cabinet on its side across the door, blocking it. He wouldn't be able to hear them coming until they were upon him, but that didn't matter now. Lee went to Corbett's desk, used the keys to open each drawer. He took out all of the drawers in the desk and looked beneath them, shone his police-issue torch inside the body of the desk looking for secret compartments, spaces behind the drawers that might conceal a package, a file, an envelope.

The desk was clean. Lee turned to the filing cabinets, rifled through them, none of them locked so he didn't spend too much time there, instead went to the cupboards, jarrah-veneer and newly varnished, smooth on their rollers and hinges, pulled out the drawers at their base and looked behind them, nothing there. In the cupboards were three dress uniforms inside dry-cleaning sleeves, three matching officer's hats in shelves beside them, Corbett risen way above the level of tactical uniform. Lee shone his torch at the back of the cupboards but each of them were flush with the walls behind.

He found the safe in the next cupboard along, behind a golfing bag. The safe didn't belong to the office, but had presumably been brought there when Corbett had taken the commander's rank. The safe wasn't large, or particularly heavy, about the same size and shape of a beer carton, and so made to be easily transportable. It was operated by a combination and a lock. Lee didn't expect any of the keys in Corbett's secretary's desk to work, but he tried anyway. Having no luck, he looked around for something to hide the safe in, but there wasn't anything strong enough. Outside the office, Lee heard the sound of fire-service sirens converging in the carpark outside, syncopating now with the sirens inside the building, the nearest tannoy to Lee, in the corner outside Corbett's corner office, beginning to cut out and crackle between each shrill wail. Lee heard voices on the same floor, entering from another stairwell. If they saw the damaged door lock then a secondary alarm would sound, and the building would be locked down. He hoped that the stairwell sprinkler had extinguished the smell of the burnt rubbish. The voices sounded breathless, a little panicked, moving toward him, two or three people, turning doorhandles, checking locks, calling out in order to identify any late workers, not hanging around, the floor clear of staff, their orders no doubt to return to the ground floor, and exit the building.

Lee thought about hiding out in the building until dawn, or until later when the drama had died down, but couldn't risk a thorough search by the fireys, looking for any point of ignition. They would assume a false alarm, but it was their job to be thorough. Lee took up the golf bag and emptied the four clubs, placed the safe at the bag's mouth, saw not only that it fitted but that the leather had been stretched previously to accommodate it. He slid the safe into the golf bag, put the clubs back inside, slung the bag over his shoulder and took one of the dress uniforms from the cupboard, carried it by the coathanger. He made sure that everything in the office looked undisturbed, lifting up the filing cabinet at the door, which he closed behind him. He put the keys back in the secretary's desk and moved through the silent offices to the stairwell, cracked the door and listened, just as boot steps echoed a final time down near the ground floor, and a door slammed shut. Lee entered the stairwell, took his time to wipe his prints off the door handle, then began to descend quietly, listening, the sirens outside the stairwell muted by the heavy fire-doors, the sprinklers having been extinguished. Lee crept down the stairs floor by floor, was nearly at the ground floor when the door opened, two firemen in their heavy yellow incident suits entered, their hats held in their hands, their faces sweaty but their voices calm and conversational. Lee stopped on the first-floor landing and listened – they were talking about a work colleague – a neat freak in the station, something about washing up. That they were chatting about work as they began to climb the stairs put Lee at ease. He took a deep breath and began to descend toward them, preparing his smile. They looked at him at the same time, no suspicion on their faces, only frustration that they had to break their conversation.

Lee turned his body to show them the golf bag, made an apologetic face.

'My boss sent me to get his lucky clubs, just in case. Heading out now.'

The two fireys stepped aside to let him pass, down the stairs and out into the ground floor corridor, which was full of firemen propping open the lift, peering up inside the shaft, one or two in the lobby, murmuring into walkie-talkies. Several police officers with their backs turned accompanied handcuffed men from the holding cells, heads bowed or looking hopefully forward. Lee looked past them to the darkness, saw the ring of fire trucks, a further ring of bored-looking coppers behind them, smoking and chatting, waiting to be let back inside. Lee sped up and joined the prisoner escorts, waited at their rear, none of them turning round. The wall of fresh air hit him, and he ducked his head, knew that it was important not to make eye-contact, hoping that the desk sergeant wasn't looking, or anyone who'd recognise the Commander's kit, and might feel obliged to ask inconvenient questions. Knowing that he was only one bladed glance away from being taken into custody himself, he shuffled behind the detainees being led toward a police transport truck, cut behind the first row of officers and administrative staff, began the long slow walk through the semi-darkness toward his Holden, feeling the tension leave his body as he approached his car, no voice or shout at his back, the sirens cutting off mid-wail, the stillness and silence deafening. Lee noticed for the first time the absence of the TRG among the uniformed men and women, standing beneath the carpark lights, beginning to move now toward the desk sergeant, who had his hands up, about to make an announcement.

Lee was watching the sergeant so intently that he didn't see the white Ford van until it was right before him, blocking his route to the Holden. The van's deeply tinted windows shimmered with reflected light, the driver invisible as the van rolled to a stop, the side door sliding open, Don Hastie standing in the doorway, looking past Lee to the coppers. He had a pistol in his hand that he pointed at Lee, waving him inside. His brother sat on the bench seat beside him, another pistol pointing at Lee, who nodded his head, stepping into the darkness just as the van began to move, the door sliding shut behind him.

60

It was dark in the van but the first thing Lee noticed, bracing himself as the Ford pulled out of the carpark onto Riverside Drive, was the familiar silhouette of the driver. The second thing was the recognition that the pistols that Don and Todd Hastie were holding had been fired recently – Lee could still smell them in the enclosed space. The brothers weren't aiming the pistols at him, however, rather at the floor, hanging loosely in their large hands, both of them exhibiting the long, chimp-like arms that he'd heard described, but had only seen the once, on the door of Club Summertime. By way of explanation, Don Hastie scratched his nose with the pistol barrel, his finger off the trigger, safety on.

'We needed to get the TRG out of Central. To set up a diversion. So we had a pretend shootout with each other, down there in Welshpool, near a servo. Let off about three hundred rounds, went through the whole armoury – the shotties, the pistolas, semiauto rifles, you name it.'

Lee didn't reply, looked instead at the driver, turning the van past East Perth train station, headed toward Bassendean, but she hadn't once looked at him, or said a thing.

'You're shaking.'

Lee looked down at his hand, gripping the seat in front of him.

Todd Hastie was right, Lee was shaking, the adrenalin leaving him in little jolts as his skin cooled, as the knots in his stomach began to loosen, as he began to breathe more freely.

'You've got big balls, son,' said Don Hastie, looking at Lee speculatively. 'You ever want to join a crew, we could put you to work. Assuming that your father's ok with it. Wouldn't want ole Daniel Brendan Southern on our case.'

'Apple didn't fall far from the tree though, did it?' Todd Hastie chimed in. 'Mongrel runs in the family, just like in ours.'

The brothers bumped fists. Lee took out his cigarettes, offered the packet, but the brothers shook their heads. 'You have one though,' said Todd. 'Look like you fucken need it.'

Lee's tremors had abated, but in the stuffy van he was sweating freely, wet hoops under his armpits, his forearms glistening. He smoked quietly, waiting for her to turn her head, meet his eyes, as one of the Hastie brothers, Lee didn't look to see which one, began taking out the golf clubs, practising his swing in the confined space.

'Careful, dickhead,' said Don to his younger brother, a familiarity in his words that suggested regular use.

'Strange fucken game, golf,' said Todd Hastie. 'I tried watching it once on telly. You should hear the commentators – gee whiz and Jiminy Crickets, what a terrific shot, eh? Jeepers creepers and howdy doodie old chap by golly what a swell hole.'

Lee tuned them out. He didn't know where the van was headed, on Tonkin Highway now, driving north into the night, and he wasn't about to ask. He felt a fool in the copper's uniform, the acrid smoke in his eyes, fixed on her profile as she drove, hands gripping the steering wheel at two and ten, her eyes never straying from the road.

61

In a darkened corner of an alley tracing the back end of a Malaga warehouse, Lee took the pair of dark overalls offered to him by Lisa. He stripped off as she stripped off, the Hastie brothers occupied with cutting through a cyclone fence concealed by the van.

Neither Lee nor Lisa had spoken. He watched her undress, shedding the copper's uniform that she'd presumably worn to see them through any potential difficulties on the road, couldn't help the pang of lust and regret when she met his eyes, nothing in there except the matter at hand.

Lee too shed the copper's uniform that she'd supplied him, couldn't help himself, held up the ID badge before dropping it to the floor. 'That bloke know you've taken his uniform, his badge?'

The question sounded pathetic to his own ears, barely masking his hurt at being played.

'Nope. He's on leave. Two weeks in Bali.'

Lee thought about asking how Lisa had gotten the uniform, whether she had keys to the man's house, whether he was another pawn in a game that he didn't understand, but that would only double down on the miserable spectacle of him standing there in his jocks, climbing into the overalls, bitterness in his eyes and self-pity his voice.

'You've got some explaining to do,' was all he said.

'I know,' was all she answered, stuffing a bin bag with her uniform, holding it out for him to do the same.

The Hastie brothers returned, Don holding the boltcutters over his shoulder like a soldier bearing arms. Todd rummaged in the canvas bag inside the van and pulled out the pre-loaded shotguns, passed one to his brother, and a revolver, and some shells, arming himself in the same manner.

Lisa took the proffered Glock – not her service weapon, but something she was accustomed to using in service. Don offered Lee a .38 revolver with a gaffer-taped handle, looked like it had done some work. Lee shook his head, which made Don Hastie smirk.

'See you both in there, eh?'

Lisa glanced at her watch, nodded. The Hastie brothers climbed through the fence they'd opened up, headed to the darkened wall of the factory opposite, scuttled toward the floodlit carpark that fronted the factory.

Lisa nodded into the belly of the van. 'Bring the golf bag. We'll need the safe. Your tools are under the seat.'

Lee took up the golf bag, slung it across his shoulder. 'Your caddy. That's fucking perfect.'

'I said I'd explain later.'

Lee reached under the seat the Hastie brothers had occupied and found his bag of tools, taken from the Holden. He shook his head, a mixture of disgust and admiration, turned and followed Lisa through the fence to the shadowed factory wall, before she broke left, the opposite direction the Hasties had gone. They walked the perimeter of the factory, new Colorbond steel, new bitumen beneath their feet, no weeds yet in the spaces between.

At the rear of the factory Lisa stopped, put her hand on his chest, opened his bag of tools, took out a spray can with a pink lid, began to shake it vigorously.

'I climb on your shoulders.'

Like an obedient dog, Lee knelt, took her weight, walked to the corner.

'Stop there,' she said, clambering up his back so that her feet were on his shoulders, the rough grip of the copper's boots biting, her hands walking across the steel until she reached the corner. She shook the can once more, dropped the lid and without looking put her hand around the corner, emptied the can, aiming upwards at the security camera that was now obscured.

'Ok,' she said as she dropped, and he caught her, his arms under hers, the smell of perfume on her neck, but already moving, twisting out of his grip. She took out her Glock and pointed with her mouth to the corner.

A small set of stairs beside a loading bay, a door at its top. They climbed the stairs and knelt. The door was solid steel, the lock and jamb reinforced with welded steel plates. Lee took out his picks and set to work. He didn't recognise the brand of lock and knew that he had to be patient. Beside him, Lisa remained perfectly still, no urgency in her posture, only glances to her left and right, the occasional glance at her watch.

Lee felt the lock tumble, and click. He kept the picks in the lock, nodded to her. Lisa slipped on some surgical gloves, tried the handle, which turned. Lee took out the picks, stood back and waited, Lisa looking at the luminous dial of her watch. She took a deep breath at one second before the hour, then the trilling of an alarm, a blue light flashing on the wall above them. From her pocket she produced a scrap of paper, a scrawled series of numbers. Lisa stepped inside the door, began punching them in. The alarm cut out, final few echoes around the inside of the factory, the blue light dying reluctantly, flashing a few more times, fading out.

Then the bark of a shotgun, the clattering and tearing of pigshot against steel, a cry of pain in the ringing silence, followed by a series of small calibre pistol shots, another shotgun blast, the ringing silence.

The gunfire didn't appear to faze Lisa, who merely nodded to Lee to shut the door, to contain the sound. He did so, then followed her down a long corridor, her gun clenched two-handed before her, as she'd no doubt been trained. At that moment he wished he had a gun too, but it was too late. The factory smelled of solvents, and of buffing wax. The smell was familiar to him, but it didn't make him feel at ease. Instead, shuffling behind Lisa, he felt a rising tide of nausea invade his guts, filling out his chest, his throat. The shadows in the corridor, the distant fluoro lights on the high ceiling, the smells of the warehouse, it all came back to him, made him wobble as he ran – the recognition that it was in this building that Lee had been held captive, almost tortured, his torturer shot and killed as he put Lee under with a needle.

Lisa slowed, listened to the breath-ragged darkness, prepared her gun. Bracing her knees low, she yanked open the plywood door and stepped into the musty showroom air, covering the ground with her pistol, then charging forward. Lee followed, out into the vast acreage of heavy shapes covered with canvas tarps, the polished concrete floor whistling and squeaking as he ran, pulling out a golf club from the slung bag like an arrow from a quiver, making ready to swing with it as Lisa approached a bank of offices. Lee remembered the largest of them where he'd been held, felt his pulse quicken again, saw the tension leave Lisa's body as she rounded into the nearest office, and disappeared.

'Took yer time,' said Don Hastie to them both. Then, to Lee, 'Remember this place, young fella? You were lucky a certain departing pervert left the front door unlocked, or we might not have got to you. You got one in yer arm, but that fella had three syringes ready to go.'

Lee listened without hearing, his eyes on Firmin, sat on an office chair, head bowed, hands bound with gaffer tape, the front of his shirt glistening with blood-spatter. The man Lee recognised as Pusey, the photographer, dead on the floor behind them, most of his neck and part of his lower jaw removed by a shotgun blast. Leaned back against the wall, as far from Todd Hastie as he could get, Lee's bouncer colleague Rowdy Tim had his hands up, would have been comical if his eyes weren't so full of fear, kept glancing at Pusey, dead and bleeding onto the concrete.

Firmin looked at Lee, tears in his eyes. 'I'm sorry, kid.'

Lee didn't understand, saw Lisa grimace, click the safety on her gun, turn it around, ready to use the butt as a hammer. The Hastie boys stood back, smiling.

'Here we go again,' said Todd.

Instead of hitting him, Lisa bent closer to the old man's ear, said in a whisper, 'Tell him what you're sorry for.'

Firmin nodded his assent, then looked at the Hasties. 'Not until you get those animals away from me.'

Don Hastie laughed. 'We'll get what's ours, mate. But I'm not gonna kill you *before* you open your safe now, am I? So speak freely, friend.'

Lisa stepped back, giving Lee a clear look at Firmin, who tried to look him in the eye, but failed. 'I'm sorry, Lee. I tried to set you up. Didn't want to, you understand, but this is bigger than me. It was me, or you.'

'It's on the security footage,' Lisa added. 'This one,' pointing to Pusey, 'and the ex-copper, the torturer from yesterday. They killed Don and Todd's mate. Firmin sent you in. The TRG were supposed to knock you off at the scene.'

'Rowdy?' Lee asked of his former colleague, who was sweating in the corner, shaking, gibbering under his breath.

'I don't know about anything, Lee,' Rowdy groaned, surprised by the volume he'd mustered, cowering again.

'I believe you.'

Lee ran the story over in his mind. He hadn't mentioned a word to Firmin about the Enright job. Finally, he twigged. 'Bamber sent me to speak to Corbett, knowing that it'd *out* me, put me in the line of fire.'

'That was my idea,' said Lisa. 'And I'm sorry for that. I wanted this to end differently, but Bamber, he baulked at killing a WAPOL commander. So we had to draw Corbett out.'

Lee felt a wave of exhaustion wash over him. 'What's Corbett got to do with the photographs? And for that matter, what's Firmin got to do with it?'

Lisa smiled, but the smile wasn't right, tinged with cruelty. 'Corbett had a photograph with his dirt file. It's in the safe that you stole. And that dead one, Pusey, on the floor. He's Firmin's son. One of his many sons, by many different women. You any closer to understanding?'

'No.'

Lisa sighed, and in that moment Lee saw past the hatred in her eyes, as she stared down at Firmin. 'Alright, you deserve an explanation. Feel free to step in, Firmin, if I get anything wrong … but back in the day, in this town, if you wanted anything done right, anything done that would never be discovered, you didn't go round asking for the right crims to do the job. You went to the right copper, who knew the right crims, and who could cover it all up, control any investigation that might eventuate. So if someone wanted a little girl kidnapped, they didn't go down the pub and ask around, they went to someone like Corbett, who in turn had a word with someone like Firmin here, who might know a crew who could do the job. He didn't have to look far. His son, Alan Pusey, and his mate, Tim Drew, took the job—'

'Stop,' Firmin begged. 'Stop. I didn't know. I *swear* I didn't know.'

Lisa laughed, but the sound was like breaking glass. 'Maybe not. But you found out, after, didn't you? You knew, later, and did nothing.'

'Yes, that's true, but—'

The butt of the Glock came down hard on Firmin's face, made a squelchy sound as it tore at skin, crunching into the cartilage of Firmin's nose. Don Hastie was right there, put his hand on Lisa's forearm, looked her gently in the eye.

'He's got to make the call, remember?'

Lisa wiped the butt of her Glock on Firmin's shoulder. The old man was sobbing, blood bubbling out of his nose, trying to speak between sobs.

Lee understood. 'The crew Firmin chose. His son, Pusey, and Tim Drew. One of them, or both of them, they were …'

'Both of them. But that one, the one with the missing neck, he was the main one. He's lucky I didn't get to him first. It was him, and Tim Drew, and later, some of their family. Their *mates*.'

'Laver. And the other Drew brother.'

'Yes, them. And it wasn't the first time, for them, was it, Firmin?'

Lisa was trembling. Lee assumed that it was repressed rage, but it was more than that. He put his hand on hers, but she wrenched it away.

'No, it wasn't,' Firmin sobbed. 'But I didn't know. I swear.'

Lee understood. There were things that Lisa couldn't say, in front of the others, without incriminating herself. Don Hastie hadn't left her side. He said quietly, 'It's time he made the call.'

'Yes, you're right.'

But Firmin shook his head. 'He'll never go for it. He's a commander. The guy's untouchable.'

'No, he isn't.' Lisa reached into her pocket, removed a stack of photographs, knelt down and began to place them on Firmin's lap. Lee couldn't see clearly, but Firmin's face settled, his breathing became gentle.

'Just shoot me now. You may as well fucken shoot me now.'

Todd Hastie walked over a phone, passed it to Lisa, who tapped out the numbers. She put the phone to Firmin's ear. Lee could hear the ringtone, the brusque answer, before Firmin began to speak.

'It's over. Your dirt, and my dirt on you. Our safes. Our insurance. They have it.'

The line went dead, Firmin began to whimper. Don Hastie was right at his ear. 'The safe combination, old man.'

Firmin mumbled it while Don wrote it down. He left the room. A minute later they heard him whistle. He returned with a box filled with cash, banded twenty, fifty and hundred dollar notes, all used. 'Lookit this. Would've taken a week to get into Fort Knox there. That's a legit bank safe, size of a fucken bus. Todd, get the gerries out of the van. Time to burn this place down.'

'No,' Lee said firmly. 'Don't do that.'

Firmin was watching him, gratefulness in his eyes.

'He'll have them all insured,' Lee said. 'You want to hurt him, you *take* the cars. They're worth more than the cash you've got there, only going to be worth more, in the future.'

Firmin's eyes lost their hope. His shoulders slumped.

'You got any pink slips in the safe?' Lee asked him.

The old man nodded. Don Hastie didn't need to be told twice. Before leaving, he passed Lee a manila envelope. From its size and shape, Lee guessed what it contained.

Lee turned to Firmin. 'Why do you have a photograph? You mentioned dirt.'

Firmin opened his mouth to speak, but Lisa raised the pistol, and the old man flinched, cowered. 'There isn't time for that.'

Don Hastie left with a chuckle, his brother following him out into the showroom, the sound of tarps being pulled.

'What are you going to do with these two?' Lee asked.

Lisa grunted. 'That one,' indicating Rowdy. 'He can go. If his boss wants to finger him, that's up to him. As for Firmin, he's going down for the murder of Don and Todd's mate, the bloke who robbed Firmin. That's all on camera. He'll be looking at life. If he doesn't take the fall for that, I've got enough dirt on him to put him away forever. You forget that I'm a serving officer. I'll make sure it happens.'

'I said I'd do it. I'll do it. Just not for the other stuff, please. I don't want to be in there, with that on me. Murder, I can carry. I'll get respect for that.'

'Shut up,' Lisa hissed. She looked at Rowdy, who had his hands over his ears, hadn't moved in minutes. 'You,' she said. 'Get lost. Keep your mouth shut, or I'll come for you.'

Rowdy stepped carefully around them, disbelief on his face, before launching himself toward the door, scurrying over the squeaking floor.

Finally, Lisa turned to Lee. Her eyes were clear and calm.

'I know there isn't time,' Lee said. 'But tell me, who ordered that the kidnapping take place?'

Lisa reached over, picked up the top photograph on Firmin's lap, passed it to Lee. Four men standing in chest-deep water at the beach, taken with a zoom lens, the image clear despite the distance. Lee recognised Firmin, Pusey and Corbett. The fourth man was hidden beneath a wide-brimmed hat, his body cloaked in a towel-poncho despite being in the water. Lee looked closer, recognised Paul Enright's tight mouth, the stub of nose.

He passed the photo back to Lisa. 'I'm sorry,' he said. 'Your own father. That is fucking horrible.'

62

Lee awoke when he heard the front door lock clatter, then the door open and close, loud on its hinges, by design. Still half-asleep, he assumed that it was his mother, who'd been at Lee's yesterday, looking for him, hoping that he was alright, knowing that he was innocent. She'd left a letter, telling him that she had to return to the South West, but to call her. He'd done so first thing when he returned, the fully restored Valiant Wayfarer ute that he'd chosen from Firmin's storeroom parked outside in the street. He'd chosen the Valiant to the bemusement of the Hastie brothers, when he could have taken any one of the Chevelles, Monaros, Pontiacs, Road Runners, Mustangs, Corvettes, Stingrays, Chargers, Falcon GTs, or any of the numerous and valuable hot-rodded '30s and '40s Fords and Plymouths.

It couldn't be his mother coming through the front door, who he'd spoken to earlier. Despite the time, with the sun just coming up, his mother had answered on the first ring, and he told her in vague terms what had happened, told her that he would come down and visit her, first thing.

The police had also been at his home earlier, and upon Lee's return a few hours ago he'd pulled away crime-scene tape from the front and back doors, cleaned the mess in his bedroom before giving himself to the remaining darkness, falling into his king-size and burying his head under the pillow.

Without needing to open his eyes, Lee recognised the sound of Lisa's boots being unlaced, the taking off of her tactical belt, the slipping out of her uniform to join him between the sheets, crawling to him and laying her head on his arm, falling asleep within seconds, Lee returning to sleep himself.

When he got up a few hours later to drink some water, he saw the calls made to his pager. He walked the phone out into the backyard, the sun not yet risen over the house behind him, the backyard still in shadow. He sat on the porch steps and looked down over the Hampton Road traffic. He called Swann first, who told him about the pristine EK Holden delivered to him in the early hours, the transfer papers stuck under the windscreen wipers. Lee organised to meet him later, to go over what had happened. The main thing was that he was no longer a suspect in the homicide. Lisa had taken Firmin to Central, escorting him to the front desk, in uniform, where he'd asked to speak to a homicide detective, because he had an admission to make. Lisa had handed the desk sergeant the tape containing the video footage of what had really happened at the Yangebup address.

Lee called Connor Baird next, to let him know that he wouldn't be coming over, to thank him for the offer. But that wasn't the reason Baird had paged him. He'd been watching the Enright company comms earlier in the night, when everything had frozen. Then, as he watched, all of the company data began systematically disappearing, transferred to a server in Sofia, and more importantly, all of the company assets, from the fleet vehicles to the properties, were removed from the system. Connor had then gone to the Enright company bank accounts, in Perth and in Singapore, and each of them had been emptied. Lee told Connor a little of what happened, and promised to call him later, to organise a meet.

Lee heard the padding of her feet behind him. He moved across the steps for her. She sat beside him, wearing one of his t-shirts. She kissed him behind the ear, put her arm around him. He turned and looked at her, and she looked away.

'It was nothing personal, Lee.'

'That's for sure.'

She squeezed his shoulders, leaned into him. 'We had fun, didn't we?'

He smiled. 'Yes, we did. But start at the beginning. How did you end up working with the Hastie brothers?'

It was accidental, as it turned out. Lisa had been watching Club Summertime because she knew Firmin had a photograph, and because Bamber had told her about a kid that worked for Frank Swann, who'd be good for doing burglaries, and who worked the door on the weekends. She'd been in the park that night watching Lee when the Hastie brothers and their friend had raided the safe. In case they'd taken the photo, or anything else incriminating from Firmin, she'd tracked them down, realised that they'd be useful. The first Drew brother, she'd taken him alone, eighteen months ago, and things had got out of hand ...

'You don't need to tell me about that.'

But she did. She'd taken Tim Drew at his house, using a pistol to encourage him out into the van. He was the first link in the chain. She'd done it alone, without Bamber knowing. She'd recently joined the police force both to get closer to Corbett and to train for that kind of thing, but it didn't help. Drew almost got the better of her when she got him to her garage, and he'd hurt her badly. It was only accidental that she'd been able to subdue him. Then the man wouldn't talk. She'd had to hurt him. It was a disgusting experience, but he was the first link in the chain, and she needed to know the others, how it'd all happened. He'd talked, finally, but he broke his bonds, came at her again, hurt her again. She'd killed him in self-defence, didn't know what to do next, had dumped his body in the bush.

'So the Hastie brothers, they helped you take the other Drew brother, then Laver.'

'Yes, for the promise of money.'

'The brothers didn't seem too upset about their murdered friend.'

'They weren't. Robbing Club Summertime was a business arrangement. The dead guy was an old cellie, he knew the risks.'

'I'm not going to ask what the Hasties did, what you did, with Laver and the other Drew.'

'Good, because I couldn't tell you. I told them I didn't want to know.'

Lee didn't believe her, something in her voice, but he didn't challenge her. Instead, he asked, 'Who was it blew up my Ford out in the street?'

'That was the ex-copper hired first to warn you off, together with Pusey. Blowing up your car was a warning. When that didn't work, they decided to kill you, on Firmin's orders, at the car warehouse.'

'You had Don and Todd following them.'

'No, I was following them. We got there just in time.'

'Last question. Why did you choose the name Lisa? You must've joined up using a real person's identity. I assume even WAPOL check these things.'

'Not as much as you might think. I chose the identity of a dead girl. Died age eight. I took her name but invented a background in Melbourne.'

'Why her?'

'We're the same age. Race.'

Lee looked at her now, felt the vulnerability in her voice. 'And?'

'She was taken by Pusey and his friends. Her body was found in Gnangara. She was the first.'

Lee reached up and took her face in his hand, wiped away a tear. 'How do you know that?'

'I can't tell you. But trust me, I know.'

Lee brought his forehead to hers, their noses touching. He wiped away another tear, felt her body tense as her dispatch radio crackled in the bedroom. She lifted out of his arms and walked away. She returned a minute later, carrying his cigarettes and lighter. She passed Lee a Stuyvie and took one for herself, lit them both.

'That was a colleague of mine. I just called her. It's all over the comms. Commander Corbett ate his gun last night.'

Lee was silent for a while. 'The final link in the chain.'

'No, not the final link. There's one more.'

'Yes, I have a rough idea of what's happened there.'

Lisa laughed. 'Your hacker friend? We've been watching him, from afar. I'm told that he's very good.'

'Not as good as you,' Lee said. 'After you learned that Firmin was on to me, that he sent Pusey and the ex-copper after me, you stayed here, to protect me. Just in case.'

'Might have, yes. It was my fault they were after you. I know you can look after yourself, but—'

'Though I'm not sure what to call you. Lisa? Jessica?'

'How about we stick with Lisa? At least until it's time for Jessica to come home.'

Lee thought about Jessica, alone in the shipping container, all those years ago, alone and afraid. How she'd carried the rage through the years. How she must know that her revenge wouldn't heal her, even if justice had finally been served. He would wait for her to talk about it, whenever she was ready.

'When will that be? You going to quit the force?'

'I'm honestly not sure. Maybe I'll take up your line of work? I don't have Felicity's head for business. I'm more hands-on.'

She laughed then, and put her hands on his chest, ran them down his sides, came to rest on his hips. Lee looked beyond her, saw that George next door was watching, while pretending to stake some beans.

'Let's go inside,' she said, 'and shower, get dressed. I've booked us lunch.'

'Good,' said Lee. 'A goodbye lunch, I presume.'

He caught the surprise, and sadness in her eyes. 'Yes, a goodbye lunch. Let's call it that.'

Lee rose as she rose, both of them bracing one another on the shaky steps, the sunlight now breaking over the roofline above them, filling out the backyard.

63

Lee took a seat beside Lisa, across from Felicity. They had the best table in the house, looking out over the ocean, protected from the direct sun, in deference to Felicity's pale skin, her eyes hidden behind dark sunglasses. There was one more seat at the table and Lee felt hands on his shoulders, turned and saw Bamber, smiling down at him. Bamber moved round the table, smiling at Lisa before leaning down and kissing Felicity, squeezing her in a gentle hug. A father's kiss, and a father's hug. They sat opposite him, knowing that he knew, and for the first time Lee saw their familial resemblance, a resemblance not there in Lisa, Jessica Enright's face.

'Does Enright know?' Lee asked.

'Not yet,' Felicity said. 'But soon. Dad only told me two years ago.'

Lee looked at Bamber, who nodded.

'That's why you stayed working for Enright,' Lee said. 'Despite everything.'

'Yes,' Bamber agreed. 'Despite everything.'

Felicity continued to look directly at Lee, speaking now to her father.

'I'm going to tell him,' she said. 'For Jess's sake.'

Bamber didn't look happy. 'I thought we agreed,' he said quietly.

Felicity shook her head. 'He needs to know.'

Beside him, Lisa's hand rested on his knee. 'Know what?' Lee asked, only now beginning to understand, the sadness in Felicity's eyes a match for the shame in Bamber's, refusing to look at him, staring down at his hands. The waiter appeared beside him but Bamber waved him away.

'It was you,' said Lee. 'You who was taken. You in the shipping container. The photographs.'

'It was a mistake. It was supposed to be Jess. But we wore the same school uniform, looked similar. The whole thing was outsourced, you'd call it now. Firmin's son, and a trusted friend. They got it wrong. It was me walking home alone that day. Jess was held back by her teacher, for misbehaviour.'

'I don't understand. Why Jessica?'

Beside him, Lisa snorted. 'I was his least favourite. And the youngest, therefore likely to garner the most sympathy. It was the bottom-of-the-harbour tax scandal, final days. The regulators were closing in. The media were beginning to ask hard questions. My father had heard that charges were about to be laid. He did it to delay. To deflect. To draw pity. And it worked. Worked well.'

'But he must've known that it was Felicity who was taken?'

Felicity looked at him, the sadness replaced by a cold anger. 'It was his first mistake. The ransom calls, then the letters. They all said Jessica. The first call he made, before he even realised, he told the police that it was Jess who hadn't come home from school, who was taken. Then he leaked it to the media.'

Lisa squeezed his hand. 'By the time I got home from school, took my time, playing down by the river, thinking I was going to be in trouble for getting detention, again, it was after dark. I came in the back door. I heard him talking on the phone, to someone. He was always talking on the phone, always sounded angry, worried, stressed out, but this time it didn't sound right. There was something strange in his voice. Pleading. I heard him say, 'Just make sure they don't hurt her. She's my baby girl.' And then, he turned and saw me, and his face dropped, and he went pale. And then we heard the sirens. And he panicked. Told me to hide in my room. Because he knew he'd made a mistake. He'd put it out there that it was me. How could a father make that kind of mistake?'

'That's enough now,' Bamber said. 'More than enough.'

Lee turned, looked at Lisa. 'But it was you they interviewed, after … Felicity's release.'

'Correct. I was coached by my father. I was eight years old. I did what I was told, said what I was told to say. There was so much that I didn't understand, but I knew one thing, and that was that it was supposed to be me.'

Lee felt sick. 'When did Enright find out about … what happened. With Pusey and his friends?'

Felicity shook off her father's hand, leaning across the table. 'I told him right away. When I got home.'

'Why didn't he do anything about it? He set up the kidnapping, but he couldn't have known …'

'Let me answer that,' said Bamber. 'Because he certainly didn't tell me. I only learned when Fe told me, two years ago. Enright had sent me packing at the time, off on holidays, up in the Philippines. I came home soon as I heard, but he never told me. Knew that even I would baulk at a staged kidnapping for sympathy. The answer to your question is the dirt that collects around a man like Enright.

He couldn't go hard on Corbett, because Corbett had him over a barrel, had evidence that Enright had staged the kidnapping, had paid Corbett to set it up. Enright didn't know about Firmin's involvement. And Corbett didn't know about Pusey and his mates, their inclinations, until later. The photographs they all kept, of Fe, was Firmin's idea. Insurance if Enright came after them. It was Jess who learned about them, after she … spoke to the elder Drew brother. This has been years in the making, son, and now you know everything about it. Which I'm not happy about.'

'Not everything,' said Lee. 'How did you find the first link in the chain, Tim Drew?'

Felicity went very still, looked down at her pale hands, wrung into a knot. 'It was by accident. I was catching a taxi into Perth, outside King's Park. The men who took me, I never saw their faces, but I remembered their smell. It was Drew's smell that condemned him. The men didn't speak either, and so I can't recall their voices. But I knew them by their smell, and without even knowing, I'd searched for them ever since. That kind of radar, sweeping in search of the men, was exhausting. It explains so much. I got in the taxi. It was mid-afternoon and I was late for an appointment in the city. The taxi driver had long brown hair. I did up my seatbelt. It was then that I noticed he wasn't in uniform, and that he'd been exercising. He wore a loose singlet and tight shorts; there was sweat on his arms. He'd likely been running up and down the steps of Jacob's Ladder. Despite the heat, the man scrolled up the front windows. I told him my destination in the city. He pulled away from the kerb, watching me in the rear-vision mirror. It started as a welling nausea behind my eyes, which closed automatically, became a roaring in my ears, blocking out all sound. The smell – rotten, bacterial – filled out my senses. Amid the shock I understood that the smell was inscribed on the man. My stomach lurched. I opened my eyes, and thumped the door. He'd been watching me, and pulled to the kerb. I gagged, then retched. My mouth filled. I spilled out the door, onto the verge. My skin prickled, my hackles were raised. I tried to breathe, but instead spilled out. The driver pulled away, not bothering to shut the passenger door, which swung, until the hard acceleration drove in the latch. I knelt on the verge, being sick, but as he drove away, I fixed on the taxi's licence plate.'

'Jesus.'

Bamber squeezed Felicity's hands, put his arms around her. Beside Lee, Lisa had tears in her eyes, wiped away with a sleeve. There was an awkward silence. The three had kept their secrets for so long, and now something intensely private had been revealed. Lee sat forward, looked at Bamber and Felicity. 'You've emptied all the Enright accounts. Taken all the company records.'

Felicity nodded, fire coming back into her eyes. 'We're taking everything. One of the things he did after the WA Inc scandal broke was put a lot in my name, all his real assets. I used those as collateral to borrow against, have been buying up stakes in his companies, stacking the board with my people. Like my father said, this has been years in the making.'

'The Bulgarian companies.'

'My … our mother, was from Sofia. We have family there. Her death was suspicious. There was a landslide in the Swiss Alps, but her body was never found. We'll never know if my father played a part in her disappearance. Witnesses we've spoken to say he went skiing that day alone. He's certainly capable of it.'

Lee looked to Bamber. 'He suspected? Knew? About you being Felicity's father?'

'I don't think so. More likely, she wanted to leave him. It was her money that started him off. But we'll never know. So instead, we're taking over his companies. Taking everything he owns. And on that ...'

Bamber looked around the table, at his daughter, at Lisa. 'We ready to go see the old man? Sooner the better.'

Felicity nodded. Beside him, Lisa stood, pulled out her chair. Bamber put out of his hand. 'Thank you, son, for everything. But you know, right, you ever—'

'I don't need to be told,' Lee said.

Lisa bent to his ear and kissed him. 'Goodbye,' she whispered. 'For now.'

Lee heard them go, behind him into the clatter of the busy restaurant, the waiter coming to him. Lee ordered a cold beer and a Jameson chaser, told the waiter he'd take it on the patio. The sun out there was fierce, and he enjoyed the burn on his skin.

64

Lee parked the Valiant at the head of the property, the '65 Way-farer's throaty engine closing down reluctantly, thumping once or twice as the crankshaft turned and the fuel burned out. He was pleased with his choice of vehicle from Firmin's lot, wanting a daily driver rather than an attention-grabber. And the thing had toe when it was needed, the engine fully restored, eating up the open road on his drives out in the country.

Lee held up a crime-scene photograph of the driveway, taken from the Enright kidnapping file, made sure that he had the right place. The rutted drive was the same, as was the weedy line that climbed the hill between the wheel ruts, the same banksia and acacia bushes grown wild since the place was confiscated.

Lee climbed the hill and walked past the old fibro house, whose asbestos panels had been kicked in, its windows smashed, casuarina needles blocking the gutters. The parched yard that skirted the house hadn't been mowed in many years, the grass long and summer-dead, grasshoppers and cabbage moths moving across the fern stems and the wild oats that were eating into the field behind. Lee followed the tyre marks, and then the footsteps that flattened the grass, before consulting his photographs once again. He found the one with the bunker door open, crossed the field until he came to a sheet of rusted corry iron, grown over with weeds. Lee put away the photographs, put on a pair of leather gloves and pulled away the iron sheet, which caught in the sea breeze and banged when it fell. Lee knelt and pulled out the cotter pin that was holding the latch, which he flipped, lifting the heavy steel door. Lee took a look around at the bush that surrounded him, but he couldn't see anyone, and stepped to the vertical shaft.

The stink of death hit him hard, and he gagged. He turned on his torch, shone it down the steel ladder, welded to the container walls, saw Pusey and the retired policeman's corpses at the bottom where they'd been thrown.

'Anyone there?' Lee called, but there was no answer. He picked up a nearby brick and dropped it down, repeated his question, but there was only the stench and the buzzing of flies.

Lee took a deep breath and began to descend the ladder, the torch in his mouth. At the bottom he sidestepped Pusey's corpse, thought briefly about the man's wife and children, remembered his observation of their house, how normal it all seemed. One day, perhaps, he would make the call.

Lee shone the torch down the length of the container, saw two still shapes slumped in the corner. He kicked the brick toward them. In the confined space, the noise was tremendous, echoing in the stifling heat. Two weeks since Laver had gone missing, more for Gavin Drew. Weeks without water down in the heat of the bunker – he wondered how long they'd lasted. Lee approached the two men, saw that they'd both opened their veins, taking the quickest route out. Beside Laver, the architect, was the nail that he'd used to open his arm, sharpened to a point on the steel floor beside him. It was then that Lee saw it, a foot away from Laver's shoulder, at the height of a kneeling child. Two words, carved into the steel, exposed by a layer of paint sanded away. The words read *ANNALISA MALONE*, but it was the scratched sad face, mouth turned down, tears falling in a line either side of the face, right down to the ground, that broke Lee's heart.

Felicity Enright had seen that face, and that name, when she was here. Even though she was just a child, she knew what it meant. That she wasn't the first.

It became the name that Jessica Enright took, when she began following the line of men, starting with the taxidriver's rego that her sister Felicity had taken, all those years ago.

Laver's head was turned toward the name, and the sad face, his sightless eyes open. Lee hoped that it was the last thing Laver saw on this earth, hoped that he'd look at it forever.

Acknowledgements

My heartfelt thanks to my publisher and editor, Georgia Richter, whose patience and insight have made this a far better book than it might have otherwise been. *I Am Already Dead* is, of course, only one of many Fremantle Press titles to be edited and published this year and yet, despite her prodigious workload, Georgia's commitment manifests in ways that make every writer feel supported, challenged and inspired to be better. Thanks always to Claire, Chloe, Alex and everyone at Fremantle Press for their ongoing support, encouragement and hard work in bringing this, and all Fremantle Press titles to the world. I'd also like to acknowledge my first reader, Mark Constable, for his detailed feedback, and help with the fine, and important details that I sometimes neglect. Thanks to my family – Bella, Max, Fairlie and Luka – for the laughs, the drama, the love and the stories. This novel is dedicated to my brother, Pete, and my sister, Kerri, with whom I have so much shared history, and who I love and admire very much.

THE FRANK SWANN SERIES

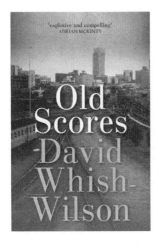 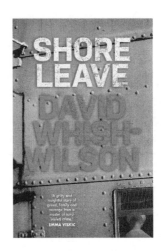

'In the Frank Swann series, David Whish-Wilson has done for Perth what Peter Temple did for Melbourne with Jack Irish.' *Westerly Magazine*

'[Perth] is indeed one of the key characters in the novel, a remote wild-west mirage with more money than sense ...' *Australian Book Review*

'Whish-Wilson has again delivered a fast-paced, entertaining and smarter than average crime novel.' *The Weekend Australian*

'David Whish-Wilson is one of the best purveyors of gritty, credible, hardboiled Australian crime fiction.' *Canberra Weekly*

'Bikers, murder, revenge, navy boys and a hot Western Australian summer all make *Shore Leave* a great read.' *AU Review*

'A gritty, fast-paced ride through late-80s Perth, complete with bikies, corrupt cops and neo-nazis.' *West Australian*

'As the plot unfolds, Whish-Wilson's text pulses from the pages at an escalating rate, building tension and suspense as the story hurtles towards its surprising resolution.' *Farm Weekly*

FROM FREMANTLEPRESS.COM.AU

THE LEE SOUTHERN SERIES

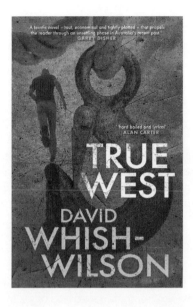

Western Australia, 1988. After betraying a bikie gang, seventeen-year-old Lee Southern flees to the city with nothing left to lose.

Working as a rogue tow truck driver in Perth, he is captured by right-wing extremists whose combination of seduction and blackmail keeps him on the wrong side of the law.

As the true nature of what drives his captors unfolds, Lee becomes an unwilling participant in a breathtakingly ambitious plot – and a cold-blooded crime that will show just how much he, and everyone else, still has to lose.

'Whish-Wilson's Western Australia is alive, its heart beating, its outback a swirl of dust and history, roads like scars, the scent of its plants as strong as the ocean's salty brine. Lee is a hell of a character ... This is compelling, thrilling, and still feels like it could be played out today in the white nationalist fringes of Australian politics.' *Readings*

AND ALL GOOD BOOKSTORES

A catalogue record for this
book is available from the
National Library of Australia

ISBN 9781760992026 (paperback)
ISBN 9781760992033 (ebook)

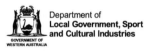

Fremantle Press is supported by the State Government through the
Department of Local Government, Sport and Cultural Industries.

Fremantle Press respectfully acknowledges the Whadjuk people of the
Noongar nation as the Traditional Owners and Custodians of the land
where we work in Walyalup.